LOVE in Revolution

By B.R. Collins

The Traitor Game
A Trick of the Dark
Tyme's End
The Broken Road
Love in Revolution

***

Gamerunner
MazeCheat

LOVE in Revolution

B.R. COLLINS

BLOOMSBURY
LONDON NEW DELHI NEW YORK SYDNEY

Bloomsbury Publishing, London, New Delhi, New York and Sydney

First published in Great Britain in August 2013 by Bloomsbury Publishing Plc
50 Bedford Square, London WC1B 3DP

A CIP catalogue record for this book is available from the British Library

ISBN 978 1 4088 1570 0

Typeset by Hewer Text UK Ltd, Edinburgh
Printed and bound in Great Britain by CPI Group (UK) Ltd, Croydon CR0 4YY

1 3 5 7 9 10 8 6 4 2

www.bloomsbury.com

Summer

One

When I was small, there was a house at the end of the town that had fallen down. We weren't allowed to play there, of course, but we did sometimes. We'd play furious, clumsy games of pello against the one intact wall, and when we were tired out we'd collapse in the shade with tepid bottles of cherry juice that stained our teeth pink. We'd argue about the bumps and curves in the wall and the angles of our shots as if we were professionals. Or sometimes we'd be too out of breath to talk, and we'd lie there in silence, listening to the breeze in the gap-toothed stones.

But there was one room in the house – or something that used to be a room – that fascinated me. It still *looked* like a room, with wallpaper on the walls, a mirror that hung crooked, a sagging old sideboard that no one had bothered to move; but one wall had been torn apart. There was a vertical crack that went the whole height of the house, and between the ragged margins of wallpaper there was a dark gap, big enough to put your hand into. After we were tired of playing pello, I'd stand in the tumbledown doorway, just looking. I couldn't help thinking about how long the crack had taken to appear – seconds? days? years? – and imagining the first moment when someone looked up from their everyday life and realised that their world was falling apart.

I always imagined that they would have screamed and run. But now, I'm not sure. I think the world can collapse around you very, very slowly, so you hardly notice it's happening. I think it can start with something small, something tiny. That's how revolutions start – with the first tremor, the first plume of dust. That's how love starts too: a shiver and something snaps, too tiny to be seen with the naked eye, hardly even felt. And it's only when the house is in ruins – when there's nothing to keep out the weather, the cold, the bullets – that you look back and wonder how it happened.

But all the same, I think I can pick a moment when my world started to end. I can see it clearly, pinpoint the first slip of subsidence, the moment when the walls shook.

It was the day Pitoro Toros, the pello player, came to our town; the day I saw Angel Corazon for the first time.

It was also the day I fell in love.

It was June. I was fifteen.

The sun was streaming in through the church windows, casting red lozenges of light on to the floor and across the pattern of my dress. I squinted through my eyelashes, making the colours blur, and then, because I couldn't help myself, I turned my head and stared at the man in the pew on the other side of the nave just behind us. He must have known everyone in the church was sneaking looks at him, but it didn't show; he was praying, apparently, his powerful shoulders hunched and his thick, famous arms braced against the wooden ledge in front of him. I breathed deeply, as quietly as I could, wondering if the air smelt different just because he was there.

Martin kicked me on the shin with his heel. 'You're staring,' he whispered, and then glanced over his shoulder, following my eyes. He bit his lip.

I rolled my eyes and kicked him back, a sharp strike on his ankle that made him wince and stifle a yelp. 'Now who's staring? Martin, you're in lo-ove . . .'

'He's here,' Martin murmured, ignoring me, with a note in his voice that was wistful and awestruck and envious all at once. 'I can't believe he's actually *here* . . .'

'And for his August and Most Beloved Majesty King Ferdinand . . .' the priest said, and cleared his throat. He must have known no one was listening, but you had to give him credit for trying.

'They say he can serve so fast you can't see the ball hit the wall,' Martin said. 'In his match against Hiram Jelek, he didn't lose serve once. Not *once*. And they say he can stop a ball dead, just with his chest. Oh, I'd love to see that . . .'

The priest slapped the altar with the flat of his hand, raising his voice. 'That he may vanquish and overcome all his enemies, especially those who with blasphemous and irreverent thoughts incite us, his people, to violence . . .'

'I know,' I said. Mama looked round and frowned at me. I lowered my voice. 'And when he played Old Man Ciro, he bounced the ball into his chest so hard it *killed* him . . .' I turned to look again, willing him to raise his head. Pitoro Toros, the Bull, three times winner of the King's Cup, one of the best pello players *ever*. And he was here, in our town, in our church . . . He didn't look like the newspaper cuttings on Martin's wall – but then, here he was in colour and not brandishing a trophy.

'He doesn't look like his photo,' Martin said. 'I wish he'd look up . . .'

'Martin! Stop *talking*,' Mama said. 'And you too, Esteya. Don't think I can't hear you both.'

We turned our faces back to the altar, struggling not to giggle. I tried to swallow the bubbles of excitement that kept rising and bursting in my throat, but they were like an itch that I couldn't scratch.

'And for all his subjects,' the priest intoned, 'above all those for whom we your servants feel a justifiable affection and pride, those sportsmen who by their endeavours express the eternal fight of good against evil . . .'

'He's making this up!' Martin hissed, half admiring, half outraged. '*That's* not what he says normally . . .'

'The son of our town, Pitoro Toros, known to all of us as the Bull . . .'

For the first time that morning our *amen* came promptly at the end of the prayer, and the priest's mouth twitched at one corner. Martin and I smiled at each other. And everywhere in the church people were catching one another's eyes and glancing conspiratorially towards the pew where the Bull stood, still doggedly pretending not to notice the attention.

'The grace of our Lord Jesus Christ, and the love of God, and the fellowship of the Holy Ghost be with us all evermore. Amen.'

'And the pello talent of our beloved brother the Bull,' Martin added, but it was drowned out by everyone else saying *amen* and the creaks and rustlings as we closed our prayer books and shuffled our feet, so that I was the only one who heard. His voice was full of longing.

'The Mass is ended, go in peace.'

'Thanks be to God,' I said, along with everyone else, and meant it. The noise swelled to a crescendo. The Bull looked up, finally, and glanced round. He had thick features, a nose that had been broken more than once and a mouth that didn't seem to close properly. It was easy to believe that he'd killed a man on the pello court. He wasn't handsome – well, actually, he was ugly – but there was a kind of glamour about him. People said he was one of the best players *ever* . . .

No one left the church until the Bull did; then we elbowed and fought to get as near to him as we could. He smirked a little – as if he'd only just noticed us – and swaggered out into the square, his hands in his pockets.

As we pushed forward Martin grabbed my arm. 'Hey, there's Leon. I thought he told Papa he was studying?' He pulled me sideways, out of the flow of people, and we stumbled to a stop in the cool shadow of the church. Leon was rolling a cigarette, leaning in a doorway on the other side of the square.

'I told you so,' I said. 'He wouldn't come to church, but I *knew* he wouldn't be able to resist seeing the Bull . . .'

I was right. You could see from the way Leon jerked his head up when he heard the voices drifting across the square. Sunlight flashed off the lenses of his glasses. He was frozen for a moment, peering towards us; then he saw the Bull. The half-rolled cigarette bent and spilt tobacco between his fingers.

'I hope Mama doesn't see him,' I said. 'Lunch will be horrible if she does.'

Martin looked at me and grimaced, but all he said was, 'Do you think I should ask the Bull for his autograph?'

The Bull was surrounded now. Someone had found a pen from somewhere, and I caught glimpses of the Bull's muscled, damage-thickened hand, writing his name over and over again. One of the Ibarra girls danced away with a scrawl of ink on her dress, just above her left breast.

'Yes,' I said, 'why don't you get him to sign your trousers?'

Martin grinned, and then tilted his head to one side, considering. 'Do you think he would?'

Just then the hubbub of voices died away. The Bull was a little apart from the crowd of admirers, talking to someone in the shadow of the fountain. He was still holding the pen – between finger and thumb, as though he wasn't used to writing – but his hand had dropped to his side: he wasn't signing his autograph. He turned on his heel, shaking his head, and swaggered back to his fans. Someone asked him something, too quietly for us to hear the words.

'Kid wants a lesson,' the Bull said.

'A pello lesson?' the other Ibarra girl asked, girlishly pleating her dress, showing her best lace-topped stockings.

'Lesson in manners, more like,' the Bull said. He glared round at the crowd as if it was their fault. A couple of people took a step backwards. 'Jumped-up little peasant. I *kill* people on the pello court. He really thinks he can survive a match against me?'

'He wants to *play* you?' I didn't see who asked, but there was the same incredulous, flattering expression on everyone's face.

The Bull's scowl dissolved slowly. He nodded. It was like seeing a rhinoceros decide not to charge, after all. He glanced down at the pen in his hand, as if he'd suddenly remembered it was there.

'Why don't you humour him?'

Everyone looked round. It was Teddy, bouncing on the balls of his feet like a little boy, his camera poised to take a photograph for the paper. His pink English face was trickling with sweat. 'It would make a splendid story,' he added. 'LOCAL HERO GIVES PELLO LESSON TO . . . no, wait, how about OUR HERO IS GOOD SPORT? Sporting in every sense of the word, old boy.'

'Oh, *please* do,' the Ibarra girl said. Her hand tightened on her dress and the hem crept even higher. 'We'd *love* to see you play.'

'I don't really feel like . . .' the Bull said, the words coming out so slowly it was as if he was trying to speak a new language.

'Yes, it *would* be embarrassing to lose.'

The words were clear, ringing off the walls like the echo of metal hitting stone. We all turned to look. There was a quiet, communal hiss of disapproval; but the boy who had spoken sat quite still, poised on the edge of a windowsill at the side of the square, a smile in his eyes. I hadn't noticed him before, but now I was looking at him I wanted to go on looking.

'Zikindi . . .' someone said, in disgust.

The boy tilted his head gracefully, as if in acknowledgement. He probably was Zikindi. He had the right colouring for it: light brown face and hair, a kind of lustrous tinge to his skin, and pale eyes. He surveyed us, like a king looking at his courtiers, and then spoke to the Bull, as directly as if they were the only people there. 'If you're afraid to play against him – he's a peasant, after all . . .'

The Bull narrowed his eyes; if he'd had horns, he would have lowered them. Then he turned away, and called into the shadow of the fountain, to the other boy, the one he'd been talking to before.

'Hey! Oi, kid!' he called. 'You sure you want a game? I don't want to send you home a cripple . . .'

'Yes.' The voice was odd: hoarse, a little too loud, and

sort of blurred, as if the tongue and mouth didn't fit together properly. It made me want to clean out my ears.

But then he stepped out into the sunlight, from behind the fountain, and the voice didn't matter. Nothing mattered.

He was like an angel.

He was blond and slim, a little dusty and grimy but blazing gold and white in the sun. He was wearing peasant's clothes but they looked like a party costume, as if just the fact that they touched his skin transformed them into something rich, something special.

'Shut your mouth, Esteya, you look like you're trying to catch flies,' Martin said.

'Shut up.'

The Bull glanced over his shoulder at the crowd, but what he saw seemed to reassure him. No one wanted to see the Bull beaten, especially not by this too-pretty-to-be-true peasant boy whom no one had seen before. He was *too* beautiful; I could see the resentment on the faces around me. They wanted to see his face smashed in – or a little bruise, here and there, at least. No one wanted him to win. Certainly not.

Except me. And maybe the Zikindi boy, who was watching too, with a crease between his eyebrows.

I looked back at the peasant boy and prayed, the way you pray for a miracle.

'Er . . . you are?' the Bull said. 'You're sure? All right, well, I'll be a bit nice to you. You play with the local kids, do you?'

'No.' The boy was staring at the Bull as if he was the only person in the world. 'Never played.'

'You've *never played*?'

'Well . . .' The boy swallowed, struggling for words.

'With my brothers when I was small. And now . . . Not with other people. I play with myself.'

A fractional pause. Then Martin caught my eye and smirked; and in spite of myself I started to giggle. A couple of people looked at us, and then the laughter spread. Even the priest smiled, dutifully, as if to make sure we knew he'd got the joke.

'I mean –'

'It's all right, sonny, it's perfectly normal for a boy of your age . . .' the Bull said, and winked, inviting another wave of laughter. 'So you should have strong wrists, at least.'

'I mean . . .' He looked round, his eyes wide, seeming to register the crowd of us for the first time. I felt his gaze slide over my face like a question and wished that Martin hadn't made me laugh.

'All right then. Got a ball, sonny? Or didn't you think of that?'

'Yes, I have a ball.' He held it out, like a child showing someone his favourite thing.

'Two, I hope,' the Bull said, and winked again. Then he plucked the ball out of the boy's hand and took up a stance in the painted square, waiting for everyone to shuffle out of the way.

I tried to push forward to see properly, but Martin pulled me back. 'You know he's injured *spectators*?'

'But –'

'Can you imagine what Mama would say if you went home with your nose all over your face? You'd be an old maid all your life, and they'd blame me . . .' Martin dragged at my elbow until I took a reluctant step backwards. Then he glanced round, briefly. 'Where are they, anyway? Oh – wait, there's Mama. I'd know that hat anywhere. Honestly, she could take someone's eye out with that . . .'

But I didn't bother to answer, because the court was clear now, and the Bull was rolling his shoulders and swinging from side to side, loosening the muscles. Everyone watched him, mesmerised. In the silence I looked sideways and saw that Martin was frowning, his lips moving as if he was trying to memorise the sequence of movements. I knew next time we played he'd insist on an elaborate warm-up.

But the boy – not that he was a boy, actually, he must have been seventeen or eighteen – wasn't doing exercises, or even standing ready. He ought to have been in the middle of the court, shuffling a little, pretending not to be overawed; but he wasn't. He was standing by the pello wall, looking at it as if it was a work of art, touching it lightly with his fingertips.

'He's completely barmy,' Martin muttered. 'He's going to get pulverised. They'll be taking him home in a sack . . .'

'Hey,' the Bull called. 'You ready or what?'

'Yes, thank you.' The boy looked round, as though he'd been interrupted in the middle of a conversation. It wasn't exactly rude, but all the same it made the Bull flush and heft the ball dangerously.

'Good.'

The Bull served.

He hadn't waited for the boy to get into the middle of the court; and he served a nasty, low little shot that was too fast to see, at least before it hit the wall. It leapt off the stone, straight into the boy's face. He jerked his head aside, just in time, and there was a hiss of excitement from the crowd. But the ball flew over his shoulder and dipped, too quick for him to get a hand to it. He spun to watch it helplessly, as it landed just inside the baseline of the court. There were cheers and applause, and laughter.

Someone – I think it was Teddy – said, 'Five love.'

The Bull stood where he was, his hands on his hips, waiting for someone to retrieve the ball and bring it back to him. There was a scuffle as the younger Ibarra girl shoved past everyone else and ran to pick it up, then ran back to the Bull with it. The other Ibarra girl glared at her.

'Ready?' This time the Bull waited, ostentatiously, until the boy was standing still and balanced, his eyes steady.

This time the Bull's serve was just as fast, but it skidded up the wall and looped high over the boy's head. He followed its trajectory, but he didn't move. Someone whistled mockingly.

It dropped a little way beyond where the first one had, right at the back of the court. A little puff of brown dust rose and sank again.

'Second serv–'

'Ten love,' the Ibarra girl corrected, and gave Teddy a vicious look.

'But . . .' Teddy frowned, and then caught the Bull's eye. 'Oh. Um. Yes. Ten love.'

'It was out,' the boy said. 'Wasn't it?'

No one answered. The Bull held out his hand for the ball, and the Ibarra girl brought it back to him. He rolled his shoulders.

'You didn't even move, kid,' he said. 'I'll give you another serve if you want, but you didn't even *try* . . . Know you're beaten already, don't you?'

'But I knew it was going out –'

Before the boy had finished speaking the Bull smacked the ball against the wall, a straight whistling blur of a serve that hit the wall then the ground, so hard it jumped back into the air, dropping and bouncing again until it fell dead at the boy's feet. He looked down, confused; it had happened so fast he'd missed it.

'It's ten love now,' the Bull said. 'What are we playing, anyway? First to twenty-five?'

'First to fifty,' the boy said, his eyes widening. 'It's always first to fifty. Isn't it?'

'Hardly worth the effort.' The Bull grinned, his nostrils flaring, and waited for the boy to stoop and pass the ball back to him. 'Good lad. Ready?'

'Wait a sec–'

This time the serve went out wide, beyond the boy's reach; but somehow, too quickly for my eyes to follow, he'd thrown himself sideways and picked it out of the air as easily as taking something off a shelf. I blinked. The Bull started to say, 'Fifteen lo–' and then stopped, staring at the ball in the boy's hand.

'First to fifty,' the boy repeated. 'A pello game is always first to fifty. That's what my papa says.'

The Bull looked at him in silence for what seemed like a long time. Then, finally, he said, 'Twenty love.'

'But . . .'

'If you catch the ball, you have to throw it again within three seconds. That's the rule. Since you're such an expert. You've still got a hold of it, so you've lost ten points. Twenty love.'

No one was clapping now. The boy looked down at the ball in his hand. His fingers were white, the nails gleaming like bone against the deep red leather. He was frowning, like a little kid trying to do a sum that was too difficult for him. For a horrible moment I thought he was going to cry.

'Stop thinking he'll play fair.'

That voice again, clear as a bell.

The Zikindi boy dropped down from his perch on the windowsill, landing lightly, like an animal. He must have sensed the collective hostility as the crowd turned to look at him, but he didn't show it. He called across the pello court, 'No one plays fair. Not ever. Get used to it.'

The other boy (the young man, the angel) stared at him, his eyes narrowed, and then turned away. He went on frowning, but now his expression had something different in it, something hard. He threw the ball sideways in a little arc and caught it with his left hand; then he held it out to the Bull.

The Zikindi boy smiled a quiet, private smile. He put his hands in his pockets and sauntered over to us, not seeming to notice the way people drew away from him, or the Ibarra girl wrinkling her nose. The Bull glowered at him, then spat silently on the ground and took the ball. Then he swung his arm around, grunting, as if he was preparing for the biggest effort yet.

And the serve was *fast*. I didn't even see it. I heard Martin say, 'Wow,' as it whistled and smacked against the stone, but then there was another duller smack, like an echo, and a thin skein of mortar dust dropping from the wall, and suddenly the Bull was diving for the ball and –

And it hit the ground, just short of the line. In.

There was a gasp from all of us, scattered, bewildered applause, and then silence.

Teddy said, carefully, as if he was trying out the words, 'Um. Love twenty.'

The Bull looked at the ball coming to rest on the line,

then back at the wall, squinting suspiciously. You could still see a faint haze of dust where the ball had hit, at the corner of a block of stone where the angle had thrown it off straight. Then he snorted and turned away. 'Go on then. Your serve.'

The boy's serve was soft – a friendly, pulling-its-punches arc that bounced gently off the flat part of a stone. But somehow it swerved in the air and dropped just a little too low, so that the Bull had to readjust his stance at the last moment. He grunted and whacked it back, off balance, but the force in it was still enough to make the boy dance backwards and hiss through his teeth as he returned it.

The square was dead silent, except for the impact of the ball and the players' breathing, echoing off the walls. I glanced down and saw that Martin was gripping my arm, just below the shoulder. It should have hurt, but it didn't. Suddenly his fingers spasmed, tightening, and I looked back at the court, just too late.

Teddy said, 'Ten twenty.'

The boy was staring at the wall again, his head tilted. The Bull was at the side of the court, breathing heavily. There was a dark island of sweat in the small of his back. He kicked the ball up into the air with his toe, reached out to catch it, and flung a hand out for it, skidded and missed. It thumped down and rolled away.

Martin breathed, 'Sacred heart, the Bull's going to *lose*.' It was a like a prayer.

Behind me, the crowd rumbled quietly. Someone said, 'The kid's fluking every shot,' and someone else said, 'You can't fluke *every* shot.'

The boy's next serve was too fast to see.

There was no applause now; hardly any sound at all.

No one knew what to do, except watch. Teddy cleared his throat and said, 'Fifteen twenty.'

The Bull won the next point, smashing the ball against the wall and down. It hit the ground in a splash of dust, and even though the kid got a hand to it he couldn't get it back; but when the crowd tried to cheer, the Bull scowled and the sound petered out thinly in the sunlight. 'Twenty fifteen,' Teddy muttered.

But the Bull lost the next point. 'Fifteen twenty.'

'Twenty-five twenty.'

'Thirty twenty.'

'Thirty-five twenty.'

The next point was a long rally, full of shots that threw flakes of paint into the air from the sidelines, both players dancing back and forth, their faces set. It felt as though they were the only people breathing – in the square, in the town, in the country. I could feel the fierce weight of the people behind me, all willing the Bull on; but I was digging my nails into the palms of my hands, praying for the angel-boy. It was as if he knew in advance where each ball would go, as if the ball and the lines and the wall itself were on his side. Everything looked like a fluke, but they were right: you couldn't fluke *every* shot.

The ball landed and skidded towards the line, bouncing like a stone skimming across water.

The Bull swiped for it, misjudged it and tried to run backwards at the same time. It was too late to get to the ball before it bounced the second time, but he grunted and threw himself towards it anyway, at full stretch. His black going-to-church Sunday-best shoes slid in the dust. He lost his balance, floundered for a split second, and then fell over.

No one laughed. It would have been better if someone had.

There was a long, long silence. The Bull levered himself up, looked down at his trousers and then rolled each ankle in turn, testing for injuries.

'Forty-five twenty,' Teddy said.

I took a deep breath. I could smell dirt and sweat – my own sweat, sharp and peppery – and the pomade Martin stole from Mama to put on his hair. The stones of the square were almost too bright to look at, with one thin edge of deep shadow at the base of the church.

The boy walked over to the ball and picked it up. He pushed his hair out of his eyes. Dust came out of it and glittered in the sunlight. The skin of his face was damp.

One more point, on serve. That was all he needed. One more.

I wanted him to win. I wanted it desperately, so much I could taste it, like thirst. But – not yet. I wanted this to go on for ever. I wanted him to lose the next point but win the next-but-one, on and on, the serve swapping back and forth between the players: so that we could go on standing here, like this, breathless and dry-mouthed, every nerve tingling, and never go back to being ordinary.

Martin took his hand off my arm. I heard the little grinding creak of his teeth as he started to bite his nails. Normally it made my skin crawl, but now it only added to the silence, like the players' breathing and the drip of the Bull's sweat on the stones.

But the boy couldn't win. Could he? Some unknown peasant kid, against Pitoro Toros, the Bull himself. Surely . . .

The Bull won the next point. The ball smashed into the

boy's solar plexus, winding him. If he hadn't seen it in time and twisted to lessen the impact, it might have done him more damage; as it was, he staggered back, flailing for balance, and gaped for breath like a drowning fish. I felt the air go out of my own lungs, and then turn solid, like a wall of glass. I couldn't inhale.

Martin grabbed my wrist again and squeezed it. I couldn't look at him, but I could feel his fingers, like a Chinese burn. I heard myself hiccup with relief as the boy finally sucked in a mouthful of air, and Martin's grip eased.

The Bull smirked, a little grimly, and served.

The next point went to the boy; the one after, to the Bull. Forty-five twenty, twenty forty-five . . . The court was so bright it was hard to see the lines; it was hard to see anything. I no longer wanted it to go on for ever. I just wanted the boy to win . . . I prayed, in my head: not *for* the boy, but *to* him. Please, please . . . I could hardly bear to watch.

The ball smacked and spun against the wall, finding angles no one could have predicted, catching the dimples and dents in the old stones as if by magic. It was so fast it made my heart race, like hearing gunshots. And the players . . . None of us had ever seen anything like it. It wasn't a game, it was a duel.

The point went to the boy. For a moment he and the Bull looked at each other, both breathless and sweating, almost smiling. Then the Bull kicked the ball, flicking it up, quick and vicious, at the boy's face. I heard someone next to me hiss through their teeth. But the boy ducked sideways, and caught it.

Teddy said, 'Forty-five twenty.'

The boy rolled his shoulders, and served.

I squeezed my eyelids shut, as if someone was going to punch me in the face. I prayed.

A clear, urgent voice said, '*Look.*'

I opened my eyes and caught my breath, because it wasn't Martin holding my wrist, it was the Zikindi boy, pushing between us for a better view. His fingers dug into the flesh between my bones and he gave my arm a little jerk, gesturing at the court. His face was damp, and there were beads of sweat on his neck, where his shirt was open. The damp skin there was very smooth, and there was a shadow in the dip of the collar-bone. In a strange, split-second shock I realised he was a girl. I raised my gaze to meet hers. She said again, '*Look.*'

So I looked.

And I was just in time to see the boy spin, his arm outstretched, twisting into his shot so that the ball spat across the court to the wall like a bullet, and ricocheted off, going high and straight. If the Bull had left it, it would have been out.

But the Bull was in the way. There was a kind of double thump. Then the Bull was stretched out flat in the dust, while the ball rolled away, and a little trickle of blood started to weep from his eyebrow.

No one moved. The boy's face was alight, as if the sun was shining more on him than on anyone else; but he was standing quite still. I felt a moment of pure triumph, blazing through me like a flame. He'd done it. He'd won.

Someone should have moved, run to the Bull to check he was all right – Papa, or the priest, or the person standing closest . . . But no one did. The pause seemed to go on for ever, as if it was the end of the world.

Then the Bull swore and sat up, shaking his head as

though there was an insect buzzing round it. He coughed, scraping the phlegm out of his throat, and spat. He said, without smiling, 'Well played.'

And then, suddenly, underneath the triumph, I felt a kind of shame.

Teddy cleared his throat and took a hesitant step forwards. He said, 'Er . . . Are you all right?'

The Bull shot him a look of pure contempt, and got to his feet without answering. He wiped his eyebrow with the back of his hand, tilted his head to one side and then the other, testing the muscles in his neck. He glanced around. For the first time I remembered that his family was there: his mother, his aunts and uncles, nieces, nephews . . . The crowd began to separate, spreading out like oil on water. I looked over my shoulder and saw the priest turn and walk away, the Ibarra girls swap a look, Mama's hat dip and bob backwards like a turquoise horn.

'Phew,' Martin said, not to anyone in particular. 'Don't think I could've stood another second of that. Would've killed me.'

The Bull had his family surrounding him now. They moved slowly away, past the tavern and down the street. The old women were talking too loudly, with too many pauses. The kids were subdued, kicking stones along the ground.

The Bull was never going to play pello again. But we didn't know that yet.

Two

The church clock chimed midday. It rang out across the square, resonating from wall to wall, and I thought I could see the vibration in the dust hanging in the air. The Zikindi girl's grip on my wrist loosened, but she didn't let go, and I didn't pull away.

The boy was still standing in the middle of the court, alone, his arms hanging loosely at his sides. Then one hand crept to his collar, fumbling, and he glanced down at his feet.

'What a player,' Martin said, shaking his head slowly. 'Wow. Can you *believe* . . . ? Just turned up out of nowhere and beat the Bull . . .'

I didn't answer. There wasn't anything I could have said. I looked sideways, and saw that the Zikindi girl had the same expression on her face that must have been on mine: glowing, dazzled, full of something too pure to smile. Her eyes were pale green-blue, and she met my gaze without blinking. We stared at each other for a few seconds; then she let go of my wrist and glanced around, like someone waking up.

The boy was crouching now, his head bowed, running one hand over the stones. He was still dripping sweat. He looked like a kid playing in the gutter.

'There's Mama and Papa,' Martin said. 'We'd better go and –'

He stopped. I followed his gaze.

Leon was walking towards us, with a patronising elder-brother smile; but when he passed in front of the boy he paused, and his face changed. His shadow fell across the boy's hands. He said slowly, 'What's your name?'

The boy looked up, and flinched. He scuffled backwards on his haunches, like an animal that didn't want to be kicked. He said, 'I'm only looking for my button. My collar button. Then I'll go.'

Leon frowned, and then crouched so that he could look the boy in the face. He stretched his hand out and patted his shoulder. 'It's all right,' he said. 'I just want to know your name.'

The boy ducked swiftly away, out of Leon's reach; but he licked his lips and finally said, 'Angel.'

'That's a nice name.' The sunlight flashed off Leon's glasses so I couldn't see his eyes. 'Where do you live, Angel?'

'Angel Corazon. From Oldchurch Farm. Over there.' The boy – the angel, Angel – pointed at the tavern, as if there was nothing in that direction but bare countryside and his farm.

'A peasant. I thought so.'

Angel stared at him, and didn't answer.

'You're a strong, hard-working son of the earth,' Leon said, leaning forward, his voice low and thrumming with drama, as if he was telling Angel a secret. 'A hero. A fighter. You're the backbone of this country. Without men like you, we would be nothing. And yet – look at you. Covered in dust, dressed in rags –'

'My button,' Angel said, in that blurred, scraping voice. 'It must've come off . . .'

Leon grabbed him by the shoulders. The tendons in his hands stood out as if it was an effort not to shake him. 'No, forget the damn button! Listen to what I'm telling you.'

I heard Martin sigh. He said, 'Odds on him saying "comrade" in the next ten seconds? Wait for it . . .'

'Do you know what you've done today?' Leon softened his voice. 'You've given us hope. All of us. You know what you are? You're a *symbol*.'

Angel gazed at him, his beautiful dark blue eyes wide and uncomprehending.

'The peasant,' Leon said, so quietly I could hardly hear him, 'rises up and defeats the bourgeoisie. Against all odds. He leaves the blood of the old order in the dust. He brings in the revolution. He *vanquishes*.'

Angel blinked. 'If I go home without it, my father will be angry. The button.'

Leon drew in a sharp breath, and then let it out slowly. The corners of his mouth softened. He said, in his normal voice, 'All right . . . what about if someone gave you a new shirt?'

'I – a new shirt?' It was as if he lived in a world where things like that didn't happen.

'Well,' Leon said, 'not exactly new, but at least with all the buttons on. Not – well, not . . .' He grimaced at Angel's shirt, at a loss for adjectives. Then he took off his jacket and started to tug at his tie.

'Oh, God, no,' Martin said. 'Please, no. Not with Mama and Papa just over there . . .'

I glanced sideways. Martin was biting his lip, but the Zikindi girl had the hint of a smile at the corner of her mouth.

Leon dropped his tie on the ground and unbuttoned

his shirt. It was too hot to wear a vest, and there were dark patches under his arms where his sweat had soaked through the material. He undid his cuffs, took the shirt off and offered it to Angel.

Martin said, 'I can't watch. When we get home it's going to be *carnage* . . .'

I said, 'It's not even *clean* . . .'

But Angel took the shirt and smiled, holding it up to the light as if to admire its whiteness. And – to be fair – it was whiter than the one he was wearing. The smile widened into a grin. Suddenly the triumph was back in his eyes: as if this was his prize for winning the game. 'Thank you, sir.'

Leon winced. 'Comrade. Please. Call me comrade.' He stood up and put his jacket back on over his bare torso, shoving his tie into the pocket. Then he paused, looking down at the stain on the ground where the Bull's blood had dripped and spread out. His eyes narrowed.

He dropped to one knee, scooped up a fingertip of bloodstained dust and smeared it on his face: two lines, across his cheekbones, like warpaint. He stood up – half laughing, half deadly earnest, the way he was when he fought with Papa – looked round at the last few groups of people, and called out, 'Death to the oppressor!'

I saw Mama's hat jump and twist behind a knot of heads, and then she came out into the open, her face set and furious. Papa said a last word to the priest and followed her, frowning. Teddy was the only person smiling; and his smile wilted as he took in the situation.

The priest said, not loudly, but very clearly, 'God damn all revolutionaries.'

Leon ignored him. 'Hey, Teddy, listen – this boy, this man, not only is he a pello genius, he's a symbol of justice

– forget the Bull, you have to write a story about this man, Angel Corazon, a true man of the people, a peasant –'

Papa said, 'Leon.'

Martin said, 'Let's go home. Come on.' He pulled me sharply sideways, so I almost fell over.

'What?' I wanted to stay; not to watch, exactly, but because of Angel, and the sunlight, and the heat from the Zikindi girl's body next to me.

'Come *on*.' He tightened his grip and tugged. 'Please. I don't want to see this. Please, Esteya.'

I sighed and let him pull me away, taking a last look at the bloodstained stones, and the church, outlined in shadow, and the Zikindi girl. Then we half walked, half ran past the tavern and down the main street. It was quiet and cool, with the window boxes dripping water. All the shutters were closed against the sun.

'Did you see Mama's face?' Martin said, putting his key into the lock of our front door and turning back to look at me. 'It's going to be horrible.'

'It won't be that bad,' I said. 'It's just Leon being Leon. Or should I say, *Comrade* Leon being *Comrade* Leon . . . ?'

'I'm sick of it,' Martin muttered. His hair had fallen over his eyes, and he pushed it back. He took a deep breath and held it for a moment; then he shook his head and tried to grin at me. 'Honestly! The best game of pello I have ever seen, *ever*, and Leon has to go and spoil it with his man-of-the-people act. All I can say is, if there *is* a revolution, I hope he gets put up against a wall and shot.'

I rolled my eyes, and he laughed, reluctantly, and went through the doorway. I heard him say, 'It will be horrible . . . I'm warning you . . .' as he went up the stairs.

But I wasn't listening. There was a movement in the corner of my eye, a flash of dark trousers and pale linen, and I turned my head. The Zikindi girl had followed us; now she was leaning in the doorway of the Ibarra house opposite, watching me. She didn't smile. Something in her gaze made my heart speed up, the way it had when her fingers gripped my wrist. I wanted to speak to her.

I opened my mouth, but I couldn't think of anything to say, except that if the Ibarras saw her they'd tell their maidservant to wash the doorstep with disinfectant. I shut my mouth again, feeling my cheeks blaze, and turned away.

To my relief, Martin was wrong: by the time they got home, Mama and Papa and Leon seemed to have said everything already, and after Leon had washed his face and put on another shirt we had lunch in a kind of uneasy peace. Mama kept her attention firmly on us – 'Stop playing with your food . . . Did you wash your hands, Martin? Esteya, is there something *particularly* interesting outside the window?' – and ignored Leon, as if she was making it quite clear that he wasn't *her* son. Papa talked about his patients, in a gentle monotone that went on and on and didn't need any answer, and Leon listened and nodded and cleaned his glasses with his tie. Sometimes he joined in, so that they talked over each other in an impersonal, dispassionate duet. It was boring, but at least they weren't arguing. I kept my eyes on my plate and thought about the pello game, and Angel Corazon, and the Zikindi girl.

'Esteya, stop fidgeting, *please*,' Mama said, shooting me a sharp look. 'Eat your food.'

I tore my bread into two pieces and pushed one into my mouth. It was like trying to eat a handkerchief. I chewed and made myself swallow.

'Too much excitement,' Martin said, nudging me with his foot. 'Delicate constitution. Can't take it.'

'And no telegraphese from you, Martin,' Mama said, and I caught his eye and smirked and kicked him back. 'Try using a pronoun once in a while . . . What are your plans for the rest of vacation, Leon? Will you be helping your father in the dispensary?'

Leon looked up, seemed to see a new smear on his glasses and took them off to wipe them again. 'I'm not sure. I might go back to Irunja before term starts.'

Papa blinked, and his mouth tightened, but all he said was, 'No doubt you miss your friends.'

'Irunja is the heart of the country, Papa,' Leon said, leaning forward and letting go of his tie, so that it dipped into the tomato ketchup on his plate. 'Here you wouldn't know there was anything brewing. But there . . . if you went there, you'd realise. The world is changing. I know you like to pretend that everything is fine –'

'Please, no politics at the table,' Mama said, but Leon didn't even look at her.

'The injustice you see there, Papa – you wouldn't believe it. The King has his palaces and water gardens and stables, like something from the nineteenth century, and there are beggars on the streets, starving workmen, policemen standing at the fountains to charge the workers for a midday drink, and if anyone complains they don't even have time to finish their sentence before they're taken away and beaten up –'

'All cities are like that, Leon. There are rich and poor. Bad things happen everywhere. But revolution is not the remedy.' Papa's egg yolk spilt out on to the plate, and he poked at it with his knife, frowning.

'And in the country – you saw that peasant kid today, so thin, and he can't have washed for *weeks* –'

'The Communists will make baths compulsory, will they?' Martin muttered.

'At least you gave him your shirt,' Mama said. 'Thereby making a spectacle of yourself in front of everyone.'

'Oh –' Leon stared at her, and then shook his head. 'That was a *gesture*, a symbol of equality. That kid will remember it, when he's a famous pello player he'll say, yes, I like the Communists, they *understand* –'

Papa raised his voice. 'Leon, I wish you would give this a rest! Not only are your politics adolescent and rather naive, they are *dangerous*. There are men arrested every day for writing things like that, or saying them too loudly, or to the wrong person . . . You have simply been lucky, so far, not to have been –'

'So we should just shut up and let the police get on with it?'

The telephone rang. For a moment we sat without speaking. Then Papa sighed and got up to answer it. We heard his footsteps in the hall, and then the murmur of his voice. When he came back he looked tired. He said, 'That was the Toros widow. I must go.'

'Probably an attack of pique,' Leon said. 'Her famous son getting beaten by a *peasant*.'

'It's not her that's ill,' Papa said. 'It's the Bull.'

No one said anything. Martin looked at me, but I couldn't tell what he was thinking. Papa sighed, kissed Mama, reached for his jacket, took his bag from the sideboard and left.

The pause went on. In the end Mama said, 'Leon, your tie . . .'

He glanced down and hooked it back. It left a trace of

tomato sauce on his shirt, a little river of red. Mama bit her lip.

'Do you think the Bull . . . ?' Martin said, but he didn't finish the question.

'Pello players are as tough as old boots,' Mama said. 'He probably wants some aspirin and sympathy.'

No one replied. I pushed my food around my plate; the little heavy ball of – what? fear? excitement? dread? – in my stomach tightened and tightened.

Leon finished his food with a blank look in his eyes. Then he sat staring into space, rubbing absently at his cheeks, as if he could still feel the tracks of blood and dust sticking to his skin.

Papa didn't come back. The silence grew and grew as we drank our coffee; it hung in the hot air like moisture while Dorotea cleared away our cups, until it felt as if there'd be a storm. As we went upstairs for the siesta I felt the sweat prickling between my shoulder blades and behind my knees. I knew I wouldn't be able to sleep, so I sat at one end of Martin's bed, while he threw a ball against the wall, over and over again.

After a while he said, 'He should be back by now. If it's only aspirin and sympathy . . . Shouldn't he?'

The silence came back, like water soaking up through a sandbag. Martin fumbled the ball and bent to retrieve it. Then he sat on the bed next to me and looked up at the mess of press cuttings pinned to the plaster. I followed his gaze. The Bull with the King's Cup. Hiram Jelek and the Bull together, winner and runner-up of the Euxara Tournament. The Bull serving, in a blur. The whitest, most recent cutting, with Teddy's headline: *LOCAL PLAYER IS THE BEST IN THE WORLD*.

'It's too hot up here,' I said. 'I'm going to sit in the garden.'

'You don't think it could be serious – that there could be something *really* wrong –'

'Martin, for goodness' sake, I don't know! Honestly . . .' I lifted my plait away from my neck and wiped the moisture off my skin. My stomach was churning, but I didn't know why. It wasn't to do with the Bull; or, rather, it *was*, somehow, but to do with Angel Corazon too, and the Zikindi girl . . .

Martin looked at me, his head on one side. He pursed his lips, as if he was about to whistle. Then he shrugged. 'Go on then. I've got homework to do.'

I went. In the mid-afternoon silence the sound of the door shutting behind me seemed to make the whole house shake. I walked softly down the stairs, past the bedroom where Mama was resting, past Leon's room, and down the last flight to the back door. Then I stepped out into the garden and stood blinking in the sudden sunlight.

I hadn't thought about what I was going to do once I was outside, only that I couldn't bear to be shut in Martin's room under the eaves, roasting. I took off my shoes and stockings and ran over the hot stones to the shade on the far side of the courtyard. Then I sat down on the bench, leant my head back against the wall and closed my eyes.

I heard a rustle from somewhere over my head and a little percussive scatter, like a shower of tiny stones.

I looked up, blinking. The Zikindi girl was sitting astride the wall above me, swinging one bare brown foot a little way away from my face.

'Are you awake?' she said.

I shaded my face with my hand and nodded.

'Is the doctor your father?'

I nodded again. I wanted to say something so that I had an excuse to stare at her, but I had no idea what to say. No one I knew ever talked to the Zikindi, apart from telling them they were on private property. I said, 'I'm Esteya.'

'Skizi,' she said, and grinned suddenly. 'Do you want to know something?' she said, as if we were in the middle of a conversation. 'I'll tell you a secret.'

A Zikindi secret. I half expected her to get out a ragged pack of cards, to tell my fortune. I said, 'Do I have to cross your palm with silver?' and then could have bitten my tongue clean off.

She gazed at me, levelly, the warmth gone out of her eyes. She swung her leg up and over the wall, as if she was about to drop down the other side, out of sight.

I said, 'Wait, it was a – I was joking – yes. Please.'

She carried on staring at me; then suddenly she laughed, shaking her head, as if I'd passed some kind of test. She said, 'I could do with some silver, anyway . . .' and spun herself round to sit with both her feet dangling in front of my eyes. They were dusty on the soles, long-toed and bony, and they were the nicest feet I'd ever seen. I forced myself to look at her face.

'Your father went to see the Bull, didn't he?'

'That's not a secret,' I said.

'I know,' she said. 'But I bet you don't know he's dead.'

For a nauseous, spinning moment I thought she meant my father. It was only when she said, 'That boy killed him,' that I realised that she meant the Bull.

'The Bull? Is . . . He *died*?'

She nodded. She had a quiet, triumphant expression in her eyes, as if she'd given me a present and was watching me unwrap it.

'Are you sure? How do you know?'

'They called the priest. And then the widow came out into the street and started howling, like a wolf.' She said it without contempt, as if she liked wolves.

'Are you sure?' I said again, but I didn't need an answer.

Skizi kicked her heels against the wall. From the sound of it I could tell her feet were hard, like hoofs, from not wearing shoes. She let the silence go on for a few more seconds. Then she said, 'It would've been worth a handful of silver, anyway.'

I looked down, into the dark margin of shadow on the ground, and thought of the Bull, flat on his back, bleeding into the dust. I'd wanted that. I'd been pleased.

And Leon, with the Bull's blood on his face: death to the oppressor . . .

When I glanced up again, she was watching me. I said, 'Why did you tell me?'

'Didn't you want to know?'

'Yes – but – why . . . ?' I gestured at the wall she was sitting on, and then towards the street. I meant, why *me*?

She shrugged.

'You followed us home. Me and my brother, I mean.' It came out like an accusation, and I wished I hadn't said it.

'Is he your twin?'

'Yes.'

'I thought so,' she said. 'Yes, I followed you.'

'Why?'

A little crease appeared between her eyebrows, and she laced her fingers together and stared at them. She said, 'I didn't think you'd mind.'

I felt a rush of heat, as if I'd stepped out of the shade. I thought of how Mama would call the police if she knew there was a Zikindi girl sitting on her wall; how Dorotea would come out, cracking a tea towel like a whip to drive her away. Leon would keep his distance and not deign to call her "comrade".

I said, 'No, I don't mind.'

She looked straight into my eyes. I stared back. Her eyelashes were short and surprisingly dark against her eyes. She had freckles across the bridge of her nose and her cheekbones, tiny flecks of brown on golden skin. I thought of my paintbox: gold ochre, Chinese orange, burnt sienna.

The church clock struck four, distant and clear in the heavy air.

She said, 'I have to go.'

'Where to? Where do you live?'

'You go to the nuns' school, don't you? With the red uniforms?'

'Yes,' I said, and suddenly prickled with sweat at the thought that she'd seen me in my uniform, my lumpy red jumper and high red socks. 'It's nearly the end of term, though . . . You –' I stopped. No, I couldn't imagine her in school uniform – in anything other than her shabby boy's shirt and ragged trousers – let alone actually *at* school. It was like trying to imagine the sky wearing clothes.

She laughed. 'Me, at school? No. But I might see you around.' She swung one leg back over the wall, ready to drop out of sight.

'No, wait – wait –'

She stopped, and waited.

I didn't have anything to say. I stared for too long. I blushed again and fiddled with my plait for an excuse to hide my face.

There was a pause. Then I heard her trousers rustle, as if she'd got something out of her pocket.

'Catch.'

She half threw, half dropped something over the wall at my feet. It thumped on the stones and darted into the shadows in the corner of the courtyard, so I had to crouch down and scrabble for it.

The ball. Angel's ball, scratched and dusty, the leather giving at the seams, the stitching darkened and rusty for the length of a fingernail. I held it in my hand, not quite believing it.

'You took it,' I said.

'He left it.'

'I don't believe you.'

Her eyes narrowed. 'Then give it back.'

I looked down at it. The ball that killed the best pello player ever. If she'd stolen it . . . The Zikindi stole everything that wasn't nailed down. That was why no one wanted to get too close – that, and the smell, and the lice . . . But Skizi didn't smell, I thought stupidly. Or if she did, it was of something good, like grass or olive oil . . . I kept hold of the ball, pressing it against my leg like a bruise. I said, 'Give it back?'

She blinked, unsmiling, then drew one knee up on to the wall and rested her chin on it.

I tried to hold her stare. But I couldn't do it. When I looked back at her she was laughing.

'Keep it,' she said. 'You know you want to.'

I felt myself smile, reflecting her grin back to her. 'Yes,' I said. 'Thank you.'

We looked at each other. The sunlight had softened from the midday glare into something richer. She had a sheen of moisture over her cheekbones, deepening the gold of her skin, like varnish. I wanted to touch her.

She raised a hand to me, in a sort of salute. Then she

slid off the wall, disappearing in one swift movement like a lizard, so quickly I hardly believed she'd been there at all.

I brought the ball up to my face and touched it with my mouth, smelling the dust and red-dyed leather. I breathed in, not quite knowing how I felt or what I was thinking. Then I went inside.

That night I couldn't sleep. It was hot; even though I'd opened my window as wide as it would go, there was no breeze coming through it. The moon was lopsided and bright white.

In the room next door, Martin's bedsprings clanked and resonated as he turned over. There was a thump and he swore, as if he'd banged his elbow against the wall. He couldn't sleep either.

There was a noise from the street below my window. A key in a lock; then the front door creaked as it swung open, then slammed. Something made a muffled noise halfway between a crash and a tinkle.

Martin's bedsprings jangled and went quiet. His footsteps crossed the room, from the far corner to the doorway. When I opened my door he was standing on the landing in his pyjamas, looking down over the banisters. He looked round at me, but didn't say anything. When I opened my mouth he shook his head at me.

There were heavy steps coming up the stairs; two, then a stumble and three more, before they stopped.

Martin said quietly, 'It's Papa.'

He'd dropped his bag on the floor when he came in; that was what had made the noise. Now he was dragging himself up the stairs again, with uncertain, clumsy steps.

Martin glanced at me, and in the moonlight spilling

through the window his face was outlined in black and white like a woodcut. 'He's drunk.'

'Don't be silly,' I said, and then stopped.

Papa was on the first landing now. He paused, and took his hat off, looking round vaguely for the hatstand that stood by the front door. Papa never got drunk; but he *was* drunk.

There was the sound of a door opening, and Leon stood in his bedroom doorway, blinking through his glasses. He was still wearing his clothes, as if he hadn't been asleep. He said, 'Papa?'

Papa looked round. 'Leon,' he said. 'Still awake?'

'Yes . . . writing a – something for my – a letter.' A silence. Papa stood still, fumbling at his tie and swaying. Leon said, 'Papa? You're . . . back home very late . . .'

'He's dead,' Papa said.

Leon took a step forward, reaching out as if he was going to take Papa's elbow to support him, but he checked himself. He said, 'The Bull? Dead . . . ?'

I saw Martin rock backwards, gripping the banister as if he was going to lose his balance. He breathed out sharply.

'Deaf, are you?' Papa said, raising his voice. 'Dead. Got a headache, slipped into unconsciousness, and then died. All in – what? – four hours. I expect you're pleased, Leon. "Death to the oppressor." Isn't that your line?'

'No,' Leon said. 'I mean . . . Papa, he's *dead*? I never . . . It was only . . . Papa . . .'

'You disgust me,' Papa said. 'You and your bloodthirsty, childish politics. You should have been there tonight. You'd have been ashamed of yourself.'

Leon stood there, watching him.

'Death to the oppressor, eh? Pray God you never know

what death looks like. A little boy, playing at violence and cruelty . . . Why don't you go tomorrow to offer your respects to the Widow Toros? That will teach you some respect.'

'Papa, you're drunk,' Leon said.

Papa raised his hand, as if he was going to hit him. He stood like that in the moonlight for what must have been ten seconds. Then he dropped his hand and laughed. It didn't sound like his voice.

'My Communist son,' he said. 'What did I do, to deserve you? If your mother could see you now . . .'

There was silence. I felt Martin look at me, but I couldn't turn my head. Leon was very still, the planes of his face pale and smooth, his rumpled shirt like marble. He stared at Papa for a long time. Then he went back into his room and shut the door.

Papa put his hands in his pockets and stood rocking gently, looking at Leon's bedroom door as if Leon was still standing there. Then he made a noise like a hiccup – a kind of hoarse gulp – and turned away. He stepped out of sight, and I heard their bedroom door opening and Mama saying, 'Darling? What time is it? What's wrong?' before Papa shut it again, muffling her voice.

I didn't want to look at Martin, but in the end I had to.

He said, 'The Bull's *dead*.'

'Yes.' I hadn't said anything; I would have had to mention Skizi. But I looked away, ashamed, because out of all of them Martin might have understood.

'You don't seem . . .' Martin cleared his throat, pressing his fingers into the banister as if he was playing the piano: something loud and slow, like a funeral march. 'Don't you care?'

I shrugged.

'We saw him get killed. I mean . . . We saw Corazon *do* it.'

'Yes.'

He looked at me for a moment longer, and then turned and went into his room; but he left the door open behind him. I followed.

Martin walked towards his bed, but he didn't lie down; he just stood there, looking up at the press clippings. Hardly any moonlight came through his window, but there was just enough to see the grey of the newspaper against the plaster.

'Do you . . . ?' He paused.

I waited.

'Do you believe what Leon says, about the revolution coming?'

I don't know what I was expecting him to say, but it wasn't that. I said, 'Sometimes.'

He glanced at me with something warm in his eyes. He said, 'I do. I think he's right. Like before a storm. You can feel something coming. Something's going to happen.' He took a breath. 'It scares me. It scares the hell out of me. It feels like the world's going to end.'

I thought of Papa, drunk, shouting at Leon; of the Bull, dead. Then I thought of Angel Corazon, and the Zikindi girl, and the pello ball under my pillow.

'It doesn't scare me,' I said.

There was a silence. Leon was moving about downstairs, making the floorboards creak.

Martin turned away, tilting his head to look at the grey grainy cloud of newspaper on the wall.

He said, 'I wanted him to lose. I was glad when he got knocked down. I liked seeing the blood.'

There was another pause, as if he was waiting for me to say something.

'I *liked* it,' he said again. 'Didn't you?'

I didn't answer.

He reached up, took hold of the nearest corner of newspaper and pulled, ripping the paper away in a great strip. He let it hang for a moment, tore it loose, and dropped it on the floor. He grabbed at the last rags of grey with both hands, scrabbling at the wall until it was clear, with only the lighter patch of plaster to show where the cuttings had been.

Then he sat down on his bed and pulled his knees into his chest.

I said, 'Martin . . .'

'Go away.'

'It'll be all right.'

'Go *away*,' he said again. So I went.

Three

The schoolyard was heaving, full of red uniforms and faces to match, already flushed and sweaty in the heat. I shouldered my way through, ignoring the snippets of sentences: 'Dead? Really, properly dead? – No, just a *little* bit dead! What do *you* think? – Honestly, where have you been? Haven't you *seen* the papers? My favourite player *ever* – Urgh, no, give me Hiram Jelek any day . . .' Yesterday afternoon, as the news spread through the town, there'd been people crying in corners, sobbing into one another's shoulders; but now everyone had settled down to enjoy the drama. Everywhere there were black ribbons and black garters and black stockings; Ana Himyana even had a huge black rose pinned to her shoulder. I pushed past her, and the silk petals rustled and skimmed my cheek. One of her friends said, 'Hey, watch it!' but I didn't look round. I heard someone else yell, 'Esteya! Is it true your father was –'

I caught sight of Miren across the other side of the yard and made a beeline for her. Good old Miren; *she* wouldn't ask about Papa . . . I threw myself down on our bench, dropping my satchel at my feet. 'Phew, it's hot. I can't wait for the end of term . . .'

Miren jumped and yelped. There was the clink of

glass on wood, a glugging noise, and then a pool of black ink spread out and started to soak into the grain of the bench. A half-empty ink bottle rolled off the edge of the seat and smashed. 'Now look what you made me do!' She was holding a soggy bit of black rag, ink dripping on her skirt.

I swiped at the puddle with my handkerchief, but it turned my hands and the handkerchief black in a few seconds without making any other difference. I said, 'Sorry . . . what were you doing, anyway?'

'Dying some toilet paper black,' she said, looking down at her skirt. She winced and hurriedly put the soggy clump down. 'For a rose. Did you see Ana's? Hers is silk, naturally, but I thought if I . . .' The toilet paper sat in a black mush, oozing ink.

I looked at it, turned the corners of my mouth down and said, 'I'm not sure it's going to work, Miren.'

She nodded. 'I had a black ribbon, but Mama borrowed it, and she said black garters with red socks were cheap and fast, and when I saw Ana's rose . . .'

I looked at Ana and her friends, in spite of myself. She was laughing and stroking her rose with her slim white fingers. She was wearing red nail polish; no one else could get away with that.

'Doesn't it look lovely?' Miren said. 'And the poor Bull . . . I've cut out every single article and photograph. I *wish* we'd been here on Sunday.'

'Why?'

'Because . . . well, you were there, weren't you? It must have been . . . so *dramatic*. The very last game he ever played . . . What was it *like*?'

I shrugged. I didn't want to tell anyone about it; or not Miren, anyway, not like this.

Miren said, poking at the black mess on the bench, 'If my silly cousin hadn't been getting married, I would have been there.'

A shadow fell across the wood, and there was a kind of whispering, over my shoulder. I looked round. Ana's friends were standing there, looking down at me. One of them said, 'Ana wants to talk to you.'

'Tell her to come and talk to me herself.'

They swapped glances; then, without a word, the smallest one detached herself and made her way back to Ana. I couldn't hear what she said, but after a few seconds Ana met my eyes and glided over, graceful as a dancer. She had something in her hand: a little flag of greyish paper, held between finger and thumb as if it might rub off on her skin. She said, 'Esteya Bidart.'

'Ana Himyana,' I said. Miren shifted nervously beside me.

'Your father was the last person to see him alive, wasn't he?'

I shrugged. I didn't ask who she meant by *him*. 'He's a doctor, Ana. He sees lots of people who are ill. Some of them die.'

She tilted her head to one side and tugged at the tiny pearl in her left ear. 'And Leon Bidart is your brother, isn't he?'

'Half-brother,' I said. I could feel the blood already mounting in my cheeks. Most people had gone home before Leon took his shirt off, but someone must have told her . . .

'He writes for the *Clarion*, doesn't he?'

'Er . . . yes,' I said. 'Sometimes. Teddy – the editor – is a friend of his, so –'

'Did he write *this*?' With a quick movement she thrust

her hand out, and the scrap of paper fluttered and then went limp again.

I took it from her and looked down at it.

The picture was of the Bull serving, his face a grimace of concentration, and there was a blurred shape in the foreground that must have been Angel's shoulder or head. It wasn't a great photo, but it showed the Bull clearly enough. The headline was: *DEAD PLAYER LOST LAST GAME.*

Distantly I heard the bell ring, but I didn't move.

Dead hero of the bourgeoisie Pitoro 'the Bull' Toros was defeated in his last ever game, by an unknown peasant boy, the Clarion reveals. In a dramatic prelude to the champion's unexpected death on Sunday, he was challenged to a pello game and was vanquished in front of a crowd of local fans . . .

I looked into Ana's eyes and swallowed. 'He might have done,' I said. 'I don't know. But it's true. Why shouldn't he write it?'

'"Hero of the bourgeoisie"?' Ana said. 'It sounds like your brother, don't you think?'

. . . a symbol of hope for those fighting against oppression . . . the King, who expressed sorrow for Toros's death, may well be uneasy at this salutary reminder of the strength of the working classes . . .

'You're not wearing anything black, are you?' Ana said. 'I suppose that means you don't care about the Bull. Or is it just that you're a Communist?'

'I said I don't know whether Leon wrote that. It might have been Teddy.'

A cool, low voice said, 'Well, Esteya, I hope it *was* Mr Edwards. Otherwise your brother would be guilty of a reckless, selfish act.'

We turned to look. Sister David was there, holding the

bell. She held out her hand for the paper, and the bell's clapper made a little clanking noise as she moved. 'Esteya, please give that to me.'

I handed it to her. She took it and read it, briefly, as if she was already familiar with the contents. She said, 'So you think there is no reason why your brother *shouldn't* have written this, morally speaking?'

'Well – he, the Bull, he *did* lose his last game –'

'I notice that there is no signature,' Sister David said. 'We can hope that your brother, not being a foreigner like Mr Edwards, would know better than to write anything so . . . seditious.' She handed the paper back and gave me a long look that I couldn't read. 'Unfortunately Mr Edwards is being interviewed by the police.'

'What?'

'Please say *pardon*, Esteya, not *what*. Mr Edwards, so I am told, was escorted from his home early this morning to answer a few questions about this article.'

'But –' I felt the pit of my stomach drop.

Sister David glanced from me to Ana, and then back again. There was something in her eyes: not quite sympathy, not quite sadness, but something close. 'Now, let's not dawdle any longer, girls. Didn't you hear me ring the bell?' She looked round, and the crowd that had gathered dispersed rapidly, draining into the schoolhouse through the door marked *PUPILS*. 'Esteya, you can wait here for a moment.'

I stood still by the bench, holding on to the bit of paper so hard I couldn't feel my fingers.

Miren and Ana stayed where they were too, but Sister David ignored them and stepped closer to me. Her eyes were narrowed against the sunlight. 'I'm not going to ask you whether your brother wrote that article or not,' she said. 'I don't want to know. But what I will say is . . . this: be careful, Esteya. Prudence is as great a virtue as courage. No one – *no one* – gains from unnecessary suffering. Do you understand?'

'Who saw Teddy being taken away?' I said. I didn't have time to be polite. 'How do you know?'

It was as if she hadn't heard what I'd said. 'Your brother has made his own choices. He's chosen to put himself in danger. But you needn't let him endanger *you*. Esteya, are you listening?' She held my look for a few seconds longer, as if she was trying to tell me something else silently. Then she walked away, looking to left and right and shepherding the littlest girls into line.

I swallowed. I could taste the egg I'd had for breakfast. The sun was too hot and too bright and there was too much noise. I thought of the police smashing down Teddy's door in the dead of night, dragging him out into the street, shoving a canvas bag over his head and driving him away. I thought of the silence, and the bag sucking in and out as Teddy breathed. He would have panicked; or worse, tried to reason with them. They would have hit him to shut him up.

And he would have been in his pyjamas. I'd seen Teddy's pyjamas, flapping on the washing line he'd rigged up between his windows. They were dark green, with a faded paisley pattern, and an iron-shaped scorch mark on the collar.

Ana said, 'How does it feel, knowing your brother is a murderer?'

I wanted to tell her to shut up, but my mouth wouldn't obey my brain.

Miren stood up, sat down, fiddled with her satchel

strap and stood up again. 'I'm just . . .' she said, and gestured at the schoolhouse door. No one answered.

'Mind you,' Ana said, stroking the rose on her shoulder, 'the Englishman was probably asking for it, wasn't he? If he was stupid enough to let your Communist brother write a cheap, nasty article like that – and then *publish* it . . .'

Something gave way. I heard myself raise my voice, the words blurring and overlapping one another. 'So the police are right to take him away, are they? If the police come for my brother, and my father because he's Leon's father too, and my mother because she happens to be married to him –'

'I'm going inside,' Miren muttered. I didn't turn my head, but I heard her hurry across the yard towards the door. Ana and I were almost the last people left.

Ana said, 'Everyone knows what happens to people who say stupid things. Your brother is lucky he hasn't been arrested already.'

'And Mr Arcos? And Bero and Jone Carkaya? And the priest from Zurian? They all had it coming, did they, for saying that the harvest's going to be bad and the poor people are discontented and the King has a lot more money than anyone else?' I heard my voice get higher.

Ana opened her mouth and then shrugged. 'I'm just saying he's stupid to risk it, that's all.'

I stared at her. I wished she hadn't said something I agreed with.

I said, 'As if *you*'d know what's stupid and what isn't. With that pathetic thing on your shoulder. What is it, anyway? A very small, rotten lettuce?'

'It's a ro–' She stopped. She glanced over her shoulder, and I followed her gaze. Everyone else had gone in. We were going to be late for prayers.

Suddenly she reached forward, grabbed something off the bench and pushed it into my face. I felt a cold, damp mass hit my cheek and wetness trickle down my neck, and smelt ink. I pulled away. She tilted her head, smiled at me and dropped the wet mess of ink-soaked tissue paper on the ground. It landed in a flat, dark splat. I put my fingers up to the wet stuff running down my face and they came away black. When I looked down there was a long stain on my jumper, already starting to soak down into my skirt. My jaw dripped.

'Now you look like one of us,' Ana said. 'Mourning suits you.'

I went to wipe my fingers on my skirt, and stopped myself just in time. I wondered what Mama would say about the stains; ink didn't wash out properly, not ever.

I looked up at Ana. She was smiling, still, and her hair was falling over her shoulder in a perfect curve, as if she was posing for a photograph.

I didn't move.

'Not *very* stylish,' Ana added, 'but then you always look a little bit scruffy, don't you?'

I knew that if I moved, I'd hit her. If I hit her, I'd be in even more trouble. I swung my hand back.

Then, before I had time to change my mind, I turned on my heel and ran through the school gates, out into the street.

I kept on running, with my satchel bouncing on my back and the sweat starting to run down my face. I wiped my cheek and the smear of moisture that came off on my hand was dark grey. I was shaking. The taste of my breakfast came back into my throat, mixed with something bitter, like lemons.

It was so hot. I almost turned on to the high street, from habit, and caught myself just in time. I didn't want anyone to see me, not when I should've been at school. Instead I went back the way I'd come and ducked into an alleyway. It was cool in the shadows between garden walls. I kept running.

And came out into the square in front of the church, in bright sunlight, so suddenly I was dazzled. The church was on my left, and to my right was the pello wall. I looked down and saw that I was standing on one of the painted lines.

There were a couple of old men outside the bar, but no one else. Everything was quiet.

I reached out and touched the pello wall with my hand, tracing the mortar between the stones. My fingers left faint inky traces. Then I sat down, with my back against the wall and my knees up, and after a while I started to cry.

I don't know how long I was there, but what made me stop crying, in the end, was the feeling that someone was watching me.

I looked up. My eyes stung in the light, and I felt the last drops of water slide down my face. My hands, where I'd been covering my face, were wet, the lines on my palms picked out in black.

At first I thought I'd been imagining it. The space in front of me was empty. I turned my head, looking from side to side. I *was* being watched; I could sense it, like something crawling up my spine.

There was a brief movement in the shadows in the doorway of the church.

Skizi.

When she saw me looking she raised her arm and waved at me. There was something odd about the gesture, something a bit clumsy, as though she'd never done it before. Then she dropped back into a relaxed, balanced stillness, as if she was made of the same stone as the church. I wasn't surprised I hadn't seen her standing there. She was like a hunter, waiting.

I stood up, wiped my face again and walked towards her. She had her hands in her pockets, like a boy. She met my gaze, as if no one had ever told her it was rude to stare, and only smiled when I got close.

'Hello,' she said.

'Hello.'

'Shouldn't you be at school?' Her tone was mocking, and she looked me up and down, taking in my crimson, ink-stained uniform. I felt my cheeks flare.

'Shouldn't *you*?'

She grinned at me. I sniffed, squelchily, and shuffled my feet. I felt like a chocolate bar left in the sun, all sticky and oozing.

'Are you being naughty?' she said. 'Did you escape?'

As if rules were inherently amusing, I thought; like banana skins, left on the pavement. Things that happened to other people. I said, 'Have you been watching me all along?'

'Yes.'

I wanted to tell her to go away, that it was none of her business, and what did she know about anything anyway? But I found myself saying, 'Why?'

'I don't know,' she said, but with a thoughtful edge to her voice, as if she was taking the question seriously, at least. She paused. 'I watch lots of people. But you're different. You notice I'm there.'

I sniffed again, swallowing. My breath kept catching and snagging in my throat, like a stocking laddering itself.

'I suppose I wanted you to notice me,' she said, without any particular inflection. 'It's nice. It makes me feel like a person.'

I laughed, without meaning to. It dislodged a fleck of snot from my nose. I wiped my face again, hurriedly, but Skizi didn't seem to register it.

She said, 'Do you know you've got black stuff all over you?'

'Black stuff? As if someone's poured a bottle of ink over me?' I said. 'No, actually it had completely escaped my attention.'

'Oh,' she said. 'Well, you have. Look, on your skirt. And your face –'

I laughed again, more easily. Skizi looked blank and narrowed her eyes at me. It occurred to me, with a strange shock, that maybe she didn't know what sarcasm was.

'Never mind,' I said. I felt better, as if the world was suddenly bearable again. A faint breeze cooled the back of my neck. I was hungry. If I hurried, I could make it back to school in time for English, and then maybe no one would think to tell Mama I'd missed the first lesson . . . I said, 'Listen, I have to go, but –' I stopped. I wanted to thank her: but what for? For watching me? For being there? For making the world all right again? It would sound so stupid.

'Where are you going?'

'Back to school. I have to. I mean . . .'

'Do you? Why?'

I looked at her, and for the first time she moved into the sunlight, so the golden skin over her cheekbones shone. I wondered, distantly, how I'd ever thought Ana Himyana was beautiful. Skizi's hair was matted, falling over her forehead in thick strands of tawny brown, and I wanted to touch it. The neck of her shirt was open and outlined in grime and the dent at the base of her neck was gleaming with moisture.

'Because . . .' I said, and then laughed. Because of what Mama would say. Because it was the right thing to do. Because of the rules. I said, 'No, you're right. No reason.'

We looked at each other, and the world seemed to turn a page: from dense black-and-white to an illustration, picked out in ochre and gold and red.

Skizi said, 'Do you want to come with me somewhere?'

I blinked, blocking out the square and the sky. When I let them back in they were still there: still dazzling, still ruleless.

'Yes,' I said. 'All right. I'll come with you.'

She tipped her head back and grinned at me. With her hands in her pockets she looked like a boy again. 'Aren't you going to ask where?'

'Would you tell me?'

'No.'

'So I won't ask,' I said.

Her grin got wider. She had crooked teeth, and I could see a gap near the back where a molar was missing. She took hold of my wrist, as if it belonged to her, and pulled me out of the shade of the church. I stumbled after her, my satchel bouncing. We ran through the alleyway, left and then right, towards the river, but Skizi dragged me round another corner before we got to the bridge, through a network of passages I didn't know. Then, in a blaze of heat, we came out into the open fields beyond the last house. The path up the hill was wide and baked hard and difficult to walk on in my school shoes. We slowed down, but Skizi kept her grip on my wrist, as if she'd forgotten about it.

I was thirsty. I thought of the rust-tasting, warmish water that came out of the taps at school, and almost wished I was there. I swallowed, and Skizi glanced at me. She said, 'Not far now,' laughing at me, as if she'd heard what I was thinking. She pointed.

In a dip on the slope was a hut, with the roof fallen in at one end and the walls crumbling at the corners. There was a sparse, sad-looking olive tree growing nearby. The land around the hut was deep with thin, dry grass and bits of stone. The Ibarras owned it, but they never bothered to come up the hill.

Skizi let go of my wrist and ran the last few metres towards the hut. She ducked under the lowest branches of the mangy olive tree and swung herself round the door, which was wedged a little way open. I stood in the sun, not sure whether to follow her or stay where I was. After a few moments she came out again, with something in her hands; but she walked through the undergrowth to the other side of the hut, out of sight, without even looking at me. I waited. Up here there was a breeze, and the grass sighed like the sea. The sky was deep blue, almost turquoise.

She came back into sight and made her way towards me, picking her way carefully round the stones as if she didn't want to risk falling over. She held out her hands. She was holding a little handle-less teacup, filled with water. I took it, drank half, and gave it back. It was pretty, even though it was broken: thin, delicate china, with a border of cobalt and gold. When Skizi saw I'd left her some water, she smiled and drank it, raising the cup to me in a kind of toast.

I said, 'Thank you.'

'There's a well, just behind the hut,' she said. 'The water's cool, even in summer.'

'Do you *live* here?'

She shrugged, but it wasn't an answer. Without a word, she went into the hut again, shoving at the door with her shoulder. I waited until she looked round, and then saw from her expression that she was expecting me to follow her.

In the first darkness, after the sunlight outside, I couldn't see anything. There was just a strange, inside-outside smell of dust and crumbling stone and sheets that had been slept in for too long. Then, as my eyes adjusted, I saw that the hut was bigger than it looked from outside, and most of it was intact, apart from the roof. The floor was stone, and the walls were whitewashed, although they were peeling and stained with great irregular patches of soot. At the far end, under the surviving roof, there was a rectangular nest of blankets, and a few things set out neatly on a board balanced on two old tins. So she *did* live here; or at least sleep here sometimes.

She was watching me through the dimness, as if she cared what I thought of it.

I said, 'Doesn't it get cold, at ni–'

I stopped, and took a step forward, staring at the wall. I'd thought they were stains, or burn marks, places where the whitewash had come off or gone black; but they weren't. They were drawings.

She must have done them with a stick of charcoal. They were rough, only sketches, some of them just a few lines. But they were . . . I swallowed, my mouth suddenly dry again. Angel Corazon, darting across the pello court. The Bull, swinging his hand back like a man about to hit his wife. Teddy, holding his camera, trying to keep score and frowning with the effort.

And me. It made me rock backwards, laughing with surprise. My own face, round and heavy-eyebrowed, recognisable at a glance but with a kind of beauty that I knew I didn't have in real life. Martin, only a blurred shape behind me, but still – clearly – Martin . . .

I put my hand up, wanting to touch one of the drawings, and then stopped myself. I still had ink on my fingers, but it wasn't just that. I took a deep breath and stared, taking in the details. The flaking whitewash and the cracks on the surface of the wall showed through the charcoal, distorting the shape of Martin's eye, leaving a dark patch on my neck like a scar.

I said, 'Did you . . . ?'

Skizi nodded, once, her eyes on my face as if I'd caught her doing something illegal.

'They're beautiful.'

She reached out and pressed the palm of her hand against the nearest picture.

'Really,' I said. 'I haven't seen anything like them.'

There was a flash of something in her face, too fast for me to identify it, and then she turned away, hunching her shoulders and pushing her hands into her pockets. Her shirt rode up, showing a glimpse of her back; it glinted gold where a stray shaft of sunlight caught it. She said, 'Thanks.'

There was a silence. The breeze whistled and sang quietly in the roof.

I took a deep breath, and let it out again slowly. 'This man here, the one with the camera . . .'

'The Englishman,' she said, without turning round.

'Yes. He . . . My brother wrote . . . He's the editor of

the *Clarion* and he published an article, saying that the Bull was bourgeois and –'

'What does that mean? Bourgeois?'

'Um . . . middle class and despicable,' I said, and almost laughed, because how was I supposed to explain class struggle to a Zikindi? 'It doesn't matter, exactly . . . But the article was all in favour of overturning the old order, and starting a revolution, and all that, anyway, and – last night, the police came and they took him – they took Teddy away. They arrested him.'

Skizi sat down on the makeshift bed, crossing her legs, and looked at me, listening.

'It was probably my brother – Leon, he was there on Sunday, he wears glasses –'

Without a word she nodded at another drawing on the far wall, one I hadn't noticed: Leon, shirtless, his fist raised in the Communist salute.

'Yes,' I said. 'It was probably him who wrote the article. It's his fault that Teddy got taken away.'

There was another, longer silence: as if she was waiting, patiently, for me to get to the point.

'He wears paisley pyjamas,' I said. 'Teddy does. They took him away in –' For heaven's sake, it was so *stupid*, to think of that . . . I tried to laugh and heard my voice crack. I couldn't go on speaking.

There was a movement behind me, and I felt warmish air on the back of my neck; but I had my hands over my face, pressing, as if I could push the tears back into my eyeballs. I felt the salt water run into my mouth.

And then there were warm hands on my shoulders, so light I only knew they were there because of the sudden heat on my skin, making it prickle under my stiff school shirt. Skizi was standing behind me, very close. I could smell dust, and grass, and something spicy, like tar or woodsmoke.

'Please stop crying,' she said.

I felt the tears dry up, as though the warmth of her hands had got into my body, burning the water away. But Skizi didn't move.

There was silence behind me: a listening, open silence.

I said, swallowing, 'It's not fair. There are all these rules, and if you break them you get punished. But the *rules* aren't fair.'

I could imagine Skizi's expression, the look that said she didn't play by the rules, she was Zikindi, she was outside all that. For a second I felt pure, blazing envy, eclipsing everything else.

Then I turned round. She took a step back, but she stayed facing me, only a little way away. In the sunlight coming from the fallen-in roof, one of her eyes was pale jade green; the other, on the shaded side of her face, was like slate. We stood there, looking at each other, until I wasn't sure if I'd said something I didn't mean to.

Her eyes creased at the corners, although she didn't exactly smile. She said, 'Don't worry about the rules,' and glanced sideways, at the picture of Angel. I thought about him playing – perfectly, fluking every shot, except that you couldn't fluke *every* shot . . . She'd told him not to play by the rules either. And then he'd won.

She put her hand out. My plait had fallen over one shoulder, and she ran a finger down the strands of hair. She did it gently, but the nerves in my scalp sang with electricity.

Then, suddenly, she grinned. 'I'm hungry,' she said, reaching for my satchel. 'Do you have a packed lunch?'

* * *

We sat in the sun to eat, bathing our feet in a trough of well-water. I wriggled my toes and compared my bare feet to Skizi's (darker, cleaner, uglier). We ate my sandwiches and drank my orange squash, and Skizi unwrapped my chocolate biscuit and ate all of it before I noticed.

Then we lay back. The sun was directly overhead, heating my eyelids and cheeks as though I was blushing. I heard Skizi rooting in my satchel, but we'd eaten everything, and after a while she gave up. She lay down next to me, and her sleeve brushed mine. I could smell her, grassy and spicy, like a plant.

I thought about the pictures on the walls of the hut – Angel, Leon, Teddy – and in my mind's eye they began to move, until I was watching Angel play the Bull all over again, except this time I was the referee, and I could make up the rules as I went . . . And I was just on the edge of realising something, of answering my own question . . .

I woke up, with a jerk. I opened my eyes and Skizi was there, watching me.

For a moment, heavy with sleep, I thought I knew what my dream had been telling me. Skizi's face was dim, her head outlined by the sun, and the shadow gave a kind of softness to her features, the gold darkened to bronze, her eyes the colour of moss. A spike of hair hung over her forehead. Her mouth was wet. Something turned over in my stomach. I stayed still, and so did she.

Then I felt a kind of panic wash over me, the way I had before, with Ana: if I let myself, I'd do something stupid . . .

I stumbled to my feet, grabbed my satchel and my shoes and socks and jumper, and struggled away down the rutted path, not looking back. All the time I was expecting her to call after me, or at least ask me where I was going; but she didn't.

I stopped after a little while to put my shoes back on. I looked back, but she'd gone inside the hut, or out of sight.

So I must have been imagining it, when I thought I heard her laugh.

Four

I got back to my form room just as the register was being called for afternoon school. I'd never lied to anyone at school before, but it was easier than I'd thought to say I'd been ill; Sister David only raised an eyebrow and told me to get a glass of water if I felt faint.

I went through the rest of the day in a kind of dream, half ashamed and half excited. I was furious with myself, and strangely shaken, as if I'd come close to some kind of accident; but there was still some magic clinging to everything. The whole world was tinted gold, blazing with sunlight at the edges. After the final bell had gone, Miren followed me through the gates, juggling her exercise books because I hadn't waited for her to put them into her satchel. She said, 'So where did you go? Why won't you talk about it? Is it a secret?'

I thought about what she'd say if I told her, the look that she'd have on her face when she said, '*Zikindi?*' and then, 'But . . . *why?*' And when I couldn't explain, she'd draw away, as if I was infectious, and she'd never be quite the same again.

I said, 'No, it's not a secret, Miren. I just went and sat in the shade because I felt sick.'

'And you know you've got something black all down

your front, don't you? And Ana Himyana was looking at you all the way through algebra –'

'Honestly, Miren, will you give it a rest? Ana threw your attempt-at-a-rose at me, that's all. And then I went and tried to get the stains out. But I *was* feeling ill.'

Miren looked satisfied, as if she'd wheedled the story out of me. Her triumph was so obvious it made me feel ashamed, as if I'd given her a compliment I didn't mean. But I *couldn't* explain about Skizi; it would be stupid to try. I didn't know myself why I'd followed her, or why I'd run away.

We got to the corner of the street, and Miren paused, as if she wasn't sure whether it was safe to let me walk home on my own. She said, 'And you're really all right?'

I was about to keep on walking, but I turned back and looked at her. Her hair had come out of its plait, and was clinging to her face in a kind of frizzy veil. She had a crumb of wood clinging to her chin from chewing her pencil, and her eyes were very wide and blank and shiny. I felt a great rush of sadness, as if I was never going to see her again.

I said, 'Thanks, Miren. I'm really all right.'

Then I leant forward, kissed her on the cheek and walked away.

Our street was very quiet, and even in the shade the stones seemed to be giving off heat. I couldn't find my key – it was probably at the bottom of my satchel, among the old hair ribbons and scraps of paper and broken pencils – so I rang the bell, glad that it wasn't Dorotea's afternoon off. When she came to the door she looked flushed and grumpy, with a pale shiny oil stain on her apron. She stood aside without a word to let me in, and then slammed the door and marched off down the passageway.

I said, 'Thanks,' to her back, and went up the stairs.

She made a noise that was halfway between a grunt and a question. Then I heard her say, 'Esteya? Will you come here a minute?'

For a second I thought she'd found out, somehow, about Skizi. But when I peered over the banisters, she was standing in the middle of the hall, staring at the little table that stood beside the drawing-room door.

I said, 'What?'

She pointed. 'Did your mother move that pot?'

She meant a little silver inkwell, an ugly, ornate thing that someone had given Mama for her thirtieth birthday, just after Martin and I were born. She kept it there so that everyone who came to the house remarked on it as they went into the drawing room. But now there was only a faint circle in the dust.

I felt a slow stirring of something under my heart, like nausea. I said, 'Don't know. Sorry, Dorotea.'

Dorotea's frown deepened, and she went into the drawing room. Through the open door I saw her shadow hesitate, then slide out of sight. She called, 'Esteya! The little statue – the gold crucifix – the *clock* . . .'

I said, 'Yes? What's happened?' but my voice sounded false, as if it was recorded. I hung on to the strap of my satchel, forbidding myself to open it, because my key *was* in there, somewhere. I wasn't even going to bother to check.

'Come here! Look – oh, dear heart of Jesus, everything valuable . . . and I was in there, in the kitchen, all the time – but how did they get *in* . . . ?'

Slowly I made my way down the stairs. I stood in the

drawing-room doorway and looked around at the gaps, the reproachful little absences that I'd hardly have noticed, if I hadn't known to look for them. I swallowed hard, and said, 'You were here all afternoon?'

Dorotea opened her mouth and shut it again, like a fish, and then dropped noisily on to the sofa, breathing heavily. 'Oh, Mary, full of grace! I could have been murdered . . .'

'Are you sure it was today?' I said. 'Maybe the things could've been gone for ages, and you just didn't notice. Maybe one of Papa's patients –'

She sat up, as if she'd had an electric shock. 'Call the police!'

'Are you sure?' I said again, feeling the dread in my stomach wriggle, like something trying to get out. 'I mean –'

'I could have been *murdered*,' she said again, and this time there was an unmistakable note of pleasure in her voice. 'Someone creeping round in here, taking everything they can lay their hands on . . . disgusting, that's what I call it! Probably –'

I said quickly, 'I'll call Papa,' but it was too late.

'Zikindi,' she said. 'Bound to be.'

I stared at her, frozen, as if the word was a curse.

Then I stumbled back into the hall and stood next to the telephone, forcing myself to breathe.

I opened my satchel, upended it on the floor and spread everything out with my foot. There were exercise books and textbooks and bits of paper and even a leathery apple core; but no key. I hadn't expected it to be there. Not when Skizi had rooted through my things, pulling out anything she liked the look of . . .

I put my hands flat on the telephone table, trying to

stop them shaking. Then I picked up the receiver and dialled: not the police, but Papa, at the dispensary. I heard myself give him a brief explanation of what had happened, as efficiently as if I were a policeman myself, not letting him say anything. Then I hung up, gathered my things and went upstairs with them in my arms. Dorotea called after me, but I ignored her.

The door of my parents' room was ajar. I pushed it open, and looked around. I didn't come in here very often, but I knew Mama kept her jewellery on the dressing table, in a little velvet-covered box. The box was there, next to her powder puff; but it was open, and empty.

I leant back against the doorway, feeling sick. I imagined Skizi walking quietly up the stairs, my key still in her hand, and casting a quick, efficient eye over my mother's things. I'd been so stupid. Everyone *knew* the Zikindi were thieves . . .

I couldn't tell whether anything was gone from Leon's room. It was as neat as a cell, with a pile of books on the desk and a pale patch on the wall where the picture of the Sacred Heart had hung. But Leon had taken that down himself.

Martin's room was so messy it looked as if it had been burgled, but the only thing that seemed to have gone was his penknife. The only really valuable thing he owned was his wristwatch, and he was wearing that.

And in my room there was nothing missing; nothing at all. I wouldn't have known that anyone had been in there – except that my ball, the pello ball that Skizi had given me, was sitting in a dent on my pillow. It seemed to be a message, but I didn't know what it was supposed to mean. I looked at it and wished it was still where it had been, in my top drawer, out of sight. I thought of Skizi going through my flaccid, off-white cotton knickers; but instead of embarrassment I felt a sharp pain in my throat, pinching my larynx until I could hardly breathe. I blinked. My eyes were stinging.

Skizi . . .

I sat down on my bed, and waited for Papa to come home.

As Mama listed the things that were missing and pointed to each gap, the policeman glanced dutifully in the right direction, nodded wordlessly and then returned his gaze to his notebook. Papa jingled the small change in his pocket, and I heard Martin sigh. He'd insisted on being there, but I could feel him shifting restlessly on the sofa next to me, as if he was regretting it.

'And there are a few other things missing,' Papa said loudly, as if he was trying to attract the sergeant's attention.

'Yes?'

'My wife's jewellery, for one thing. Nothing priceless, but some items of great sentimental value.'

'Jew-ell-er-y,' the sergeant said, making a great show of writing it down.

'Luckily I don't keep any cash in the house,' Papa said. 'But I understand the thief went through every room – even my younger son's penknife was taken.'

'*Army* knife, Papa,' Martin said. 'My Swiss Army knife, that Grandpa gave me.' He added, to the sergeant, 'It's really Swiss. I think it's worth quite a lot actually.'

'Ar-my . . . knife . . .' the sergeant said. I felt Martin nudge me, but I ignored him.

There was a silence. Finally Mama said, 'Do you think you can catch them?'

I looked down at my shoes, clenching my toes so hard it hurt.

'Well . . .' the sergeant said. 'Probably not. The thing is, there was no forced entry. Just opened the door and waltzed in, you see. Could've been anyone. Not easy things to sell, silver boxes and the like . . . Got household insurance, have you?'

It took me a second to understand what he was implying. When I raised my head, Martin was leaning forward, his cheeks flushed, just about to open his mouth. Papa shot him a look.

'As I've explained, my daughter Esteya dropped her key in the street, this morning, when she was feeling ill. Anyone could have picked it up and decided to help themselves to our things.'

'Ex*act*ly what I was saying, sir,' the sergeant said, and scratched the inside of one nostril with his thumb. 'Could've been anyone. No evidence. Careless of your daughter, I'm afraid.'

'It certainly was,' Mama said. I didn't look at her.

'But . . . well, I sympathise with your loss, of course, sir,' the sergeant said. His voice was greasy and ironic. Papa's jaw tensed and he took a deep breath, as if the words had an extra meaning only he understood. 'But . . . I wouldn't hold out too much hope.'

'This is ridiculous,' Mama said, standing up and straightening her skirt. 'We know perfectly well that there are Zikindi hanging about the town. It seems to me that you would do very well to start with them.'

I swallowed, feeling the heat start to creep over my cheeks, like mould.

'Zikindi?' The sergeant was being deliberately stupid; I didn't know why, but I could see it in his eyes.

I looked at my shoes again, scared someone would notice my face.

'Zikindi are thieves, blood and bone,' Mama said. 'Everyone knows that, surely? Even people who appear to know very little else.'

'We-ell,' the sergeant said, looking at his notebook, as if he hadn't noticed her tone. 'Undesirables, certainly, and we *will* be asking them to move on, but as for your little silver boxes and suchlike –'

There was the noise of a key in the front door, a foot-step, and then the drawing-room door opened and Leon stood in the doorway, sweaty-faced and in his shirt-sleeves. 'Hello. What's this, then? The end of a whodunit? Who's dead?'

The sergeant looked round at him, and the dislike showed on his face, as if the veneer had finally worn through. 'Sorry to say there's been a burglary,' he said. 'And you must be –'

'My son Leon,' Papa said, and cleared his throat. 'Well, thank you for your effor–'

'Papa, you let him into the house?' Leon's upper lip curled, as if he could smell something bad. 'I hope you don't expect the police to do anything except keep a sharp eye out for their own interests. Oh, and beat people up, of course.' He added to the sergeant, 'Teddy home yet?' and then to Papa, 'Better go round to see him as soon as he is. He'll be in need of a bit of work.'

'Leon,' Papa said, 'please don't –'

'*Oh*,' the sergeant said. 'You're the one who likes playing at Communism, are you? We've heard about you.'

'*Playing* at –' Leon began.

'*Leon!*' Papa said. 'Go and check your room to see if anything's missing.'

'No need, sir,' the sergeant said. 'Got all your details. Anything else comes up, let us know. You can send your son down the station, if you want. Kill two birds with one stone.'

'I beg your pardon?'

The sergeant frowned, scratching his head. 'Oh, nothing meant by it, sir, only a joke. Just – well, thievery and the – what's the phrase? – the redistribution of wealth aren't that different, are they?' He nodded to Leon. 'Better watch what you say, sonny. Got away with it so far, but no one's luck lasts for ever.'

There was a silence. Leon took off his glasses and wiped them on his shirt.

Martin said, 'Is it true that Teddy – that Mr Edwards was . . . ?'

The sergeant rolled his neck, making the tendons crack. He said, 'Mr Edwards is having a word with my colleagues down at the station, about an article he caused to be published.'

'"Caused to be published"?' Leon muttered. Mama flinched, but no one else reacted, as if we were all hoping the sergeant hadn't heard.

'Well . . . if that's all . . .' He shut his notebook and pulled the elastic band round it with a snap. 'Good evening, Dr Bidart, Mrs Bidart . . . I'll let you know as soon as we hear anything . . .'

Papa moved the corners of his mouth into a smile and crossed to the door to show him out. I heard him say, 'Thank you for coming, and do excuse my son – students, you know, he's at a rebellious age . . .' Then the front door opened and shut again.

Martin shook his head and hissed through his teeth, glaring at Leon, 'Great idea, Leon! Just insult the police, why don't you? To their faces. Why don't you draw a bullseye on your shirt and invite yourself to the station for target practice?'

'Be quiet, Martin,' Mama said, her voice cracking like a whip. 'Esteya, I cannot credit your stupidity in losing your key! I'm disgusted and disappointed in you both. And as for you, Leon –' She stopped, catching herself, and shrugged.

Papa came back into the room. He looked round at us, dropped into the nearest chair and dabbed at his eyes as if they were hurting. After a while he said, 'I looked after his brother's little girl, when she was ill. Poor little thing. I tried my best, but she was too far gone . . . They had no money, they hadn't wanted to call me in, until it was too late . . . They've never forgiven me.'

'And now they have a reason to hate Leon too,' Mama said. She sounded waspish, but her face was white and strained.

'They don't need *reasons*,' Leon said. 'They're the self-serving skivvies of a corrupt regime, and –'

'Be *quiet*!' Papa said. He took a deep breath and looked at Mama. She returned his gaze, without saying anything.

The silence went on and on. In the end Martin said, 'I'm hungry.'

'Yes,' Mama said, 'I suppose you'd better wash before supper. Esteya, you've got ink all over your hands. I hope you haven't left black fingerprints all over your school uniform . . . Leon, perhaps you could try to look a little more respectable . . . ? And Martin, you've been playing pello in your good shoes again, haven't you? Honestly, I don't know why I bother . . .' Her voice sounded too thin, as if she couldn't catch her breath. She made her way to the door, holding on to the furniture to support herself, like an old woman. 'Go on, children. Do get a move on.'

Leon went out without a word, his hands in his pockets, and Martin followed him, more slowly. I stood up too, but the floor felt soft and wobbly, as though I was standing on a plate of jelly. My stomach ached. I said, 'Sorry, Mama.'

'Oh, Esteya . . .' She glanced at me, and then sat down, very suddenly, on the nearest chair. 'If only you hadn't been so silly . . . we probably shan't get anything back, and that horrid policeman . . . and Leon being so –'

She broke off, and ran her forefingers delicately under her eyes. I realised, with a surge of sickness, that she was crying. I said again, pushing the words out, 'I'm sorry . . .'

'Run away, Esteya,' Papa said. 'We're all a little overtired, with the upset. Go and wash your hands for supper.'

I swallowed, took a last look at Mama and went out into the hall. I shut the door behind me and then sat on the stairs, my head in my hands. I was too tired to wash my hands; too tired to move. I wasn't hungry anyway. I never wanted to eat again. It was all my fault. My fault, for being so stupid, for trusting Skizi, when everyone *knew* the Zikindi were thieving bastards . . . I thought of all the spaces in the drawing room, where Mama's little cherished things had been; and of the sergeant's face when he called Leon a Communist, with that malicious, triumphant edge in his voice – the same tone he'd used when he'd said, *Mr Edwards is having a word with my colleagues down at the station* . . . Now the police had noticed Leon, and that was dangerous. Maybe Papa should never have called them. But if Skizi hadn't robbed us, he wouldn't have needed to. And if I hadn't let her steal my key . . .

The thoughts went back and forth, like a ball smacking against a wall over and over again.

And it was only then that it occurred to me that maybe I should have told my parents about Skizi. I thought of how easy it would be, really: a few days of fury from Mama and cold disappointment from Papa, distaste from Leon, bewilderment from Martin . . . and the police would get back everything she'd taken, and beat her up a little bit to make sure she moved on, and then everything would be sorted out. That's what Miren would do, or Ana Himyana, or . . . well, anyone else. That was how things worked.

I closed my eyes. I saw the walls of Skizi's hut, with lopsided sunlight streaming from the hole in the roof, so the drawings were picked out in random gold: Leon's glasses, Teddy's camera, Angel's beautiful face.

Distantly I could hear my parents arguing, muffled by the door: Mama raising her voice and Papa trying to calm her down. I kept my eyes shut and thought of Skizi.

Then I went upstairs to wash my hands, letting the taps run so I couldn't hear my parents' voices.

I woke up in the middle of the night, jolting out of sleep, and I was on my feet and at my window before I realised I was awake. I stood looking out into the street, bracing myself against the window frame, and took deep breaths of night air, feeling the sweat drying on my skin. Something had woken me. It might have been a nightmare, but somehow I was sure that it was something real: a noise, or someone calling my name, something that meant something . . . But everything was quiet.

I waited until I felt chilly. There was nothing but silence. I took a deep breath, and another, and then slowly I turned away from the window and sat down on my bed. But I wasn't sleepy: whatever had woken me up had woken me up completely, like a bolt of electricity. I leant my head against the wall, wondering if Martin was awake, if he'd heard it too.

And then, suddenly, I realised what the noise was. The front door.

The front door, but no one had come up the stairs. So . . .

I stood up, but I couldn't make myself open my bedroom door. I was cold, properly cold now; but I felt foolish too, half dressed, as if it made a difference that I was in my nightdress. I grabbed my cardigan and wrapped it round my shoulders, and shoved my feet into my shoes. It helped a little, not to be barefoot. Then, gritting my teeth, I went out on to the landing and looked carefully over the banisters. It was dark, and nothing moved; there was just silence.

I wished Martin had woken up. I thought about knocking on his door, but I didn't want to make any noise. I was shaking. I went slowly down the stairs, my skin prickling as I listened; but there was still nothing, no movement or sound. There was only the moonlight, steady and silent, giving everything a faint silver edge.

And when I got to the bottom of the stairs, everything was so dark and quiet that my heart slowed a little. There was no one here. There was only a pale rectangle on the telephone table, grainy and blurry-edged in the darkness. When I picked it up there was just enough light to read *Papa* in thick black ink. Leon's handwriting.

I fumbled, tearing at the envelope, my hands clumsy and sticking to the paper. For a moment, when I got the page out, I thought it was blank. I reached out, finding the light switch with my fingers, and then had to close my eyes as the world leapt into bright yellow, dazzling me. I waited a few seconds, squeezing my eyelids tight against the light, and then opened them. I blinked and looked down at the bit of paper in my hand. The writing on it was thin and spidery, hard to read.

Dear Papa, it said, *By the time you read this I will be on the train to Irunja. It's two o'clock in the morning, and I can't sleep, so I'm leaving now and I'll wait at the station for the early train. I want to be sure that if anyone comes looking for me, I'm not there.*

The relief went to my knees and my heart and my hands all at once. I leant back against the wall, hot and trembling, and heard myself laugh in a quiet alien chuckle that went on and on. I sounded like a madwoman, even to myself, but I couldn't stop. All of a sudden I saw how stupid I'd been, to be afraid that someone had come for Leon; because they pounded on the door, didn't they? They didn't care if they woke the whole household up and caused a panic, and they didn't let people leave notes for their parents . . .

I don't know when I'll see you again. The Party needs me, Papa – more than you do, anyway, or my stepmother. I know you're afraid of my getting into trouble, but don't be. I'm working for a better world, where no one will be dragged away in the middle of the night and tortured and never seen again. You have to let me do that.

Will you tell Esteya and Martin that one of my friends has promised me tickets for the final of the King's Cup? Maybe they can visit me in Irunja then.

With a sudden shock, I realised I was reading someone else's letter. I imagined Mama's face if she saw me, and put it hastily down on the telephone table.

Right now, Leon would be waiting at the station – or outside it, sitting on his suitcase, probably reading a copy of *The Communist Manifesto* by moonlight. He was safe, and we were safe, and even if the policeman came back tomorrow to arrest him, no one would get hurt. I felt the giggles of relief bubble up again. I'd been so scared . . .

I turned around to go upstairs. The little side table caught my eye, and I paused, looking at the space where the inkwell had been. The circle in the dust was blatant in the electric light. Dorotea hadn't even bothered to wipe it away.

I thought I was feeling glad that Leon was safe; but somehow, without anything changing, I knew it wasn't gladness. It was fury. I was so angry I could hardly breathe.

Skizi. This was all her fault.

I couldn't believe the cheek of it. How had she *dared*? The guilt and the hurt faded, until I couldn't feel anything but rage.

It was as if I was watching myself from outside. I saw myself open the front door and step out into the street, head held high, fists clenched at my sides. The door swung noisily shut behind me, but I didn't look round. I saw myself stride away, towards the church, following the monochrome streets, my footsteps ringing out in the dead silence. When I got to the church, I turned left, down the alleyways, trying to remember where Skizi had taken me. I wasn't sure exactly where I was going, but I kept walking and I wasn't afraid, even when I could hardly see anything. I came out by the river and made my way up the hill, through the long grass. Now I could see the path, wide and pale in the moonlight, with low, odd shadows, and the hut and its olive tree, in front of the moon. I sped up, breaking into a run, and my bare feet felt slippery in my shoes.

When I was a few metres from the hut I stopped to catch my breath. Up here the breeze was stronger, and the olive leaves rustled, whispering to me. I was still shaking with anger. I took deep breaths, but my heart was racing and I couldn't get it to slow down.

I walked through the grass to the door of the hut, careful not to kick the blocks of stone that were scattered around. I heard something on the ground scuttle away as I came close. The door was ajar, and it opened loudly as I pushed it, scraping on the ground. I heard a movement from the other end of the hut, where Skizi's bundle of blankets had been.

I said clearly, 'Get up. You dishonest, thieving Zikindi scum.'

There was a patch of paler grey that raised itself, and I saw the glint of her eyes. 'Esteya?' Her voice was thick with sleep; it made her sound very young, like a child.

'You stole my key,' I said. 'You let yourself into our house and took my mother's jewellery and Martin's knife and all the little valuable things. You're a *thief*.'

There was a silence. The world was developing, very slowly, like a photograph: now it was clearer, with subtle, hardly perceptible hints of colour. Skizi was sitting up, her hair over her face, her eyes catching the light.

She said, 'Yes . . . ?'

It took me aback; I'd expected her to deny it. I took a deep breath and tried to remember what I'd been planning to say. 'Well, I want them back. Now. They're not yours. It was a wicked – a wrong – a *horrible* thing to do.' I heard my voice, and wondered why I didn't sound convinced by my own words. 'Give them back *right now*.'

Skizi raised her hand to push her hair out of her eyes

and leant forward, watching me through the dimness. She said, 'Do you need them?'

'No, but – no, but they're not yours. You *stole* them.'

'Yes, I suppose so . . .' she said again. Her voice was quiet and level, as if she didn't understand what I wanted.

I strode into the middle of the room. The holes in the roof threw a pattern of moonlight on the floor, like angular lace. I said, 'Where are they? Where have you hidden them? I want them back *this instant*.'

'All right,' she said. 'If you really need them.'

But she didn't move. I could see her properly now. She was still wearing her grimy shirt. Her neck was only a little bit darker than the cloth.

There was a silence.

She said, 'It must be really hard, fighting to survive in a world where you don't even have a gold crucifix or a little silver box shaped like a heart.'

There was a part of me that wanted to laugh; a part of me that noticed, surprised, that she *did* know what sarcasm was, after all.

I said, 'I could have told the police about you.'

'But you didn't,' she said, and I didn't know whether it was a question.

'Of course I didn't.'

'Why not?'

I stared at her. I said, 'Did you *want* me to?'

She shrugged. 'No, of course not. But most people would have done. I thought you might. I hid everything, just in case.'

There was a silence. I wished I was still angry; it had made everything so simple.

She said, 'If all you wanted was your things, you wouldn't have come here. You'd have told the police.'

'All right,' I said. 'I want Martin's knife, that's all. The folding knife. It's not worth anything anyway. Please. Just that, and I'll go. I won't come back, if you don't want me to.'

'That's all you want?' she said. 'Really all you want?'

I didn't answer. She got up, went to the corner of the hut and knelt on the floor. There was the sound of wood creaking as she levered up a half-rotten floorboard, and she dipped her hand into the dark space beneath it. Then she stood up again and held something out to me.

I took it. It sat heavily in my hand, the metal cool to the touch. Martin would be glad to get it back; I wondered how I'd give it to him, without letting on about Skizi.

'Thank you,' I said. It should have seemed strange to thank her, when she'd stolen it in the first place; but it didn't.

She smiled without meeting my eyes, and touched the knife in my hand with the tip of her forefinger. There was a shaft of moonlight catching her cheekbone, like silver. It made me think of my mother's jewellery.

She said, very softly, 'I didn't take anything of yours . . .'

'I know,' I said.

Everything was very still. Neither of us moved.

I leant forwards, without letting myself think, and kissed her cheek. I just had time to notice that her skin was smooth and cool and slightly damp; then she turned her head to look at me, and her mouth brushed against mine.

I rocked backwards, almost losing my balance; instinctively, to stop myself falling, I grabbed her shoulders and held myself upright. I started to say, 'Sorry –'

And then she was kissing me: fiercely, awkwardly, as though she was thirsty, as though she couldn't wait. Her mouth was hot and tasted of nothing and sent shivers down my back. She was holding me, one hand on my head, one on my waist, so that I couldn't get away, even if I'd wanted to. I heard myself try to speak, idiotically, but she took no notice and there was no time, no space to insist or breathe or think.

I don't know how much time passed before we both ran out of air. Then we separated and stood looking at each other, breathing hard. I started to laugh. Skizi watched me, her mouth in a kind of half-smile. When I stopped finally, she put her hands on my face, tracing the shape of my cheeks, running the ball of her thumb over my mouth. I thought of her drawing my face, how this and that were almost the same thing.

She kissed me again. This time she was tentative, very gentle, as if she was listening for my response; and it was me who was fierce, taking control, not letting her get away.

Somehow, sometime after that, I think Skizi drew me over to her bed. Or maybe it was the other way round.

I made my way home just after dawn, leaving Skizi half asleep and wrapped in blankets against the early-morning chill. I was so tired that I'd come out of the other end of it, like a tunnel, and I was blazing with a kind of electricity, as if I'd give off sparks if someone touched me. I felt like an angel, or a god, as if everything was possible. I didn't have a key for the front door, but I knew I could climb over the back wall, get in through the back door and go upstairs without waking anyone. No one would ever know, unless they could read it in my face. I took deep breaths, wondering whether anyone could see me and *not* know.

When I went past the church I stopped, my eye caught by something on the wall of the pello court. I stood, my arms wrapped around myself, and looked at it.

Words: huge, two-metre-high words, in red paint, and the Communist fist stencilled beside them.

It said: *WE RISE.*

I stood there and looked at it, feeling as if I'd written them myself. *WE RISE.*

And I thought: *Yes*. Yes, we do.

Watch us. We rise.

Autumn

Five

That summer went on longer than usual, baking the earth hard and filling the air with a great veil of dust that shone gold and ochre in the daytime and left a halo round the moon at night. There was no rain, and the sun was merciless, burning clouds away as soon as they appeared. Papa kept getting cases of heat exhaustion – one little boy died of it in August – and the fountains in the town square ran red and brown and then dried up completely. By October you could see fatigue on everyone's face, and hear the beginnings of desperation in the farmers' voices.

But I couldn't have cared less about the weather; except that, if I'd thought about it, I would have been glad that it was warm enough at night to sleep in Skizi's hut, and so hot during the day that we could swim in the river without minding the icy mountain water. We spent whole days and nights together, hiding or running away whenever we saw someone who'd recognise me, and nothing else mattered. I went home for dinner, but the meal passed in silence mostly. In the evenings Papa was too tired to talk much, and Mama's efforts petered out when no one answered her. Even Martin was quiet and pensive, watching me and pretending not to. After a few days of trying to follow me, he'd given up asking where I went. I thought he spent every day alone in his room, or playing pello with one of the stuck-up boys from his school, but I wasn't sure, and I didn't ask. I knew he wouldn't tell Mama that I was sneaking out every night and only coming home to wash and eat, and didn't care about anything else.

And Skizi . . .

Skizi was perfect.

It was the beginning of October, and we were sitting outside the hut. The sun had gone down, and the sky was turning a deeper and deeper blue, as if the world was expanding like a bubble. There was a breeze from the west, blowing cool air into our faces. Skizi had her knees drawn up, and her hands linked between them. I couldn't help stealing looks at her, because she was so still, and so beautiful. After a while she turned to look at me, without smiling, and her gaze was so level and intimate that I had to look away. I could feel her staring at me, and the heat rising in my cheeks.

'See?' she said, with a laugh in her voice. 'All this staring gets annoying.'

'I'm not annoyed.'

'What are you then?'

I shot her a glance, and the gleam in her eyes softened. I thought she was going to touch me, but she just went on looking at me, with a strange half-smile.

'I'm nothing,' I said, at last. 'Stop it.'

She laughed properly then, and dug in her pockets for her tin of dog-ends and cigarette papers. 'Cigarette?'

'No, thanks.' I wanted to kiss her, more than anything, but even now I didn't quite dare to do it – not just like that, while she was concentrating on something else, like constructing a cigarette from the dog-ends she'd picked off the street. Even now, when we kissed, I felt a pang of surprise and helpless pride that she let me near her. I turned my head and forced myself to keep my eyes on the darkening blue-to-black sky. I heard her light the cigarette, and smelt smoke.

'I have to go soon,' I said.

'So go.'

I swallowed. 'I don't know when I can come back.'

She glanced at me and shrugged. 'Come when you can.'

'School starts next week, and . . . and this Sunday it's the King's Cup final, I have to go to Irunja with Martin, Leon got us tickets . . .'

Something flickered in her face, but all she said was, 'Lucky you. You'll see Angel Corazon play.'

'Will I? I didn't know.'

'Against Hiram Jelek or Francois Mendoza. You didn't even *know*?'

I remembered how I'd been before last year's King's Cup: obsessed, scouring the papers for every article, every photo, begging Papa to let me watch the final on the Ibarras' television with everyone else. But this summer I'd hardly noticed; and the only time I thought about Angel Corazon was when I saw his face on Skizi's wall. I said, 'Angel Corazon . . .' and felt a faint surge of excitement, like an echo.

Skizi bent her head again over her cigarette. She said, without looking up, 'I'd like to see that game. It should be good.'

I watched my hand reach out for hers and then stop. 'I wish you could come.'

'No, you don't,' she said. 'You wouldn't want anyone to see me with you.'

'I wouldn't mind . . .'

She looked at me, half smiling, and then tapped her cigarette ash carefully into the grass. 'It's all right. I understand. Look at me. Who wouldn't be ashamed?'

'I'm not. Really, I'm not.' I didn't know if it was true.

She laughed. There was a silence, and I heard the church clock strike the half-hour. I was going to be late, if I didn't hurry.

'Imagine what your parents would think of me. Your mama.'

I shrugged and looked away. It was true that I didn't want anyone to know about Skizi; but not because I was ashamed. I just didn't think anyone else would understand.

She laughed again softly. She'd never heard my mother speak, but somehow she could mimic her to perfection. She said, 'Esteya! What on earth are you doing, with that Zikindi boy? No – oh, heavens! – that Zikindi *girl*? Oh, the shame, the *shame* . . .'

'Shut up.'

'I never thought a child of *mine* . . . Oh, I can't bear it! How could you, Esteya? What have I done, to deserve thi–'

'Shut up!' I was on my feet, dragging her up to face me, my fingers digging into her shoulders. I shook her, hard. 'Stop it. Stop it! You don't know what you're talking about. You don't know *anyth–*'

She tried to wrench herself away, clawing at my hands with her nails. 'You think it wouldn't be like that? You think she'd invite me in for tea? Please, come in, you twisted Zikindi bi–'

'Shut *up*!' I said, and slapped her.

The shock of it stopped us both in our tracks; we stood still and quiet, looking at each other. For a second I hoped, shamefully, that she'd hit me back, and then we'd be quits. But she didn't.

'I'm sorry,' I said. 'Skizi, I'm sorry –'

'It's all right,' she said, shrugging. There was a faint hand-shaped shadow on her cheek, only just visible in the twilight. 'I asked for it, didn't I?'

'No, you didn't. I mean – yes, but –'

'Really, it's all right. It's not the first time someone's hit me.'

I opened my mouth, but my throat had tightened and I didn't know what to say.

'Stop looking like you killed someone,' she said, turning away. 'For God's sake, Esteya, stop *caring* so much. Take it easy. Otherwise you'll never survive.'

'I can't help caring,' I said. 'And I *am* sorry.'

'More fool you then,' she said. 'You're doomed.' It might have been a joke, or it might not.

I said, 'I love you.'

She turned back to look at me, but I couldn't read her expression. There was a silence, as if she was giving the words time to settle. Then, still expressionless, she leant towards me and brushed her lips over mine. It was so brief it wasn't a kiss, but something else. It made me shiver.

'Doomed,' she said again. 'You're doomed.'

The train to Irunja was packed and baking, humid with evaporated sweat and too many people breathing at once. Leon had promised to meet us at the station, but even so Mama's face was tight and unsmiling as she waited on the platform for us to leave. Martin waved as the train jolted slowly into motion, but she only stared at us, lips pressed together, motionless. The night before she'd begged Papa not to let us go, and they'd argued until the early hours of the morning. Martin and I had listened, crossing our fingers, as words echoed up the stairs: *bread riots . . . don't like the things I hear on the radio . . . dangerous . . . only children . . .* We never heard any of Papa's answers, but he won anyway, in the end. We'd only had a few hours' sleep before we had to get up again, and now I felt so light-headed and odd that I almost wished Mama had persuaded him to change his mind.

I leant my head against the window and closed my eyes, feeling the vibrations resonate through my skull. I thought of Skizi, asleep, curled up in just her shirt and with her hair all over her face, the way she'd been the last time I saw her. A flower of warmth unfolded in the base of my stomach and spread downwards.

Martin said, 'Esteya,' and elbowed me in the ribs.

I opened my eyes, ready to snap at him, but he was pointing at the newspaper someone had left on the floor. There was a picture of Angel Corazon, with a footprint over his face, and an article that took up the whole page. The headline was: *THE DEVIL'S OWN LUCK?*

I looked at the photo. Even in grainy black-and-white, he was beautiful. I remembered the way he'd moved, the way he'd known exactly where the ball was going, every time. Angel Corazon . . . even the name had a kind of magic.

'He didn't lose a single point, his last match,' Martin said. 'Not a single point. Imagine.'

'It'll be harder against Hiram Jelek, though . . .' We stared at each other, and for a moment I remembered what it had been like before I met Skizi, when I could think about other things. Martin grinned at me, and I grinned back. 'Wow, Martin – we saw him play his very first match, his first game *ever*, we were there . . .'

'Yes, when we're old and grey we can tell people about it,' Martin said.

'And today . . .' I left the pause hanging, because it was too much to say that he might win the King's Cup. It was tempting fate.

We looked at each other for a few seconds longer, almost laughing with excitement. I wished Skizi was there, but I was going to see Angel Corazon again, see him play pello, and that was something . . .

Martin's smile faded, and he turned his head, as if he didn't want me to see his expression. He said, 'Esteya, where have you *been*? Even when you're at home, you aren't really *there* . . . I miss you.'

'Nowhere,' I said.

He turned back to look at me, opening his mouth, but before he could speak there was a noise from the other end of the carriage. I heard a scuffle and a shout, and then the door burst open and a kid in a ripped shirt flung himself through, almost falling to his knees. Two policemen came in after him, swinging their truncheons. The noise in the carriage faded. Everyone was watching, their faces closed and tense.

The nearest policeman said, 'You haven't got a ticket. Get off the train, you little bastard.'

The kid glanced over his shoulder, tried to speed up, and caught his foot in the strap of someone's suitcase. He tottered for a moment, then fell forward, landing heavily, only a few feet away from me. He had a red patch on his forehead that looked like it would be a bruise, later. He couldn't have been older than I was. He said, 'Please . . .'

The other policeman took a deep breath, looked round at the people in the carriage, and said, 'Hey, mate, let's just leave it, OK? He's only a kid . . .' His face was gaunt and unshaven and he had purple bags under his eyes. There was a rusty brown stain across his shirt, just where it said *IRUNJA POLICE*.

The policeman nearest us snorted, and charged down the aisle. He grabbed the kid's collar and twisted, so that the kid choked and swung round, scrabbling at his neck. 'Get – off – the – bloody – train!'

'But – I want to go to –' The kid struggled for breath, his eyes watering. No one in the carriage moved.

The policeman half lifted, half pushed him down the aisle, past where we were sitting, and through the door behind me. I didn't turn round. There was a metallic kind of bang, and a gust of air and dust blew into our faces. There was a scream too: a brief, cut-off kind of scream.

And silence. It was real silence, somehow, even though it was filled with the clank and rumble of the train's wheels. No one looked at the other policeman. We kept our eyes lowered, our faces deliberately blank. For a moment the air crawled on my skin, like the heaviness before a storm, unbearable; but slowly, unbelievably, the sounds in the carriage bubbled back to normal, and that terrible expectant silence was gone. Or . . . not quite gone. But hidden.

We looked out of the window for the rest of the journey, without speaking, trying to pretend nothing had happened.

The streets of Irunja were full, packed with people sweating in the heat and elbowing each other, everyone fighting to get to the arena. Every bar had a notice in the window

– *TELEVISION HERE* – and people spilling out of the doorway, clutching their drinks. Leon's grip on my wrist tightened, and he pulled me closer to him, as if the flood of people could sweep me away. On the other side of me, Martin had looped his fingers through the belt-loop of my shorts, and every time he took a step the waistband cut into me. It was hard to breathe in the crush. Leon was swearing quietly under his breath.

Martin said, 'Well, Irunja isn't how I remembered . . .'

I glanced at him and shrugged. Irunja wasn't how I remembered it either – last time it had been quiet, cleaner, with fewer beggars and no overflowing drains – but then neither was Leon. I wondered what Papa would say if he could see Leon like this, pale and thin and with a dark, louring look in his eyes that he hadn't had at home, even when he was at his most fervent.

'See the banners?' Leon said. 'That's the arena, there.'

They were red and green, two long, thin flags hanging slack in the heavy air. I felt my heart give a funny bounce. Red and green, Hiram Jelek and Angel Corazon. I glanced around and imagined the roar of this crowd, the people in the bars, the *noise*, when the game started . . . I caught Martin's eye, and he stared back, as if he was too excited even to smile.

We had to batter and push through the crowd, as if it was a wall; but finally we went past the guards checking tickets, past the policemen, who looked us up and down with their hands on their guns, and got to our seats in the stand on the north side. Leon wiped his glasses on his shirt, glancing round. He looked tired. When he caught my eye, he smiled, but as if it was a duty.

'Thanks for the tickets, Leon.'

He shrugged.

‘Papa said he hoped none of your professors saw you and disapproved.’

‘My prof–’ Leon started to say, and then stopped suddenly, as if he’d caught himself before he made a mistake. ‘Oh. Yes. No, well . . . they’re working us pretty hard, but, well, pello, you know . . .’

Martin had turned his head to stare at him; now he narrowed his eyes. ‘You do still *have* professors, at the university?’

‘Of course. Don’t be stupid,’ Leon said, peering over the shoulder of the woman in the seat in front, trying to read her programme.

‘And you are . . .’ Martin said slowly, ‘you are still studying at the university?’

Leon’s jaw clenched, but he carried on staring at the woman’s programme. He said, ‘Hmm . . . Hiram Jelek has to be the favourite . . . but Angel Corazon, well . . . yes, of course, Martin, why wouldn’t I be?’

‘Just . . .’ Martin looked at me, swallowed, and didn’t finish his sentence. We both knew that Leon was lying: there was no point talking about it any more.

And then the referee appeared, in neat black and white, with his notepad and his striped flag and the white silk bag that held the ball. He was followed by an official who stood in the middle of the court with the King’s Cup in his hands and announced something. The crowd was roaring so loudly no one could hear what he said, but it didn’t matter because there was a drum roll, and someone drew aside the curtain over the entrance to the tunnel of draped red-and-green silk that led from the changing rooms.

I saw the announcer’s mouth make the shape of ‘Angel Corazon’.

My heart pounded in the roof of my mouth and behind my eyes, as if it was inside my skull.

He came out into the arena, blinking a little in the sunlight. He was smaller than I remembered, and more muscular. He was wearing clean clothes with a green sash, and even though the noise was deafening he hardly looked at the crowd, just stared at the wall and then at the ground. But he was still beautiful.

'Hiram Jelek,' the announcer said. I didn't think it was possible for the noise to get louder, but it did.

Hiram Jelek had been one of my favourite players, before I'd seen Angel play. He was big but elegant, with a film-star moustache and dancer's feet. He bowed to the crowd, his hand over his heart, and a few wilting red flowers pattered down on to the clay around him. Someone – a woman – shouted, 'Marry me!' and a younger woman shouted, 'No, marry me, she only wants you for your money!' The crowd laughed. Hiram Jelek winked, and said something to the referee, who guffawed as if it was terribly witty. Then he turned and shook hands with Angel, adjusting his red sash with the other hand. He wore it over his shoulder, with panache. I noticed suddenly how many people in the stands were wearing red.

'Five minutes warm-up,' the referee said, still beaming at Jelek. He nodded to the other official, who passed Jelek a string bag of warm-up balls. Angel stood still, his face set, waiting for Jelek to take his place on the court. I could see his hands trembling.

They started to warm up. The noise of the crowd faded a little. The balls bounced back and forth against the wall, fast but straight, and both players shifted lightly from foot to foot between shots. They looked like friends having a knock-up; but you could see the tension in

Angel's shoulders, the gleam in Jelek's eye when he broke off to wave at someone in the stands and inclined his head when the crowd applauded. I didn't want to think he was doing it on purpose, to put Angel off, but there was something in the quirk of his mouth, under that flamboyant moustache . . . Leon leant his chin on his hands, frowning; on the other side of me, Martin whistled tunelessly through his teeth, as if he was sizing up the players' form.

Martin said, 'He looks tense, doesn't he?'

'Big occasion,' Leon said, without looking round. 'Lone peasant standing up against the full weight of the established order . . .'

Martin started to say, 'Oh, for heaven's sa–' and then subsided, rolling his eyes.

'He beat the Bull,' I said. 'And the Bull beat Hiram Jelek.'

'Yes, but only a couple of times, years ago,' Martin said. His tone was reasonable, academic, and I wanted to hit him. 'You have to say Corazon's the underdog . . .'

Now they were practising serves. I watched Angel, and the cold hole in my stomach got bigger. He didn't look good. His serves were clean, but straight and slow, and he was frowning every time.

Martin nudged me with his shoulder. 'It's only a game, Esteya. Relax.'

'He had nothing to lose, before,' I said, and my voice sounded hoarse. 'Now he's under pressure.'

Jelek served with his last ball, and nodded to himself, looking satisfied. He walked to the sideline and stood with his hands on his hips, watching Angel. His smile broadened, and he bent, picked up one of the flowers on the clay and tucked it jauntily behind his ear.

'He's going to lose,' I said. 'Angel's going to lose.'

Martin shrugged. 'Yes, I know,' he said.

The referee rapped on his desk, and the crowd settled to a kind of murmur. 'Ladies and gentlemen, the final of the King's Cup is about to start.' He cleared his throat, and glanced at the royal box, which stood on stilts at the back of the west stand. 'Due to unforeseen circumstances, His Majesty has been unable to join us, but . . .' He faltered, and then gestured rapidly at the players, beckoning them forward to bow anyway. They swapped a look, then Jelek shrugged and bobbed his head at the empty box. Angel frowned, and looked around, as if he was waiting for someone else to tell him what to do. The murmur of the crowd got louder, and now there was a strident, cheated note in it: they'd been looking forward to the King's grand entrance. It was traditional. And now the players had to bow to nothing . . .

Leon said, 'The King's a coward. Scared he's going to get shot. Scared someone'll notice how fat he is, and cart off his carcass to feed the hungry masses . . .'

Martin said, 'So who's going to present the Cup, at the end?'

The crowd muttered and subsided slowly. Angel nodded to the box, still looking as if he didn't understand what was going on. Then he walked back to the middle of the court. My heart was banging against my ribs, and the atmosphere was already simmering, as if the crowd's resentment only increased their excitement. I took a deep breath, scanning the rows of people opposite.

There was a still, pale face that caught my attention: a grimy, golden, intent face, with dusty hair falling over the forehead, and narrowed blue-green eyes . . .

Skizi.

I felt my heart stop, and start again; and as if she felt my gaze, she looked straight into my eyes, and smiled.

The referee said, 'First game, Mr Jelek to serve. And . . . play.'

Six

I stared at Hiram Jelek, the blood rushing in my ears, my eyes refusing to focus on the ball in his hands.

Skizi, here.

How did she . . . ? Part of me wanted to know how she'd got a ticket – how she'd got the *money* for the ticket – but the rest of me didn't care. She was here, and suddenly my heart was racing even faster than it had been, and my bones were singing.

The crowd quietened down, and I heard the grunt and smack of Jelek's serve. Someone's shoes skidded on the clay, and the ball thudded on the line. I saw it through a haze. The official called, 'Out,' but his voice and the applause at the end of the point were muffled, as if I had cotton wool in my ears. Skizi, here . . .

I kept my eyes on the court, my face blazing, praying that Martin wouldn't notice anything.

'Ten love,' the referee said.

I didn't even know who had won the point. I turned my head and looked at the blackboard. The girl chalking up the points was simpering, brushing her hair back over her shoulder, trying to catch Jelek's eye. *CORAZON v JELEK, 0–10.*

Then I looked again at Skizi. She was watching, still as

stone. Most people were looking at Jelek, who was about to serve again; but she was staring at Angel. I wondered if we two – we four, with Martin and Leon – were the only people rooting for him. Surely he had family here, or friends . . . ? But I scanned the front rows of the stands, where they would have been – where Jelek's glamorous wife and younger brothers were sitting – and there was no one wearing green. I suddenly wished I was.

I clasped my hands in my lap, squeezing until it hurt, and watched Jelek serve.

He served well. It was lethally fast, and it spun off the wall and went wide, just clipping the sideline. Angel moved, but not fast enough, and he seemed to catch his foot on something. He stumbled sideways, too late.

'Fifteen love,' the referee said, and the crowd cheered.

Angel managed to get his hand to the next serve, but his return was straight and slow. Jelek had time to adjust his stance, twist backwards and then put his whole weight into smashing the ball straight back at Angel's face. Angel made a surprised, frightened noise, like an animal, and ducked. Everyone laughed; and it *was* funny, or should have been. Someone called out, 'Careful of your good looks, mate!'

The ball bounced a good two metres inside the court, and rolled to a stop. The referee said, 'Twenty-five love.'

'What's *wrong* with him?' Martin hissed. 'He looks like someone drugged his coffee.'

I shrugged. My mouth was too dry for me to speak.

Jelek took the ball from the official, rolling his shoulders, and then stood for a few seconds flexing his wrist and bouncing a little from foot to foot. Angel stared at him, a crease between his eyebrows, and I felt a surge of frustration, that after all the other matches he'd played he *still* wasn't used to a bit of gamesmanship . . . I wished Skizi would call out to him, the way she had when he played the Bull.

Finally Jelek served, and it was as good as I expected it to be. This time Angel lunged for it, stumbled, and fell over his own feet. He dropped to his knees on the clay, catching himself awkwardly on his hands.

'Thirty love,' the referee said. His voice was very flat.

The crowd had started to mutter restlessly: the excitement was turning to resentment. They'd paid to see a proper match, not some clown who couldn't find his backside with both hands . . .

Angel stood up. His face was very white, and I could see his hands still shaking, even from where I was sitting.

Jelek got ready to serve again.

'I don't want to watch this,' Martin said. 'This is going to be horrible . . .'

He was right. I didn't want to watch it either. Instead I looked at Skizi, staring and staring, trying to imprint her face on my retina. I thought of what she looked like when we slept together – mouth open, a crease between her closed eyes – and the shape of her body, small breasts, thin sinewy limbs . . . I thought about the smell of her bed, the musty blanket and indoor–outdoor smell, and about the drawings on her wall, beautiful and primitive, like cave paintings . . . I shut my eyes and tried to remember exactly what it had been like the first time we kissed. It made my heart beat faster just to think about it, and the hard, cold weight in my stomach softened. Somewhere a long way away the crowd applauded half-heartedly, jeered a little, muttered and unwrapped sweets and flapped their programmes. There was the thud of the ball, then a pause, another thud, shoes skidding on clay, more muttering . . . The referee said, 'Thirty-five love . . . love thirty-five . . . thirty-five love . . . forty-love . . .'

'He hasn't got a *point* yet,' Martin said. 'Come on, Corazon, go for his head, like you did with the Bull . . .'

I tried not to listen. Skizi, I thought. Skizi . . .

'Forty-five love,' the referee said, as if he was bored, and then, 'Game, Mr Jelek.'

Martin caught my eye, and grimaced. 'Best of five, Esteya,' he said. 'There's hope yet.'

'Not the way he's playing.'

'He's only a kid, anyway. Maybe he'll win it next year.'

I shrugged. Opposite me, Skizi was watching Angel. She looked very serious, as if she was praying. Suddenly I realised that the grass stains on her shirt were in a wide band, across her chest, like a sash: she'd stained her shirt on purpose, because she hadn't got any green material. I felt a surge of something like amusement and jealousy, mixed.

'Second game, Mr Corazon to serve. And . . . play.'

To my surprise, he served well, and Jelek only just managed to get his hand to it. It smacked against the wall and came back wide, where Angel could lunge for it and send a gentle little lob looping back against the wall. It grazed the stone – just *brushed* the stone – and then dropped, dead weight. Jelek had run forward, but he swiped at the ball too soon, and hit it too hard. It shot past Angel, and bounced beyond the baseline.

The referee cleared his throat, and said, 'Ten love.' He sounded relieved.

The crowd cheered, although there was an ironic note underneath the encouragement.

'There, you see?' Martin said. 'It'll be all right. He was just nervous.'

But he was still nervous; in fact, he looked even more tense, as if that point had reminded him of what he was playing for.

He lost the serve on the next rally.

I glanced sideways. Martin was chewing his bottom lip, his chin propped on his hands. On the other side of me, Leon was glowering. And in the stands opposite, Skizi was sitting still, so still . . .

At least now I'd stopped hoping. I forced myself to breathe slowly, not to feel anything, while Jelek tore Angel apart. Jelek wasn't even playing that *well*; it was just that Angel was like a rabbit transfixed by a weasel. I watched in a kind of miserable trance. That game passed very quickly. The final score was fifty fifteen.

The excitement had gone out of the crowd now. They'd wanted to see Jelek win, most of them, but not like this, not so easily. A couple of people shouted insults as the players had their break. Angel glanced up, hunching his shoulders as if the words were missiles. And if it went on like this, someone probably *would* throw something – an apple core or a tomato, if he was lucky; a penny or a glass bottle, if he wasn't.

'Time, please. Mr Jelek to serve. And . . . play.'

I watched the players walk back to the middle of the court, and wondered dully whether we'd be able to get an earlier train home than the one Mama had decided on.

Jelek's serve was sloppy, and spun away out of the court. His second serve was a little better, but it was out too. It was Jelek's first double fault, and the crowd whistled and booed, as if they couldn't believe that now *he* was playing badly too.

A man in the stands opposite, just in front of Skizi, stood up and shouted something. He brought his hand up, jerked it forward in what I thought was the Communist salute, and then –

But it wasn't the Communist salute.

And the bottle he'd thrown spun end over end so fast I only caught a glimpse of it, curving through the air towards the players.

No one seemed to see it. No one reacted. The world stood still, and the only thing moving was the bottle, flashing in the sunlight, blurring, lethally fast. From where we were sitting, you couldn't tell which player it was aimed at – where it was going to land, which face it was going to smash –

I saw Skizi's mouth open, her whole body jerk forward as she yelled. I couldn't hear her voice, but her lips made the shape of, 'Angel!'

And somehow, magically, he looked round.

I have never seen anyone move as fast as Angel did at that moment.

Suddenly he was there, next to Jelek, with his hand in front of his face as if he was shielding his eyes from the sun.

And the bottle was in his hand, intact.

There was a moment of stillness. Jelek stared at him, his eyes wide. Then he glanced up at the stands, taking in what had happened. His mouth opened, and then closed again. He cleared his throat. In the silence it made a hoarse, dry sound.

He said, 'That would've hit *me* . . .'

'Oh,' Angel said. He hunched his shoulders and bowed his head, as if he'd done something wrong.

'Bloody hell,' Jelek said. He looked at the stands and back at the bottle in Angel's hand. 'Bloody hell,' he said again, shaking his head. 'If you can do *that*, then what the hell . . . ?' He started to laugh.

Angel frowned, and he followed Jelek's gaze, staring at the bottle in his hand as if he was seeing it for the first time. He said, in a small voice, 'I just . . . thought . . .'

Jelek was still laughing. And slowly, with a kind of warm rumble, the audience joined in. Angel raised his head, and you could see that for a moment he thought everyone was laughing at him. Then the cheers began, and someone in the top of the stands started to chant: 'Ang-el! Ang-el!'

Jelek's grin faded, but he slapped Angel on the shoulder and winked at the audience, as if Angel was a fan who wanted his picture taken with him.

The referee blew a short blast on his whistle. The audience subsided, but they were still clapping, and Angel was looking round with an incredulous expression in his eyes. You could see he was confused – as if, as far as he was concerned, he hadn't done anything special – but he had colour in his face now, and a spark in his eyes.

And Hiram Jelek, I noticed, was looking definitely tight-lipped.

'Love all,' the referee said. 'Mr Corazon to serve.'

Angel served. It was a soft, wide-angled serve, that seemed to bounce off a hidden dent in the wall, and just clipped the line. Jelek hit it back, with a grunt, and Angel's return was straight and low. The rally went on, shot after shot, the longest of the match so far. Jelek was suddenly having to fight; and he didn't like it. He grunted again and smacked the ball, aiming for the corner of the court, and it flew over the line and hit the referee's chair.

'Five love,' the referee said.

And slowly, without doing anything spectacular, Angel

went on getting points. I wouldn't have recognised the way he played – nothing fluky, nothing clever – but it worked, all the same. Ten, twenty, thirty . . . Jelek was getting rattled, and he made mistake after mistake, while Angel just kept on playing.

And between the points, there was a new note to the audience's noise: a kind of hum of surprise and pleasure. They might see a decent game, after all . . .

'Forty five,' the referee said.

Angel served. It was his first really fast serve. Jelek didn't move: he just stared at the little puff of paint where the ball had landed on the line, and shrugged, shaking his head.

'Forty-five five.'

And the same serve again, precisely; except that this time Jelek scowled, and spun on his heel to walk back to his bottle of water and his towel.

And the audience erupted.

'Game Mr Corazon,' the referee must have said, but no one heard him. 'Mr Jelek leads, two games to one.'

'My God,' Martin said, shouting above the noise. 'I can't believe it.'

Leon turned and said, 'It's just Jelek, being surprised that he can play at all. Once he's got used to the idea, he'll start playing properly again. You watch.' He added, almost to himself, 'They always underestimate their opponents, the upper classes . . .'

But Jelek didn't get used to the idea. When they walked back into the middle of the court he seemed distracted, and when the audience yelled he looked round, scanning their faces. He kept smoothing his moustache.

And the next game went quickly. It was funny, because Jelek wasn't exactly making mistakes any more; it was more that he seemed to be moving too slowly, not quite matching Angel's pace.

'Forty twenty,' the referee said. His voice had taken on a new authority.

The shouts of 'Come on, Hiram!' and 'Come on, Angel!' built to a crescendo and then died away. There was quiet again, only broken by the claxon of a police car a long way away.

Martin whispered, 'Breathe, Esteya.'

Angel served. Jelek returned it. Then Angel sent it skimming vertically up the wall – it looped high over Jelek's head – and it dropped just inside the baseline. In.

'Game Mr Corazon. Two games all . . .'

The noise smashed into us, so loud my ears were hurting.

The referee let the players take a longer break than normal. Jelek took a gulp of his drink, gargled and spat, then wiped himself vigorously with the towel; but Angel only wandered over to the wall of the court and stood staring at it, without even remembering to have a drink.

The referee took a deep breath, and said, 'Final game. Mr Jelek to serve. And . . . play.'

Angel turned and walked back to the middle of the court, still staring over his shoulder at the wall, as if he was trying to learn it by heart. Jelek stared at him for a long time. Then, with his jaw clenched, he took the ball from the official and served.

Jelek wasn't in the lead any more, but he wasn't the best player in the country for nothing. When he served you could see, just from that one shot, that he wasn't going to go away.

But Angel was playing well now. No, not *well*. He was

playing . . . unbelievably. It took a player like Hiram Jelek just to hang on to him. Everything seemed to be on his side: the ball, the sidelines, the wall . . . He did things that looked impossible, shot after shot, so even the people who hadn't seen him play before started to realise that he wasn't fluking anything. It wasn't the devil's own luck; it was genius.

But Jelek was good, and he didn't give up.

The roar at the end of each point was deafening; and then it dropped into a silence so dense that it seemed as loud as the noise had been. I couldn't breathe. My throat was dry and aching, and I realised I'd been shouting, along with everyone else. I couldn't look anywhere but at the court, at Angel . . .

The serve swung back and forth. Twenty twenty-five. Twenty-five twenty. Twenty twenty-five . . .

When the score finally changed – thirty twenty, Angel's serve – the roar was so loud I felt the vibrations in my bones, like thunder right overhead. I was yelling too, but I couldn't hear my own voice. The stands were trembling under our feet, as if the noise could split them apart like a ship in a storm. Two more points, two more points . . . but there was no room to think, only to watch with my heart in my mouth, holding on to Martin's hand as if I was in danger of being washed away. My pulse was shaking my whole body, saying: oh please, oh please, oh please . . .

'Quiet, please,' the referee shouted, pounding on his desk with his fist over and over again until, gradually, the crowd subsided.

And then the silence was like nothing I'd ever heard before.

I didn't want to watch – I *couldn't* watch – but I

couldn't close my eyes or look away either. Angel took the ball from the official, took a deep breath, and then served. He snatched a little at the serve, as if he didn't want to think about it too much, but Jelek wasn't quick enough to do anything more than smash it back against the wall. And neither player seemed to want to take a risk: shot after shot went into the middle of the court, bouncing at an easy height.

It was Jelek who made the first move: suddenly, as if he'd had enough, he sent the ball spinning off the wall and into the far corner of the court. But Angel was there, smacking it back, dancing out of Jelek's way to avoid a collision.

I held on to Martin's hand, hardly realising I was doing it, while the shots got more and more outrageous, the returns harder and harder.

Martin hissed, 'Esteya, let go of my hand, will you? I might need my fingers, one day.'

Jelek's next shot took the pace out of the ball, so it bounced off the wall and dropped dead weight to the ground. Angel did well to get to it, but he didn't even seem out of breath. He knocked it upwards, almost vertical, so it brushed the wall and looped back over his head towards the back of the court. I thought it was going long, but Jelek jumped and smashed it back before it bounced.

And missed.

'Forty twenty,' the referee said.

Angel served. Jelek returned it. And then – as if he was just playing against the church wall somewhere, mucking about with a friend – Angel knocked the ball against the wall, straight and low, and sent it wide. It shot sideways, almost parallel with the wall, and hit the line in a puff of white dust.

Jelek stood in the middle of the court, his shoulders sagging.

The devil's own luck, I thought. But it wasn't luck.

The referee said, 'Final game and match, Mr Corazon.'

It was like being in the middle of an explosion. The noise clawed at my eardrums, shook my bones, made the stands shake, like an earthquake. I was shouting – I couldn't help myself – but I had my hands over my ears, trying to keep out the uproar.

And Skizi was shouting too, with one fist in the air, as if she was giving the Communist salute.

It went on for so long I thought it might never stop. But in the end it faded: not stopping, but receding a little, as if the tide had gone out.

Jelek had gone over to his chair and was wiping himself down, flicking the towel furiously, as if he wanted to hit someone with it. But Angel was standing in the middle of the court, his mouth open and eyes blank, totally still. He didn't even look happy; just completely stunned. A few photographers had raced to the front of the stands, and tomorrow Angel would be on the front of all the papers.

'He looks like the village idiot,' Martin said. 'Honestly, he's practically dribbling.'

The referee got down from his chair and nodded to the official, who disappeared into the red-and-green tunnel and then re-emerged, holding the King's Cup. It was smaller than I expected, but the wide, two-handled bowl shape was familiar. I could have drawn the King's Cup with my eyes shut.

And when Angel saw it, he unfroze. A slow, wonderful smile spread over his face, and he made a tiny movement with his hand, as if he couldn't wait to touch it.

Martin asked again, 'So who's going to present it? If the King isn't here?'

And the same question seemed to have occurred to the crowd, as the murmur grew louder again, with an aggressive, mutinous note to it. Jelek glanced round, up at the box, and then shrugged. *He* didn't care; it wasn't as if *he'd* won the Cup . . .

The referee said something quietly to the official, and then announced, 'Ladies and gentlemen, I will now, as His Majesty's appointed delegate, present the –'

But he didn't finish the sentence. The buzz of anger got louder and deeper. The crowd was supporting Angel now: after the game he'd just played, they couldn't believe the *referee* was going to present the Cup . . . An apple core flew from the back row and landed damply on the baseline of the court.

And then there was a bottle, and another, smashing on the clay like little glass bombs. The referee drew back, pulling the official with him, and glanced over at the ranks of policemen who had been guarding the ticket gates. They had their hands on their truncheons, and one of them nodded at the referee.

But the crowd on the east side was overflowing the stand, surging and pushing at the barriers, catcalling and raining pennies and bits of rubbish on the court. A tomato hit one of the policemen, and he swung round, scowling.

I was glad Skizi was in the stand opposite, not on the east side, where the trouble was. In spite of the sun I felt cold.

The referee took the Cup from the official, and said, 'On behalf of His Majesty, it's my duty and honour to present the –'

Angel took a step forward, beaming. But the noise from the east stand was overwhelming. The barrier was being battered down, and at the back of the stand there was a group of young men throwing everything they could get their hands on. The policemen were shuffling and glancing around, as if they were waiting for an order from someone.

There was a shout from the royal box.

The referee turned to look; so did the players, and the policemen.

One of the young men – a kid really, a skinny, shaggy kid in a brown shirt – had climbed into the box somehow, and now he was standing on the throne, dancing a little jig of defiance. He shouted something, his whole face distorted, and then swung his arm back and threw a coin. One of the policemen cried out and stumbled back, blood running down his face. There was a crack, as if one of the stands had given way, and the kid in the box dropped to his knees, with a dark patch on his shirt.

Not everyone noticed. The barrier fell with a crash, and people surged on to the court, shouting, pushing the policemen, trying to grab their weapons.

But I saw the blood spread out from the bullet wound in the kid's chest, and the policeman at the far end of the line look down at the gun in his hand in amazement, as if it had fired on its own.

Martin said, in a small, tight voice, 'Oh, God.'

Leon turned to look at us, his glasses flashing. 'You two should go back to the station *right now*.'

But no one was leaving the arena. The policemen were panicking, shouting to each other, threatening the crowd. And then someone – you couldn't see his face – threw himself into the line of uniforms, screaming and flailing, a broken bottle in his hand, and it was as if something snapped. There were shots – I saw three people drop to the ground – but now the crowd's blood was up, and they outnumbered the policemen twenty-five to one . . .

It was a battle. I sat still, frozen. I felt as if I might be sick. At the other end of the court I caught a glimpse of Angel and Jelek being hustled into the red-and-green tunnel, away from the danger. So Angel wouldn't even get to touch the King's Cup, after all that. Somehow it still seemed to matter.

The stand around us was emptying. I realised that there were people climbing out over the back and sides of the stands, leaping to one of the neighbouring roofs or dropping a couple of metres past the barrier down to the street. They were shoving each other, scrabbling and pushing to get to safety.

I swallowed. I said, 'It's not *that* dangerous, is it?' My voice sounded high and thin.

Leon said, 'You have to get out, both of you. Go straight to the station. No – go straight to my rooms, in the university quarter. They're number twelve, in the building opposite the Royal Museum. You'll be safe there.'

'What are you going to do?' Martin said. He sounded hostile, so I knew he was afraid too. 'Stay here and lead the revolution?'

'Be part of it, anyway,' Leon said. He grinned, and the grin scared me more than the shots had.

'Don't be stupid. It isn't a revolution,' I said. 'It's just a fight. Isn't it?'

'Go on. Go,' Leon said, and stood up. He took his glasses off and put them in his pocket.

'All right,' Martin said, and took hold of my arm. 'Come on.'

'But –' I looked across at the stands opposite, but I couldn't see Skizi. My heart twisted, squeezing out the blood, and I felt dizzy. Where was she? I couldn't leave her here, I couldn't leave . . .

'Come *on*! What's the matter with you? Let Leon stay and get killed if he wants to, he's hopeless, we can't do anything about him . . . Please, Esteya.'

'I – I thought I saw someone I –'

Martin didn't answer. His grip tightened on my arm and he dragged me sideways, towards the bottom corner of the stands, where we could drop down into the street. I stumbled after him. I could feel tears running down my face. Skizi – where was Skizi?

And then, before I had time to struggle or pull away from him, Martin half lifted, half pushed me over the barrier, and I dropped painfully, landing in an awkward crouch that punched the breath out of me. Then he was beside me, and the noise had faded, and we were in a quiet street, full of people running away.

Seven

I didn't know where we were, or where we were going, but Martin took my hand, held it tightly and walked as if he knew the way to Leon's rooms without even having to think about it. I couldn't stop crying. Once he turned and looked at me as if he was about to say something, but in the end he closed his mouth again and gave my hand an extra squeeze.

'They were shooting those people,' I said. 'With real bullets. They *shot* them. That kid in the royal box . . .'

'Yes,' he said, and pulled me sideways, down a narrow street that smelt of drains. I realised, without caring, that he'd kept us off the main streets, where the crowds would be.

'I want to go back,' I said. 'Please, Martin . . .'

He gritted his teeth and pretended he hadn't heard.

'Please. Leon's there. I don't think we should leave th– him . . .'

'Shut up, Esteya. We're not going back. I don't want to get shot.'

'It's our duty! Stop being such a coward. We should be there, with the –'

He swung round, and his face was white and furious. '*What*? Our *duty*? To be with the working classes, while they get massacred? God, you sound like Leon! I'm not a coward, I'm just not stupid. You want to kill yourself, you can do it nice and neatly at home with one of Papa's scalpels, not get battered to bits or shot here. Now, you dare say another word, you *dare*, and I will never, ever forgive you.' He paused and took a breath. 'Understand?'

I swallowed, and nodded.

'Good.'

He sped up, so I had difficulty keeping up with him, and we went the rest of the way without speaking. I had a sharp hook of fear in my chest, dragging me back towards the stadium; but I tried to ignore it, and followed Martin.

The building opposite the Royal Museum was shabby and dark inside, with peeling paint and the tiles missing from the floor of the hall. It was silent too, with a dead, echoing sort of silence as if no one had lived there for years. We walked up the stairs, and the cold air brushed against my face like cobwebs.

Leon's door was closed but unlocked. Martin pushed it open and grimaced at the smell. There were dirty plates on the table, a couple of tins with crusty spoons and a half-empty bottle of vodka. The curtains hung half open, and there was a fly buzzing at the window. Martin looked round, shaking his head. 'Nice,' he said. 'Who would've thought students lived in such style?'

I went over to the window. There was a desk in front of it, covered in papers. *Your country needs you. A war is starting. An underground war is starting. Your comrades need you. A ~~secret war~~ ~~fight for~~ Leon Bidart. ~~Mr Bidart~~ Comrade Bidart, Secretary of the Communist Party. Comrade Bidart, ~~the nation's darling~~* . . . There was a pile of textbooks under the windowsill, but their spines were grey with dust.

I said, 'I'm not sure he counts as a student, any more. Not of medicine, anyway.'

Martin came over and stood beside me. He took a deep breath.

'Papa is going to go mad,' he said. 'I *knew* there was something up.'

The door behind us opened, and we spun round. There was a pale young man in the doorway, holding on to the door frame as if he had trouble standing upright. He said, 'Who are you? What's going on?'

'We're Leon's brother and sister,' Martin said. 'Who are *you*?'

'Oh,' he said, and rubbed his eyes. 'Hello. I'm Karl.'

Martin glanced at me. 'Er . . . oh. Like Marx?'

'As a matter of fact, yes,' Karl said, and gave a little fragile smile. 'My *nom de guerre*. As a tribute to the great man.' He yawned. 'Where's Leon?'

'There was some trouble at the King's Cup final,' I said. 'He stayed.'

'Trouble?'

Martin said, 'Shooting. The police against the crowd.'

All Karl said was, 'Oh. Again . . .' But he glanced at the far end of the room, with a kind of stifled excitement in his face. I followed his eyes. Through the murk I could just see a huge photograph tacked to the plaster over the mantelpiece. It was of a man who looked like an office clerk, in collar and tie, with a sagging mouth. Karl glanced at me. 'Our Glorious Leader,' he said. 'He's in prison. But when the revolution comes . . .'

Suddenly, as if on cue, there was the sound of shooting: a couple of single shots, and then the long rattle of machine-gun fire. It was a few streets away, maybe further, but Martin and I both jumped and took another step into the middle of the room.

Karl laughed, and hurried past us. He pushed the window open with a grunt and leant out, looking this way and that down the street. He said, 'It's over by the Queen's Park – must've spread . . .'

I sat down on Leon's chair, feeling sick.

'There've been riots all week, haven't there?'

Karl said, 'Ye-es . . .' still staring out of the window, as if he hadn't really heard what Martin had said.

'The King wasn't at the final,' Martin said. 'That's why the shooting started. The crowd started throwing things on to the court. Then the police – they looked sort of . . . ready, like they knew there was going to be trouble, like they were expecting something to happen . . .'

'They were,' Karl said. 'We're rising. They know that.'

'Yes, but . . .'

'No buts.' Karl drew his head back in. He was grinning, and he didn't look quite so harmless any more. 'You know what? This could be it.'

'It?'

The grin broadened, and he swung back into the middle of the room. 'You had better stay here. If Leon comes back, tell him I've gone to headquarters. Tell him to find Nico – no, of course, he's in prison . . . Never mind.' He hurried out without waiting for us to answer, and the door shut behind him with a squeak. The room was very quiet. Far away there was another burst of shooting.

There was silence. Martin pushed aside a dirty plate and sat down on the table.

He said, 'What do you reckon's happening?'

I didn't want to think about it. Ever since I'd heard the

guns, I could see that boy with blood on his chest, dropping to the ground; only he had Skizi's face.

Martin poked one of the spoons, then lifted it up, wrinkling his nose when the tin came with it. Then he paused. 'I can hear shouting.'

I listened. He was right, and it was getting closer. There was the smash of glass too, and whistles, and drums . . .

I stood up and walked over to the window. My knees felt soft and watery, and I had to hold on to the window-sill just to keep myself upright.

Martin came over and stood beside me. I could feel the heat coming off his body, and smell the stuff he put on his hair. The shouting flared up into a sudden roar, and when I looked round there was a trickle of men running out of one of the side streets, spilling into the road. They had handkerchiefs over the bottom half of their faces, like bandits, and one of them was clutching his head and dripping blood on to the paving stones. None of them was Leon.

Then, like a flood, there were more and more people running out into the street. Someone called out, 'They've got us cornered, the bastards!' and someone else yelled, 'What happened to those bloody rifles?'

I looked sideways. The clattering noise got louder, and with a shock of recognition I thought I knew what it was. Then they came into sight, and I *did* know.

Cavalry.

The King's Cavalry. They looked wonderful, like a pageant: in blue and gold, with their sabres drawn and glinting in the sun. Even their horses had an arrogant look in their eyes.

Martin breathed, 'Mother of God . . .'

I pulled away from the window, leaning back against

the wall; but not even the wall seemed stable any more. I remembered Karl saying, 'This could be it . . .'

'Esteya,' Martin said, and reached out for me, as if he wanted to hold on to something. 'Look. They're . . . look.'

It took an effort to turn my head. I didn't want to look; I wanted to stare into the corner of the room until the grimy flower-patterned paper was imprinted on my memory. But something in Martin's voice was irresistible.

The far end of the street was packed with people. There were lots of young men, with their faces covered, but there were old men too, and women . . . I saw a one-legged man on crutches, and a woman wearing a silky, expensive-looking dress and no shoes. And there were kids too, a group of boys, a little girl who kept looking round . . . It wasn't just people like Leon and his friends, it was *everyone* . . .

The man in the centre of the cavalry called an order, and slowly, without hurrying, the line of horses advanced. The crowd pushed and shuffled backwards, but there was nowhere for them to go. There were still people spilling out of the side street.

The line of cavalry stopped ten or twenty metres away from the crowd, and the crowd stayed where it was, murmuring uneasily. The young men pushed to the front, armed with broken bottles and police rifles.

The cavalry officer said something to his men, and they sheathed their sabres. My heart leapt, but it was only so that they could unsling their own rifles and point them at the civilians.

No one moved. The street was silent.

Very quietly, Martin said, 'We shouldn't be by the window.'

'No,' I said. But we stayed where we were.

There was a little disturbance in the crowd, and I flinched; but it was only the barefoot woman – no, girl, she was younger than I'd thought – in the silk dress, pushing her way to the front. She stepped out into the open, right in front of one of the rifles, and stood there for a moment. She had something in her hand: a green branch, dotted with red flowers. The crowd behind her rustled and whispered.

She walked slowly towards the line of cavalry. They still had their guns pointing at the crowd. I prayed for her to stop before she got too close, before someone panicked and shot her, but she kept on walking. It seemed to take for ever for her to cross the empty space.

She stood in front of the officer, and held out the branch.

He looked at her. His hand went to his sabre. My heart stuttered.

Then he shrugged, smiled, took the flowers, and bent to give her a kiss.

Martin turned away, his eyes closed, and dropped into the nearest chair. He'd gone white. He put his hands over his face and started to laugh.

I drew away from the window and sat down too. I felt sick and shaky, as if I'd been out in the sun too long. There were voices from the street, faint laughter that echoed Martin's.

Martin said, 'Technically that's probably a mutiny.'

'Better than a massacre.' As soon as I'd said the word I wished I hadn't. I stood up again and paced to the window, then to the mantelpiece, where I stood looking at the picture of Our Glorious Leader, without seeing it.

If only Skizi was in the street outside . . . but she wasn't. And that meant she was somewhere else, somewhere where the shooting might not have stopped . . . In my head, that girl offered those flowers over and over again: but the officer didn't take the flowers and kiss her, he drew his sabre and cut her down . . . And over and over again I saw the boy who'd been killed in the royal box, and Skizi's face.

'Where's Leon, anyway?' Martin said.

'How should I know?'

'No reason.'

'Then stop asking bloody stupid questions!'

Martin squinted at me, as if I was something very far away and hard to see. There was a silence. He peered at one of Leon's plates and scratched the rim with his fingernail.

I went on pacing, for what seemed like hours. When I looked out of the window again there was no one left, except the man who'd been dripping blood. He was in a doorway now, slumped against the frame with his eyes closed and his whole shirt stained red. He looked like he was asleep. The shadows had advanced so that there was only a narrow strip of sunlight on our side of the street. Nothing moved, not even the dust or the curtains in the windows opposite. My heartbeat made my ears ring.

I went into the corridor to find the lavatory, and took my time washing my hands, because it was something to do. When I came back Martin was asleep.

I couldn't believe it. The world was falling apart around us, and he'd gone to sleep. He was snoring gently with his mouth open, and I wanted to slap him. How dare he? Skizi could be *dead* . . . I reached out to shake him, and then stopped.

Skizi could be dead.

I had to find her. I had to.

And now Martin was asleep. He might not even wake up before I got back.

I went to Leon's desk, found a piece of paper and wrote: *Dear Martin, Gone to look for Leon, won't be long, don't worry, I'll be careful. See you soon. Love, Esteya.* I was afraid the sound of the pen would wake him, but he didn't stop snoring.

Then I left it on the table, propped up against an ancient tin of beans, and slipped out of the room.

The street was quiet and cool, but the tension was still in the air, and I could feel the windows looking down on me from both sides, as if they were people. I stayed close to the buildings, ready to duck out of sight if I needed to. For a moment I glanced up at the building I'd come from, wondering whether Martin would come after me; but I told myself that it would be all right, that he might not even wake up, and even if he did he was sensible enough to stay there, where he was safe. More sensible than *I* was . . . I stopped and closed my eyes, and saw the note I'd written superimposed on my eyelids. *Gone to look for Leon.* As if Leon needed looking after, as if it would be any use if I did find him, as if Leon would let anyone distract him from the revolutionary struggle –

As if I cared half as much about Leon as I did about Skiz–

I opened my eyes, and the daylight hit my retinas. I did love Leon, yes, of course I did, it was just that –

Skizi was everything. I couldn't live without her.

I heard the words in my head as if someone else had said them, and they hit me like a punch. I heard them again, appalled, afraid. I couldn't *live* . . . It was true. I'd known before that I loved her, but *this* –

I took a deep breath, looking straight ahead. It doesn't matter, I thought. How you feel doesn't matter. Just – *find her*.

Now.

I started to walk. There was a sound like a clock ticking, getting louder as I walked down the street towards it; it made me uneasy, as if it was counting down to something. When I looked round I realised it was the man in the doorway, still dripping blood on to the ground. There was a thin line of it running into the gutter.

I felt cold. I didn't want to cross the street to him. I wouldn't be able to help anyway; he probably needed stitches, and aspirin and iodine . . .

I crossed the street, running through the band of sunlight as if it was a searchlight, and threw myself into the doorway. I bent, shook his shoulder and said, 'Are you all right?' My voice cracked and gave out.

He didn't need stitches, or aspirin, or iodine. And he wasn't all right.

He was dead.

I thought, stupidly, that I'd never seen a dead body before, and wondered if I should be interested. But it wasn't anything special, it was like looking at an empty suitcase. It made me feel queasy, but that was all. I had blood on my hand from his shirt, and I scraped it on the wall, trying to get it clean. But even when the stain had come off, my hand didn't feel right. I kept on wiping it over and over again until the skin was red and raw. It hurt, but that didn't matter; I just wanted to get the man's blood off me.

There were shots, a long way away, and I came back to

myself with a jolt. What was I doing, standing here, wiping my hand on the wall, while Skizi . . . ? I spun round and started to hurry down the street. I had to find her. What if she was slumped in a doorway somewhere, like . . . ?

I got to the end of the street, and stood staring down the narrow side street. Suddenly I realised how big Irunja was, and how hard it would be to find someone. I had no idea where to start looking. All I could do was go back to the arena. If she wasn't there, at least I'd know she hadn't been hurt straight away, when the fighting started . . .

Now that the sun had dipped behind the buildings it was chilly, and I remembered suddenly that it was October, not summer any more. I wrapped my arms round myself and started to walk. I wasn't sure of the direction, but I thought I recognised the streets, and the smell of drains. Once I saw a policeman, but I ducked into an alleyway, my heart pounding, and when I peered out again he'd gone.

It took me longer than I thought it would, although I was hurrying, and even when I caught sight of the arena I couldn't find the entrance. I turned down narrow, dim street after narrow, dim street, and it was only when I saw the same house with ox-blood shutters that I realised I was going in circles. I heard myself laugh, although it wasn't funny. How stupid . . . The arena's red and green banners flapped and sagged above me, so close I could see the hems on the cloth; but there was just a blank wall in front of me. Where was the entrance?

I went up to the wall, looking to left and right, but there were houses built up against it, so I couldn't follow it round. But there were cracks in the bricks, and crumbling mortar, and if I jumped I might just be able to get to the top. I couldn't go on wasting time like this; I had to get over that wall.

It didn't work. I jumped at it, scrabbling for handholds, but my shoes wouldn't get any purchase on the bricks and I dropped back to the ground. My hand stung where I'd rubbed the blood off. I wanted to curl up on the ground and cry.

But I didn't. I took my shoes and stockings off, and tried again. This time my toes managed to grip the gap between the bricks, and I flung myself upwards, grabbing for the top of the wall, gasping for breath. I felt myself slipping – it wasn't going to work – and I thought of Skizi on the other side, and suddenly my fingers were closing on the top of the wall, and I was hanging there, digging my feet into the crumbling mortar, and I knew I was going to do it.

I found myself kneeling on the top of the wall, the edge digging into my knees. There was sweat running down my face, and my heart was beating harder than it had when I saw the policeman. It was hard to keep my balance, but I shuffled my legs out from underneath me and slid awkwardly down the other side. The stands were in front of me, the space underneath dark and littered with bits of food and greaseproof paper. When I landed something scuttled away from me into the shadows.

I walked round the back of the stands, trying not to make any noise. It was so quiet – dead quiet, as if the walls of the enclosure kept out every little sound.

There was no one here. It was strange, after the pello game, when it had been so full, so noisy. Now it felt like the end of the world.

I stepped into the middle of the court, looking round. There were dark stains on the wooden seats, and the barrier of the east stand had been bashed into pieces. There were no bodies; they must have taken them away already. From this angle I couldn't see inside the royal box, and I wondered if they'd remembered that he was there, the boy they'd shot . . . But it didn't make any difference: he was an empty suitcase, I thought, just an empty suitcase . . . There was still a thin line of sunshine at the side of the court, but my teeth were chattering with the cold.

Skizi wasn't here.

I walked across the clay to the ticket gates. They were hanging open, with a chain and a broken padlock trailing on the ground. There were tickets on the ground, smeared with red.

It was so silent. It felt like a practical joke, as if someone was waiting to jump out on me, yelling, 'Made you look! Thought it was real, didn't you?'

But no one did. It was as if it *was* real.

And a long way away I could hear gunfire again. It went on and on, machine guns and single shots, and after a while sirens joined in, and the wailing spread and echoed off the walls around me. I thought it was coming from the north-west, the direction of the Queen's Park and the Palace. That was what Karl had said, anyway.

I realised with a shock that I hadn't even thought about Leon. Where was he? Was he with Karl and the other Communists, trying to start a revolution?

Martin would have woken up by now. I ought to go back. If I didn't, he might come looking for me, and if he got hurt, or –

No. Martin was safe, and Leon would be safer without me.

I had to find Skizi. That was all that mattered.

I didn't know where to go next. But if she was hurt, if she was in danger . . .

I gritted my teeth and hugged myself, trying to stop shivering. Then I walked out through the ticket gates and turned right, towards the north-west, and the gunfire.

Eight

The streets were still deserted, so deathly silent that the gunfire was almost comforting. I hurried towards it, walking as quietly as I could, desperate to see someone – anyone. I felt like the last person left in the world.

There was a faint, bitter smell in the air, and it caught the back of my throat and made me cough. It smelt like our All Souls' bonfire the time Martin dropped a rubber ball in the heap of leaves and forgot about it. It was a threatening, urgent kind of smell; it made me speed up, although I wasn't sure why. I ran past the closed shops and shuttered windows. The red flags and banners – there were a few green ones too, but not many – flapped uneasily in the breeze. There should have been King's Cup parties on the streets, people celebrating, going over every detail of the game; but there was nothing but the growing shadows and the whiff of smoke.

The firing was closer now, and I could hear shouting, glass smashing, police whistles. I felt light-headed, and my knees had gone watery again. If Skizi was in the middle of that . . . And for the first time I thought I might not be able to find her, or that even if I did, she might get hurt anyway. Hurt, or –

No. I was going to find her.

It was hard to make my legs move, but I crossed the road and stood at the corner of a side street, looking down it. At the far end, through the narrow gap between the buildings, I could see movement, and the flash of red and brown. The air was hazy, as if I was seeing everything through dirty glass.

I carried on walking, stumbling on broken bits of pavement, as if the nerves in my legs weren't working properly. When I got close to the end of the street I stood in the shadows, looking one way and then the other. The smoke rasped in my throat again and made me want to cough, but I swallowed hard, not wanting to make a noise.

There was a barricade, piled with chairs and tables and mattresses; and on the near side of it there were little groups of men in shirtsleeves, holding rifles. I saw one pouring liquid out of a petrol can into milk bottles, pausing to wipe his hands on his trousers. Next to him there was a woman holding two rifles, trying to brush her hair off her forehead with her arm. The man said something to her and she laughed. For a second I felt a kind of blinding envy: I wanted to be there, holding a rifle in each hand, part of what was going on . . . Then I heard another burst of firing, and everyone ducked. There was a thump, and the barricade juddered as if someone was trying to knock it down from the other side.

At the other end of the street, to my right, there was a larger group of people. They were young, all about Leon's age, and they were sharing food and drinking from vodka bottles. A few young men were sitting in the doorway. If you didn't look too closely, it could almost have been a King's Cup party; but they were all tense and unsmiling, as if they were waiting for something. In the centre of the group there was one man with rolled-up sleeves and a red cap, leaning forward and talking in a low voice. I stood still, staring at his back. There was something familiar . . .

Suddenly two people ran out of one of the side streets parallel to the one I'd just come down, shouting and waving long swathes of green, like banners. Everyone looked round, and I saw the face of the man who'd been talking. It was Karl. He stood up and called out, and I saw two more men spilling into the street, one of them wrapped in another green flag; he was dragging the other, who had a green sash over his shoulder. I saw something in his hand glint silver in the last of the sunlight, the familiar shape of a two-handled bowl, the King's Cup . . .

Then he looked round, and I caught sight of his face.

It was Angel.

And the man who was with him was Leon.

He was laughing, with a high, hoarse note in his voice that didn't sound like amusement. He pushed Angel forward and doubled over, putting his hands on his knees. He said, 'Sweet heart of Jesus, we nearly got shot . . .' and went on laughing.

Karl shrugged, and folded himself down again on to the pavement. He said, over his shoulder, 'Sit down, Comrade, and pull yourself together.'

Leon stood up straight and said, still with an edge of hilarity in his voice, 'Hey, don't you realise who this is? This is Angel Corazon, Comrade. This is the great man himself.'

Angel glanced round, and crossed his arms over the King's Cup, to protect it.

A few people swapped looks. Then someone said, 'Leon . . . he's a pello player. He's not even a Communist.' He turned to Angel. 'Are you?'

Angel shrugged, and his hands tightened on the handles of his trophy.

There was a kind of silence, filled only with the firing from the other side of the barricade. Then the woman with the two rifles walked over, shaking her hair over her shoulders. She said, 'Angel Corazon? Are you really?'

Angel nodded. But she didn't seem to see; her eyes were on the King's Cup, and she stretched out one of her arms as if she wanted to touch it, as if she'd forgotten about the rifles she was holding. Then she grinned at Leon, and turned to Karl. She said, 'He's right, Comrade. What a man to have with us! The people love him – or they will now . . . Our hero. A true man of the proletariat . . .'

Leon grinned back at her. Angel looked from him to her and back again, his mouth a little open.

Karl said, 'Let's make sure the revolution actually happens, before we worry about matinee idols for our propaganda, shall we?'

The revolution? I leant back against the wall, my legs shaking, a kind of sob rising in my throat. They all seemed so serious . . . But this was just a bread riot – a disturbance – not a *revolution* . . .

I closed my eyes. What was I doing here? I ought to go back to Martin. I'd never find Skizi, and if the police caught me with Leon and his friends . . .

Distantly, I heard Angel say, 'I just . . . I'm good at pello, that's all . . .' but no one answered him.

A clear, light voice said, 'Let's get on with it then.' I opened my eyes again. It was the woman, talking over her shoulder as she walked back to the barricade.

'Yes . . . where is everyone?' Leon said, polishing his glasses on the cuff of his shirt. He was covered in dust and dark stains; it didn't look as if he'd get them very clean. 'What's the plan?'

The glint went out of Karl's eyes, and he looked into the middle distance, biting his lip. 'Most people seem to be concentrated in the main streets. They're hemmed in by the police, but they'll break out. The army was mobilised, but they seem not to want to fire on their own people, which is good. The police are armed, but they're outnumbered fifty to one. God, Leon, *so many people* . . .' he added, and then shook his head. 'Amazing. But the important thing is, the police don't have enough men to worry too much about us, here. Except for –' There was another burst of gunfire, and he grimaced. 'Well. A few of them. But we've got relative freedom. We can take advantage of the situation.'

'And do what?'

'The obvious targets,' Karl said. He walked away from the other men, and Leon followed. In a lower voice, he said, 'The prison. And the Palace.'

'Jolly good.'

'That pello player of yours . . . you really think he'll be useful?'

Leon hunched one shoulder, considering. 'Well . . . maybe not now . . . but if we need a rallying point, a personality . . .'

'Yes,' Karl said, nodding. 'And if we can say he was here, with us, behind the barricade . . .'

'Exactly.' They grinned at each other. I clenched my jaw and looked at Angel. He was on the balls of his feet, biting the rim of the King's Cup like a kid. His eyes were wide, and he jumped every time the firing reached a crescendo.

'The prison then?' Leon got a red handkerchief out

of his pocket and started to tie it round, to cover the lower half of his face.

'Yes. Get a rifle. They're in the cellar of the house over there. God bless Elena and her soldier boyfriends . . .' He laughed, but I couldn't tell whether it was a joke. He raised his voice, and called, 'Elena! You ready? You and Ricky coming?'

The woman glanced at him and nodded. She sauntered over, one hand in her pocket, the other swinging her rifle. The group of men started to get to their feet, passing the bottle of vodka to each other and swigging from it. The last one tipped it up vertically and then threw it casually towards the barricade. It didn't go over; it smashed on the near side, and a man jumped backwards, swearing.

I stood where I was, watching. My heart had slowed down. I felt almost safe; as if I was invisible. It was like watching a play.

The noise behind the barricade rose again, but no one paid any attention. Leon had disappeared into one of the houses, and everyone was on their feet. Karl was staring down one of the streets and muttering as if he was calculating the quickest way to the prison. I drew back into the shadows. There was no point staying here; I had to find Skizi.

There was a kind of rumble from behind the barricade; then, as if in slow motion, it started to collapse. A table half slid, half toppled to the ground, so that its legs were pointing at the sky; and the chairs and the mattress that it had been resting on trembled and started to edge forwards. The police were breaking through. I opened my mouth, but my throat had closed and I couldn't make a sound.

And then, suddenly, there was a policeman clambering

over, wielding a rifle; only no one had seen him, no one had time to turn and –

He started shooting.

The first bullet only ricocheted off a wall, chipping a cornice. I saw Karl turn, and look around for the nearest cover. Then the others started to notice, and ducked into doorways, pushing each other out of the way. But it took so *long* . . . and now the man was sliding down this side of the barricade, and behind him there were more, ten or twenty, all with guns – mostly rifles, but one policeman had a different model that I realised, with a dull surge of fear, was a sub-machine gun.

I stood frozen. I wanted to run, but I couldn't. Leon hadn't come out of the house, and I prayed that he'd stay in the cellar, hiding, although I knew he wouldn't.

They all opened fire; and the Communists returned it.

A few of the policemen spun to the ground, as if someone had lassoed their arms or legs, and blood blossomed slowly on their uniforms. But when I looked round I could see more bodies not in uniform; and the line of policemen advanced, the man with the machine gun in front, covering the others. The noise was deafening: as if just the *sound* of a shot could kill you . . . I leant against the wall, squeezing my hands over my ears, but it was no good.

I saw Karl look round at the bodies, and then he stood up, and yelled, 'Run! We haven't got a chance! Don't fight, *run!*' And he dashed across the street, to the side street, and disappeared round the corner.

One by one, a few people followed him; then, all in a rush, the others ran too, scattering into the side streets, yelling to each other, skidding and stumbling. Someone ran past me, brushing my shirt with his rifle as he struggled to sling it back over his shoulder as he went. I flinched as someone else went by, swearing and smelling of smoke.

I thought: Leon. Leon was in that house, and if he came out now, with his handkerchief over his face, and his rifle in his hand . . .

The woman – Elena – had been crouching in a doorway, taking shots at the policemen; now she stood up, called, 'Karl! Karl, see you at the prison!' and started to run. She ran down the street, zigzagging to avoid the spray of bullets. I thought I could hear her laughing and whooping, as if she was running through a thunderstorm; she jumped over a body like a kid leaping a puddle, full of energy, having fun . . . Then she fell to her knees. She stood up and started to run again; but now I could see a dark patch on her trouser leg, and she was running oddly, throwing herself forward and flailing at the air with her arms as if she couldn't keep her balance. She dropped her rifle, and for a moment she picked up speed. Then she tripped, and she fell flat on her face in the middle of the road.

The back of her neck was just a red bubbling mess. A thin slick of blood spread out underneath her.

Somehow I still expected her to get up: she'd tripped, that's all; she probably hadn't done her shoelaces up properly . . .

But she didn't move.

And the last of the Communists disappeared into the side streets opposite me, and the policemen spread out, brandishing their guns and shouting insults, and I realised I was the only person left.

I started to run, too late.

While I was standing still, no one had noticed me; but

as soon as I moved, I heard someone shout and fire, and there were bullets filling the air like little whining wasps, pinging off the walls. But it didn't seem real. The police didn't shoot at people like *me*: I hadn't done anything, I was only here for the King's Cup, I was a nice middle-class girl, it was all a mistake . . . I kept running, feeling unreal, like one of those dreams where you can't move properly. My feet hurt.

'Hey, you! Stop! Stop running right now!'

Part of me wanted to stop, because surely they wouldn't shoot me, if I stopped and told them my name and address and just *explained* . . . but I'd have to explain why I was there, behind the barricade, and give them Leon's name, and Karl's, and –

I kept running. Now everything hurt, and my heart was hammering in my head, as though it might spill out of my mouth. If only they'd give up, and forget about me . . . but they didn't. I could hear them running after me, panting with exertion, and the occasional rattle of bullets off the walls on either side. The man with the machine gun must have gone after someone else. That was something; if he hadn't, I'd have been dead by now.

But I couldn't last much longer.

I got to the end of the street, flung myself round the corner and looked desperately for somewhere to hide. But the doors were all closed, and the windows were all shuttered, and the street stretched out wide and empty in front of me. I went on running, keeping as close to the wall as I could. Behind me there was more shouting, and then a pause. With a surge of relief I stopped and looked over my shoulder, thinking I'd lost them, but the policemen were in a cluster, the one in front raising his rifle . . .

I spun round and ran. My back prickled with

anticipation and fear. They were going to shoot me. They were going to –

I heard – no, felt – a movement behind me. I'd gone past another turning – I should have turned, but I was running too fast to think clearly, and now it was too late – and now there was someone else chasing me, someone –

Someone between me and the policemen's bullets –

Someone calling my name.

I looked round.

And at the same moment whoever-it-was caught up with me, grabbed my arm and pulled me sideways, down the next street and into an alleyway, half pushing, half dragging me, and the hand on my arm was so tight it hurt, as though I really had been shot. I had time to see a grimy grass-stained shirt, a blur of skin, and then we were running together down the alley and left and left again and right and there was a door that was mostly boarded up and she pulled at the corner with one hand and we fell through into the dark and –

And I fought for breath, gasping, and when I managed to fill my lungs again it came out as a sob, I thought it was a laugh, and then she had her arms round me and I was still sobbing and I couldn't stop.

'Esteya, you *idiot*,' she kept saying, over and over again, like she was hushing a baby. 'You bloody idiot, what were you doing . . . ?'

'Looking for you,' I said. 'What else?'

And then I gave in to the tears and just let myself cry.

When I stopped crying, the last of the light had faded and we were sitting in complete darkness. It was cold, and I was glad of the warmth of Skizi's body next to me.

Through my sniffles I could hear her breathing, and the soft sound of her hand stroking my back.

She said, 'All right now?'

'Yes, thanks.' I leant my head into the hollow between her shoulder and her neck, smelling her musty indoors–outdoors smell, and the tang of sweat. More tears came, and I let them run down my face silently. If something had happened to her . . . I swallowed. 'I was scared for you.'

'You should've been scared for *you*. Idiot.'

'What happened? Martin made us leave the arena, and you were still there, and I thought –' I stopped, because I didn't trust my voice to hold out.

'I ran away.'

'Where to?'

I felt her shrug, and she blew her breath out impatiently. 'Oh, come on, Esteya. I know trouble when I see it. I'm used to having to keep an eye out for myself. Not like you, you –'

I said, 'Idiot.'

'Porridge-brain,' she said, at the same time, and I caught the glint of her teeth as she smiled. 'But honestly, Esteya . . . What were you thinking? Martin was right, you ought to have gone somewhere safe and stayed there. You could've got yourself shot.'

I shrugged. 'I wanted to find you.'

She shook her head, and I felt her face burrowing into my hair, just above my ear. The warmth of her mouth made me shiver.

'Anyway,' I said, 'what were you doing there? How on earth did *you* get –' I checked myself. 'I mean, how did you manage to get –'

'How did *I* get a ticket?' she said, mocking my tone.

She shifted, so that she was sitting up straighter and I had to move my head. 'How did a dirty little Zikindi like me get hold of a –'

'You know that's not what I meant.'

'Does it matter? How I got the ticket?'

'No, of course it doesn't! Forget it.'

There was a silence. She said, 'I sold one of your mama's things, if you must know.'

Suddenly, out of nowhere, I was so tired I wanted to close my eyes and never open them again. I said, 'You're right, it doesn't matter.'

The silence came back, cradling us, rocking us, like the sea. I closed my eyes and drifted. I was almost dreaming. But faces kept surfacing in the blackness: the boy in the royal box, the man in the doorway, Elena . . . I remembered Leon, with a jolt of guilt. Please, God, let him have stayed in the cellar, hiding . . .

'What a game, though,' Skizi said.

For a second I thought she meant the fighting. Then I understood, and started to laugh.

'What?' she said. 'Wasn't it amazing? Angel Corazon – what a player . . .'

I kept on laughing, so hard I could hardly speak.

'What? Esteya, what's wrong? Are you all right? What's so funny?'

'I've seen three dead people – no, more than that,' I said. 'Today. I'd never seen anyone dead, and then today . . . I was chased, and shot at, and I've never been so scared in all my life. And you sit there and say – you – you say . . .' I took a deep breath, and forced the words out through my giggles. 'And you – you're still talking about the pello game . . .'

There was a pause. Then she said, 'But it *was* amazing, wasn't it?'

I nodded, still spluttering, and I felt her start to laugh too, as if it was contagious. I said, 'Yes, yes, it was. It was amazing. You're right. What a game.'

She leant her temple against mine, and I felt the vibrations in my skull as we laughed, helplessly. I turned my head so that my mouth was resting against her cheek, and I could feel her breath on my neck.

She kissed me, and then shifted, as if she was going to get to her feet. She said, 'Where's Martin then? Did he find somewhere safe?'

'Leon's rooms, opposite the Royal Museum. Martin's probably . . .' I stopped. He'd be furious.

'Better take you back then.'

'But . . . I want to stay here, with you. I mean – you can't – I can't tell Martin about –'

'Yes, I know, Esteya, but I'll be fine. It's you I'm worried about. I'll take you back, and then you must get the first train home as soon as you can. I don't know what's going to happen here.'

It felt good, to have her looking after me – as if she really wanted to keep me safe, as if she really *cared* . . . I nodded, too tired to reply.

'Come on then. On your feet.'

She pulled at my wrists, taking my weight, as I stood up. Then she let go of me, and I heard her move to the door and open it. A faint trace of light shone through the gap, just enough to make her eyes gleam. I could smell smoke again.

'All right,' she said, peering out into the street. 'Can you find the way back to Leon's rooms, if I go with you?'

'Probably,' I said, and giggled. I felt light-headed, dizzy with fatigue.

She looked back at me and shook her head. 'This is

serious, Esteya. Honestly, try to concentrate . . . I suppose it's in the university quarter?'

'Yes.'

She nodded, and held out her hand, as if I was a little girl. I took it, loving the familiar cool, dusty feel of her skin. I wanted to stay here with her, for ever.

'I can smell burning,' she said, turning her head from side to side.

'Can't we stay here?'

She pulled me forward into the street. 'Let's go.'

'I thought you might be dead,' I said. 'I couldn't stop thinking about you.'

She glanced at me, without smiling. 'Come on,' she said. 'And Esteya . . .'

'Yes?'

'What have you done with your shoes?'

I thought I'd be able to find my way back to Leon's rooms without too much trouble; but in the dark the city looked different, and the streets were full of a strange, heavy silence that made me too uneasy to concentrate. Twice we retraced our steps to avoid the shouting that we could hear in the distance. My feet hurt, and Skizi walked too fast, holding my hand so I had to keep up with her.

After an hour, I thought we were lost. We were at the corner of a little street, opposite a church; it had scuffed, wonky pello lines painted in the little square in front of it, and the wobbly bits looked familiar, even in the dark. I said, 'Skizi . . .'

'Yes, I know.'

We looked at the church in silence, and she took a long, deep breath. She said, 'Do you have any idea at all which direction we should be going in?'

'No. I'm sorry.'

'It's not your fault.' She sighed again, and looked from one side to the other, as if she was trying to remember which way we'd gone last time. 'If I knew where we were, I could probably work out where to go. But . . .'

There was a silence. I thought I ought to help her, but I was so tired.

She glanced at me, and rubbed her face with the palms of her hands. 'All right. We'll walk in one direction until we get to something you recognise.'

She set off, without looking back, and I stumbled after her. I was afraid I'd fall asleep on my feet, or start to cry. But after a while I went into a sort of dream, and the tiredness faded into a sort of trance. I stared straight ahead, at the golden, flickering sky, and let my thoughts drift.

I woke up, with a start, because Skizi was doubled over, coughing. I ran the last few steps towards her. 'Are you all right?'

She caught her breath, nodded and spat. The spittle gleamed reddish in the light. 'It's the smoke, that's all.'

The smoke. Of course, the smoke. I'd been smelling it for so long I'd stopped noticing; but the air was thick with it, itching in my throat, and when I swallowed I could taste it. And that was why the sky was glowing, why the windows in the street gleamed orange at the edges . . . I said, 'What's burning?'

'A barricade?'

'No.' I took a step forward, as if it would help me to see more clearly. I could hear shouting, and the faint crash of glass, and shooting, and screams . . . I said, 'No. It's a building. They've set fire to a building. A big one.'

'But . . .' Skizi narrowed her eyes. 'If we're where I

think we are, then there's nothing in that direction but the Queen's Park, and the –'

'The Palace,' I said, and we looked at each other.

Skizi opened her mouth, and then started to laugh. She said, 'Come on,' and grabbed my wrist and started to run.

It hurt to go with her – my feet stung every time they hit the pavement – but my tiredness was gone. It was stupid, it was mad, to run *towards* the fire; but that didn't matter. The Palace, on fire . . .

We stopped at the gate to the Queen's Park. There was no need to go any further: through the railings we could see the flames on the Palace roof and pouring out of the windows, throwing sparks upwards. And against the fire there were black figures, standing still and watching, rifles slung across their backs. There seemed to be hundreds of them. I thought I could hear screaming, but no one moved, beyond passing a bottle or lighting a cigarette; and I might have been imagining it.

I heard Skizi say, 'The Palace . . .' She made a noise like a laugh, full of disbelief and admiration.

I said, 'They said they were going to attack the prison.'

Skizi leant her forehead against the railings, and I saw the gleam of her teeth. 'Maybe they already did. Or maybe the guards just gave up and let everyone out. Better than being shot.'

'But –'

'Do you think the King is still in there?'

'Of course not. If he was in there, he'd be –' I stopped, but the word hovered in mid-air. I didn't even need to say it. I swallowed.

Skizi turned to look at me. 'What's the matter?'

I sat down, without meaning to. I wanted to be sick.

Everything was . . . They were burning the Palace, and everything was . . . I closed my eyes. It wasn't just a bread riot, it was . . . I said, 'I'm scared.' It was almost the right word, but not quite.

'We're safe here. No one's seen us.'

'No, I mean . . .' I thought of Martin, asking me if I thought there'd be a revolution. I understood how he felt now. 'What's going to happen, Skizi? It's all going to be . . . different . . .' But I couldn't explain how I felt. It was like trying to describe vertigo.

'Yes,' she said, and I felt her crouch down next to me. She stroked my hair. 'It'll be different. But don't worry – once the fighting's over, it'll be good. Equality and freedom and no more hunger or people being dragged away in the middle of the night. That's what Leon says, isn't it? And men and women being equal, and gypsies and Jews and Zikindi all being equal too . . . Don't be scared. It'll be all right, I promise.'

Her voice had the same dreamy tone that Leon's did. I tried to laugh. 'I didn't know you were a Communist.'

I felt her stiffen and stand up. I opened my eyes and she was glaring at me.

'You don't understand, do you? You don't have a clue. I'm not a Communist, I just don't like being hungry and cold and having to run away from people because I'm Zikindi. I don't like knowing the police could take me away and no one would ever see me again and no one would *care*. I don't like it that you're ashamed of me –'

'I'm not ash–'

'I don't like it that people would hate us both if they knew! Why can't you understand that? Do you *want* things to stay as they are?'

'No, of course I don't.'

'So stop being so *weak*.' She spun round and pointed at the flames. 'That's the old world, burning! And it deserves to burn! Can't you see what it means – for everyone, for *us*? I don't want to have to hide any more, I don't want *you* to have to hide –'

I stared at her. I'd never seen her like this. I said, 'I didn't know you cared.'

'Of course I bloody care!' She held my gaze, and slowly the anger went out of her face. 'Of course I care.'

I got to my feet unsteadily, and took her hand. She didn't move.

I said, 'I love you. I love you, I love you, I love you –'

She turned and ran, tugging at my hand. I stumbled after her, cursing my bare feet. She pulled me into an alcove, and pushed me up against the wall, in the shadows.

I said, 'I lov–'

She kissed me, cutting off the words. Her hands slid round and dug into my back. She was pressed against me so hard I could feel the stones in the wall behind me, and the cold seeping through my shirt. I was shivering. I felt a drop of water land on my forehead, and another and another; it was starting to rain.

She broke away, slid her mouth down over my chin, burrowed her face into my neck, and then kissed down my collarbone to the neckline of my dress. I said, 'Skizi . . .'

'Stop talking.'

'D'you think this is the revolution? Really?'

'Yes,' she said. 'Right here, just us, together. Me and you, against a wall.'

'No, I meant –'

Somehow I knew she was smiling. 'I know what you meant. Stop talking.'

And then she moved her hands, and I stopped thinking about the revolution, and the smell of smoke and the rain on my face faded into nothing, and all I could think about was her, her, her.

Winter

Nine

It was cold the day we came home from Irunja, the rain pelting against the windows of the crowded train. The sky was as grey as the ash that was still settling, days after the Palace burnt to the ground. And the rain went on and on, until it turned into sleet, weeks later, and then snow, as if winter had arrived early the day of the revolution and refused to go away. Martin said it was because the Communists had forgotten to appoint a Minister for Weather, but he never said it very loudly.

Christmas was cold and muted – Leon stayed in Irunja, too busy to come home, although he spent the afternoon of Twelfth Night with us, and he didn't talk about bourgeois religiosity with the same venom as normal. He looked tired, and he didn't mention politics until Papa asked him how his new job was going; then he smiled without using his eyes and said, 'Papa, we're building a new world from scratch, how do *you* think it's going? It's –' he hesitated – 'hard work.'

'What do you do all day?' Martin said. 'I mean, it's all very well, building a new world, but what do you actually *do*?'

'Paperwork, mainly,' Leon said. 'I'm in the Ministry

for Information. Well. I suppose I *am* the Ministry for Information.'

'How lovely,' Mama said. 'A pity you had to give up your studies, though.'

There was a silence, and she stroked the teapot with the tip of a finger. It was an English teapot, blue and white, that Teddy had given her because he didn't have room for it in his suitcase when he packed to go home, just before Christmas. He'd come to say goodbye, cradling a cardboard box in his arms, with the teapot and the cups to go with it. I'd been standing at the top of the stairs, and I saw him fumble and drop it as he tried to put it into Mama's arms. The teapot was the only thing that survived the smash, and when Teddy had crouched down to sort out the wreckage he'd started to weep into his hands, desperately, as if someone had died. I'd never seen a man cry before, and now whenever I looked at the teapot all I could think of was Teddy, sobbing on his knees in our hallway.

In the silence Leon said, 'I should get back to Irunja. I'm so busy I hardly have time to sleep.'

After that, he wrote, sometimes; but that was the last time we'd seen him. And then it was February, and we were waiting for spring, and for everything to get better.

We were sitting outside in the schoolyard, in the freezing cold, waiting for the bell to ring so that we could go inside again. I leant my head back against the wall, and then jerked it away from the stone when I felt the cold soak through my hat and into my scalp. I narrowed my eyes against the grey light, wishing I could be somewhere else.

Next to me, Miren was turning a pamphlet over and over in her hands, as if it was a precious relic. It was one of Leon's, that he'd sent with his last letter: it had a picture of Angel Corazon on the front, and the title *NEW HOPE*. He'd got Angel to sign it for me. His letters were in rough, childish handwriting. *To Esteya, form Angel.* I thought of the last time I'd seen Angel – that smoke-smelling street in Irunja, in the sunshine and gunfire – and it seemed worlds away, as if it couldn't possibly be the same person who'd signed the grainy, badly reproduced paper that Miren was touching so carefully. I was glad he'd survived, but . . .

I shut my eyes completely, but all it did was intensify the cold. I hadn't seen Skizi for nearly a week, and the last time I had, we'd sat silently for a long time, too cold even to move. When I tried to kiss her, she'd smiled faintly and turned her cheek away. She was thinner, and her golden tinge had gone, leaving her the colour of dirty cream. She smelt stronger too – because she was too cold to wash, I supposed – and she seemed not to want me to get too close. I hoped that was why, anyway. I dreamt of sneaking her into our bathroom for a long, hot bath, but I knew it wouldn't work, and it was too dangerous. If Mama caught us . . .

I was shivering so hard I could hear the seams in my coat cracking with the strain. I opened my eyes again, trying to imagine the wall opposite without its hat of grimy snow. I prayed for the clouds to open, because at least if it was actually snowing the nuns would let us back into the schoolhouse.

Miren said, 'Gosh, isn't it *cold*?'

I shifted from buttock to buttock, trying to warm myself up. Over on the other side of the schoolyard, Ana Himyana was flirting with the guard, fiddling with the red band she'd tied her plait with. He grinned, leaning on his rifle, and then checked his watch. None of them liked the schoolyard shift, out in the cold; Ana Himyana was probably the only thing keeping him from shooting someone out of sheer boredom.

Miren said, 'Maths next. I'm so *sick* of maths. Honestly, no Spanish, no history, no literature, no catechism . . . Not that I miss catechism . . .'

'Stop going on, Miren,' I said, without looking at her.

'What's the matter with you?' she said, putting the leaflet down on the bench next to her. 'You haven't been nice to me for *months*.'

I looked at her, taking in her red cheeks, the clear drop trembling on the end of her nose and the expression on her face.

I said, 'I'm sorry. I just . . . Sorry, Miren.' I glanced over at the guard again, wishing he could stand somewhere else, out of sight. It was stupid; they were supposed to be here to check on the nuns – to make sure no one taught us 'imperialist fictions' instead of the truth – so why did he have to be outside with us? To prevent a counter-revolution by a bunch of schoolgirls? To stop us escaping?

Ana Himyana said something, and he laughed, throwing his head back.

Miren turned her head to follow my gaze, and said, 'My papa says there isn't anything else for them to do, and the government just wants them to feel important. So they get rifles and badges and then they stand around flirting with people like Ana.'

I clenched my teeth. 'Miren. Stop saying things like that. He might hear you. Or . . .' Or someone else might; it didn't matter who. I didn't know why she made me feel so jumpy, but there was something about her voice, flat and earnest, as if no one could possibly disagree with what she said . . . I shut my eyes again, wishing I could shut my ears as well.

There was a shout from the schoolhouse – a male voice, followed by two women's voices, overlapping into a mess of vowels without any words. I opened my eyes and turned to look. A guard – the oldest one, with a paunch and a grey beard – was pulling one of the nuns into the schoolyard, in a flurry of black and white. She had her head down, so I couldn't see who it was, but behind her was Sister David, her face flushed, raising her voice. She said, 'Let go of her at *once*! How dare you lay hands on her like that! Get *off* –'

I felt Miren stiffen, and the noise in the schoolyard faded.

The guard dragged at the nun's arm, pulling her upright. She was shaking; she fumbled with her veil, pushing it away from her face. It was Sister Paul, one of the youngest nuns. She used to teach the catechism classes, and gave us sweets if we got all the answers. She said, 'I only – thought that – it wasn't *right* –'

'You know it's not allowed! I'm here to make sure none of your subversive politics gets – none of your bloody *religion* –'

'This is a convent school! I'm a *nun*!' Sister Paul said, her voice high and breathless. She jerked her arm out of his grip. 'I refuse to cut these children off from the love of Our Lord, simply because evil has taken over the country and –'

'That's enough,' Sister David said. She said it quietly, but somehow it cut through everything, leaving a silence with sharp edges. 'Sister Paul, please control yourself. Mr Aznar –'

'*Comrade* –'

'Comrade Aznar. Please excuse my sister-in-Christ – she is still learning to appreciate the glory of our new revolutionary government. I assure you she won't be any more trouble to you.'

He chewed his bottom lip, licking strands of his beard away from the corner of his mouth. Finally he looked Sister Paul up and down, and said, 'Yes, well, don't do it again. The Ministry of Education would have my balls –' He stopped himself, as if he'd realised he was talking to a nun, but Sister David only smiled at him.

He turned and rolled his shoulder, adjusting the rifle strap. 'All right, well . . . Bloody hell, it's cold out here –'

'The glory?' Sister Paul said, and took a step towards Sister David. 'The *glory* of our revolutionary government? The *glory*?'

Sister David looked at her, and then turned on her heel. 'Did you leave your form alone, Sister? You should be getting back to them –'

'You think – glory? *Glory?*' It was as if she couldn't say anything else: as if the word was stuck in her throat and she was trying to get rid of it. She ran after Sister David, caught her arm and swung her round. 'How *dare* you, Sister? How dare you say such things, when you're wearing the habit of a religious order? You know as well as I do that it's evil, they're murderers and thieves, how can you bear to defend them? You should be ashamed! You're betraying everything, the Church, Our Lord himself, *everything* –' She shook Sister David's arm. 'You want us all to stay quiet, just go along with it, and it's *evil*, we have to say something, it's our duty, how can you *bear* . . . ?' She ran out of breath. Her eyes were wide and there was saliva in the corner of her mouth.

Comrade Aznar was staring. He cleared his throat and glanced over his shoulder at the other guard. No one said anything. Finally, in the silence, Sister David said, 'Thank you, Sister, that's enough. Go and compose yourself.'

Sister Paul was crying now. She shook her head.

Sister David took a deep breath. Her face looked calm, but she was shaking, and I didn't think it was because of the cold, or not just because of the cold. 'Remember your vows of obedience,' she said, with a softer note in her voice. 'We will talk about this later. Now go inside.' She turned to Comrade Aznar and said, 'I apologise for her, Comrade. I'm sure you'll understand that it has been rather a strain for us recently.'

Comrade Aznar screwed up his face, sniffed and said, 'Well, just make sure nothing like this happens ag–'

But he didn't have time to finish his sentence. Sister Paul flew at him, her breath catching and squeaking in her throat. He reeled back, swearing, but she went after him in a flurry of black cloth, spluttering tears and pounding her fists against his chest. There were words mixed in with her sobs: 'Go away, go away, go *away* . . .'

'Sister – control yourself –' Sister David tried to drag her away from him, but she wasn't strong enough. There was the noise of a seam tearing and a yell from Comrade Aznar. Suddenly there was blood running down his face and Sister Paul was laughing in a high, hysterical tone that made my stomach contract. Sister David was grabbing for her arms, but Sister Paul kept throwing her off. Her face was stretched and wet, and her eyes were fixed on Aznar.

'Get off me – don't you touch me again, you bitch!'

Aznar had one hand up to his forehead, and blood was trickling down between his fingers. His other hand was on his rifle.

'Go away – leave us alone – this is *our* school, you don't have any right –' She pulled away from Sister David, and tried to run at him again, her fingers curled as if she wanted to claw his eyes out. Her mouth was open. She looked mad, possessed.

He recoiled, and now his rifle was level, pointing at her. He looked scared, even though he was the one with a gun. 'You take one more step –'

'Sister, please, *please* stop this –' Sister David's voice was high and breathless; I wouldn't have recognised it.

'*Get out of our school!*'

And then there was a scuffle, a flap of black and white, and a gunshot.

I felt Miren jerk next to me, and for a strange dislocated moment I thought someone had shot *her*. Then, in the silence, Comrade Aznar stepped backwards, his rifle wobbling in the air as if he couldn't hold it steady, and I saw Sister Paul kneeling on the ground in front of him, her head bent and her hands clasped over her stomach. She was coughing. Aznar said, 'Oh . . . hell . . .'

And then the other nun started to cry, and it was Sister Paul, and I realised that meant –

The one who'd been shot was Sister David; she must have tried to get between them, to stop Aznar firing . . .

Slowly the noise in the schoolyard rose. I heard Miren take a deep breath and start to sob. Someone, somewhere, was shrieking. But Ana Himyana was the only person who moved. She crossed the yard to Sister David, bent down and then looked up at Aznar. She said, 'Call Doctor

Bidart, please, Comrade. I'm sure no one will mind if you use the telephone in Sister David's office. It's next to the hist– the political-awareness classroom.'

Sister David said, 'Thank you, Ana. Would you be kind enough to help me up, please?' Her voice was tight but the words were clear. I felt a surge of relief: if she could talk, then she'd be all right, wouldn't she?

Ana helped her up, and in spite of the strain on her face Sister David stood up straight, or nearly. There was a shiny patch on her black habit, spreading outwards from her stomach. She said to Aznar, gasping a little, 'I think perhaps these children should be given the rest of the day off. If you would see to it . . . and Sister Paul needs to go to the infirmary. May I ask you to see to that too?'

Aznar nodded, without meeting her eyes. He mumbled, 'Sister, I didn't mean to . . . you know, it was just that . . . listen, I . . .' but then he petered out.

Ana and Sister David hobbled back into the building, and Sister Paul followed them.

Aznar turned round and said loudly, 'Right, you lot. Go home.' Then he strode over to the other guard and started a loud conversation about the best place to buy cigarettes, as if nothing had happened. But his rifle was still in his hands, and still shaking.

Miren took hold of my hand tightly. I squeezed back. I felt her turn her head to look at me, but I didn't want to meet her eyes. If I met her eyes, it would all be real.

After a long time, three girls from the form below me stood up and made their way to the gate. They had their arms round each other, and two were crying. The other one was staring around with blank eyes, as if she'd lost something.

Slowly the schoolyard emptied. Miren and I stayed where we were. In the end we were the only ones left. I could hear raised voices from the infirmary window, and heard someone say, 'Bidart.' They were talking about Papa; and right on cue he was there, hurrying through the school gates with his bag in his hand. For a split second I didn't see him as my father, but a thin, greying stranger. He walked straight past without seeing me, and I wanted to cry. I said, 'Papa . . .' but he still didn't hear. He almost ran into the building, and the door swung shut behind him with a bang.

Miren stood up. She said, 'I'm going home then.' She looked at me with a strange expression, as if there was something she wanted me to do.

I nodded. I wanted to say something, but I was scared I'd burst into tears. I wished Papa had just *seen* me.

And Sister David . . . All of a sudden I remembered what she'd said to me, months ago. *Be careful, Esteya. Prudence is as great a virtue as courage. No one* – no one – *gains from unnecessary suffering* . . . But she'd stepped between Sister Paul and Aznar's gun, hadn't she? I gritted my teeth. Why had she done it? What a stupid, *stupid* thing to do . . .

'Are you . . . ? Esteya?' Miren said. 'Are you all right?'

It shouldn't have happened. The revolution was supposed to *stop* people getting shot. Aznar wasn't a policeman, he was a People's Guard, he was meant to protect us . . .

Be careful, Esteya.

'I'll be going then,' Miren said. She sniffed and wiped a drip away from her nose. 'Um . . . see you tomorrow . . .'

I smiled at her, although I could feel it wasn't very convincing. I said, 'Yes, see you tomorrow.'

She walked away. After a while I got up and went out through the gates. I didn't look back; although later I wished I had, because the next day the school was closed, and it never opened again.

I should have gone home, but I couldn't bear the thought of it. Martin would still be at school, and imagining explaining to Mama what had happened made my throat tighten even more. But I was too cold to stay where I was.

Skizi. I had to see Skizi.

Just the idea of her helped a little. As I made my way through the quiet streets and out into the open fields I was hurrying, thinking of the warmth when she put her arms round me, the comfort of her hands on my back. I wanted to close my eyes and let her kiss me, blotting out the image of Sister David with that wet patch on her habit, Sister Paul with her eyes wide and ferocious, flying at Comrade Aznar . . .

I trudged up the hill. I could see smoke coming from the chimney of Skizi's hut and trickling out through the holes in the roof above the hearth. Normally she didn't light a fire in the daytime in case someone saw; but I didn't blame her, today.

When I pushed the door open Skizi was in a nest of blankets in front of the hearth. The air was thick with smoke – the chimney didn't draw properly – and it smelt acrid and resinous. The fire was spitting and hardly seemed to give out any heat.

Skizi looked up. Her face was pale and blank, as if the muscles had frozen. She blinked. 'What are you doing here?'

'They sent us home.'

'This isn't your home.'

I shrugged. I stood where I was for a moment, waiting for her to invite me in. I wanted her to ask what had happened, but she didn't.

Skizi went back to staring into the fire. I came into the hut, feeling the smoke sting my eyes, and sat down next to her without taking my coat off. I wanted to reach for her hand, but it was hidden inside the knot of blankets.

There was silence. I wondered how long Skizi had been like this, sitting staring into the fire, motionless.

I said, 'Are you all right?'

She nodded, without looking at me. After a while she said, 'I'm cold.'

I put my arms round her, rubbing her back through the blankets. She seemed to shrink away from my touch, and I stopped. The blankets smelt damp, as if they hadn't been properly dry for months.

In the end I said, 'One of the guards shot someone. Sister David, who teaches maths. There was a sort of – well, a sort of fight, and –'

Skizi stiffened, but all she said was, 'Dead?'

'No, only in the stomach, but –'

'She'll die, probably. People do, from stomach wounds. Everything leaks out and poisons them. You should know that; you're a doctor's daughter.'

I swallowed. All I could think of to say was, 'Oh.'

She leant her head on my shoulder, and I felt her breath come and go on my neck. After a while she said, 'Sorry.'

I tightened my arm round her. I wished I had something to say – something to make her laugh, or take my hand, or just look at me. The way I felt about her made me ache, worse than the cold. I felt my throat start to hurt, but I was scared to cry, in case she said something scathing – or worse, nothing at all. I clenched my teeth and tried to remember what it had been like in the summer: long lazy days when we hardly said anything at all, and it didn't matter. Now it felt as though the silence was a reproach.

I said, 'Have you been here all day?'

'Of course,' she said, and huddled closer into her blankets. 'Where else would I be?'

'Well, you might've . . . gone into town for food, or . . .' I looked up at her shelf of tins. It was almost empty. She'd need some more, soon.

'I don't like going into town,' she said. 'People won't serve me, even when I can pay.' She wasn't complaining, but I knew she was telling the truth. 'Anyway, there's nothing to buy. The shops are all empty.'

'Don't be silly,' I said, hating the way my voice came out. 'Of course the shops aren't *empty*. We have loads of food at home. I'll buy you food. What would you li–'

'Bloody hell!' Suddenly she threw me off, and she was on her feet, wrapped in blankets. She stared at me, her top lip drawn back, showing her teeth. 'When was the last time you were in a shop, Esteya? So *you'll buy me food*, will you?' She mimicked my voice, high and pathetic. 'The shops are empty. The only reason you and your bloody family have food is because your brother is a bloody Communist. Take a look around, for God's sake! *You* have meat and cheese and bread and potatoes and . . . and *chocolate* – but who the hell else does? Your friends at school? The priest? Just think about it. No one wants to get on your bad side, in case you go running to your pet Minister of Information or whatever he is. And don't you –' her voice cracked – 'don't you *dare* tell me not to be *silly*. You stupid, self-absorbed, *lucky* little –'

She stopped, breathing hard, as if she'd nearly said something terrible. For a moment we stared at each other. My insides felt frozen, heavy and rigid.

Then, like something finally breaking under a weight, she dropped to a crouch on the floor and put her hands over her face.

I heard myself say, 'I didn't know. You're right, I'm stupid.'

She laughed, and went on laughing, until I realised she wasn't laughing at me. I got up, knelt next to her and put my arms round her. When I squeezed she flinched, and hissed as if I'd hurt her, but when I went to pull away she caught my hand and held me there. I wasn't sure, but I thought she was crying.

'It's such a mess – it was supposed to get better – and I thought, I really thought . . .' Her voice was thick and blurred.

'It will get better,' I said. 'It will. I promise.'

'Oh yes?' She was laughing again, sobbing with laughter as if she was in pain. 'You know there's still a notice in the town hall that says: no dogs, no alcohol, no Zikindi? And in one of your brother's pamphlets it says we're a problem the Communists are going to solve. And the bloody guards – now they're shooting nuns . . .' She sobbed helplessly, and this time it definitely wasn't laughter. 'And I'm freezing cold, I'm *dying* of cold, and I'm hungry, and –'

She stopped, shaking her head, and rubbed her face against the cloth of my coat, like a cat. Her cheeks left wet marks on my lapel.

I held her tighter, and she winced. She glanced up at me quickly – almost warily, I thought – and then away again. She stroked my hand with a fingertip, her mouth softening as if she could feel my gaze.

'What's wrong?' I said.

'Nothing,' she said, too quickly. 'Well, I'm hungry and cold, like I just said.'

'Why don't you want me to touch you?'

'I do,' she said. 'I'm just shrammed, that's all. A bit stiff. You know. It's so *cold* . . .'

I twisted to stare her straight in the eyes. She looked away. I pulled the corner of the blanket gently away from her neck, and bent to kiss the skin I could see. It was cool and smelt sour and smoky. Then I tugged at the blanket again, and at her collar, until I could see the contours of her collarbone, and the edge of a bruise blooming purple and blue between her breasts. My stomach turned over. I started to unbutton her shirt, but she pulled away. She said quietly, 'Don't. It's cold.'

'What happened?'

'A couple of men from the town. The butcher wouldn't serve me, and then when I came out of the shop, they were there, and . . .' She shrugged.

'Did they . . . ?' I stopped. I couldn't breathe.

'No. Don't worry. It wasn't . . . it happens. It's not the end of the world. It's not like it happened to *you*.' She wasn't being sarcastic; she really meant it.

'When?'

'A couple of days ago. There were some guards there, but they didn't do anything. I mean . . . they didn't help.'

'Let me see,' I said, and this time she let me unbutton her shirt. She was shivering, and her nipples were puckered and sticking up. There was a bruise – a chain of bruises – twisting across her ribcage like a purple scarf, ending in the middle of her collarbone. Here and there the skin had been broken, and the scabs looked thick and painful. It made my own skin tingle to look at them.

I laid my hand on the bruise, very gently, and Skizi caught her breath and hissed through her teeth. For a moment I felt a surge of guilt that was so strong I couldn't speak. This was all my fault, somehow. I should've been able to protect her. How could I have let this happen?

I said again, 'It'll get better. I promise, Skizi. I'll make sure it gets better.'

'Course,' she said, with a hint of a smile. 'With you on my side . . .'

I swallowed. She was right: there wasn't anything I could do. For a moment I wondered whether I could get Leon to send a box of food, like the one he'd given us at Twelfth Night – a leg of lamb, bars of chocolate, jam, potted shrimps, a pineapple . . . I knew it would take days to get to us, and then Mama would ration it out, at mealtimes; but just for a moment I let myself imagine turning up with the food in my arms, and Skizi's face lighting up.

I said, 'Wait here.' I buttoned up her shirt again and wrapped the blanket round her, pulling the folds gently up to her neck.

'Where are you going?'

'I'm . . . Just wait here,' I said.

'You're coming back?' Something in her voice tugged at me. She sounded younger than normal, helpless, like an animal.

'Yes,' I said. 'Just wait here. Keep warm. I'll be back soon, I promise.'

I got up, went out into the field and ran down the hill, towards home.

Ten

I didn't know where Mama was, but the house was empty. I stood in the hall, listening to the silence. The air seemed to taste of dust and damp, and everything was still. For the first time I was glad that we'd had to send Dorotea away. I went into the pantry, and started to gather things into a tea towel. My heart was pounding, but my hands were so cold it was hard to pick things up. The last dregs of a jar of honey had crystallised. I wondered how long it had been since Skizi ate something sweet and put it into my bundle.

Once I thought I had enough – or rather, once I'd taken everything I thought I could get away with – I ran upstairs to collect a cake of soap and a towel. Then I came back downstairs again, and filled a bucket with coal. There wasn't much left, but Papa could always get more, and Skizi needed it more than we did . . . Finally I was ready. I eased myself out through the front door, trying not to drop anything, my arms full and already aching from the weight of the coal.

Ana Himyana was at the corner, talking to another guard. She'd changed out of her school uniform: now she was in brown workmen's trousers and a thick jumper, her hair pushed up into a red beret. She looked unreasonably glamorous, like the star of a film. I pulled back into our doorway, squeezing my eyes shut and hoping she hadn't seen me.

'Hey! Esteya!' Her voice had a familiar, amused note in it, as if we were friends. 'Are you running away to seek your fortune?'

I was going to have to walk past her. I gritted my teeth and hurried down the street so that she wouldn't be encouraged to go on talking to me. As I passed her I said, 'No, I'm – I'm just visiting a – a friend of mine . . .'

Ana laughed again, and stepped out in front of me. I stopped, because she was in my way, but she didn't move. She reached out and plucked the soap off the top of the pile of things in my arms. 'Oh, rose,' she said. 'How lovely. Do you always take soap to your friends, or is this one particularly dirty?' She gave me a radiant smile.

'It's none of your business,' I said.

'Oh, Esteya! Your repartee is so *withering*,' she said, putting a hand on her heart and pretending to swoon. The guard – he had a dark, narrow face and a thin moustache, and I disliked him already – chuckled and wiped his nose with his forefinger.

'Get out of my way.'

'There's no need to be so –'

'Get out of my way, or I promise you'll regret it.' I just meant that I might lose my temper; but something like fear flashed in her face and she stepped sideways.

'Sorry, Esteya,' she said, 'I was only teasing,' and handed the soap back to me.

I stared at her, and suddenly I remembered what Skizi had said: *no one wants to get on your bad side, in case you go running to your pet Minister of Information* . . . I swallowed. 'You watch yourself, Ana Himyana,' I said, hardly recognising my own voice. 'If you put a foot out of line – if you do *anything* – I'll tell Leon, and the Party will know about it. So be very, very careful.'

She held my gaze for a moment, and then her eyes dropped. She said, 'I didn't mean . . .' Her voice tailed off. The guard wouldn't meet my gaze either.

I walked straight past them, feeling my blood buzz in my cheeks. I felt like a witch who'd called down a curse on someone. It made me feel queasy and excited at the same time.

Then I turned left, past the church and into the alleyways, and I was so eager to get to Skizi that I forgot all about Ana.

Skizi was curled in her blanket in front of the fire, but now even her head was hidden, and only a tuft of greasy-ish hair was sticking out of the folds. She was shivering. The fire had almost gone out, and the smoke was hanging in the air like a cold fog. She didn't move, even when I said her name. It was only the crash of the bucket of coal dropping on to the floor that made her emerge, blinking.

I smiled at her, crouching to put down the bundle of food. I flipped open the corners of the tea towel, like a pedlar displaying his wares. 'Look,' I said, and I could hear the pride in my voice. 'Cheese and sausage and a tin of sardines and olives and half a loaf of bread and – well, this *was* honey, once, but I'm not sure what it is n–'

Skizi sat up. She said, 'What's in the bucket?'

'Coal.' I waited for her to smile, but she didn't. 'I thought – I know the hearth in here is a bit small, and it'll take ages, but we can heat enough water to fill the hip bath, and then you can – I brought some soap –'

'How kind,' she said.

I looked down at the food, spread out in front of me,

and suddenly it seemed pathetic: there was too little of it – or too much, I wasn't sure which. I cleared my throat. 'Don't you . . . I thought . . . aren't you . . . ?'

'Don't I want it?' She stood up, wrapping the blanket round herself, and came towards me. She reached out and nudged the jar of honey with her toe. 'Oh yes,' she said. 'Of course I want it. I'm not proud. I don't mind accepting charity.'

'Skizi, it's not –'

'Nice, is it? To be a good, sweet little ministering angel? Nice to be able to raid your larder and give it all away. Wish I could do that.'

I stared at her. I forced myself to say, 'It's not charity.'

'No? What is it then? What do you want in exchange?'

'I . . . Skizi, I love you, it's a – a present –'

Her eyes narrowed. If I hadn't known better, I might have thought she was going to cry. 'Oh, for God's sake, Esteya! Stop saying that. You don't love me. I make you feel good, that's all. You like feeling superior, you like playing at being in love, you like it when we –'

'That's not fair! I *do* love you –'

'You don't know anything about me. How old am I, Esteya? Where was I born? Where are my parents? What –' her voice cracked – 'what the *hell* am I doing living here, in this hut?'

I dug my nails into the palms of my hands until all I could feel was the pain. 'You never said, so I thought – I didn't want to ask –'

'Yes, I'll take your food. I'll even let you heat water for me to have a bath, and I'll wash myself with your pink soap and smile at you and pretend to be grateful and afterwards, because I feel sorry for you, I might let you kiss me and undress me and . . . but don't think it's because I love you, or even like you particularly. All right? I'll be nice to you because I'm hungry, and I want to be warm and clean, and . . . but you're smug and self-satisfied and you make me bloody *sick* –'

She stopped. She was staring at me, and her own face was appalled.

I closed my eyes.

When I opened them again nothing had changed.

'You don't have to –' I swallowed. 'But – why did you . . . Never mind. I'm sorry.' I turned on my heel and stumbled towards the door. If I could only get out, and out of sight, before I started to cry . . .

'And take your bloody coal with you.' Her voice was thin and tired.

I looked over my shoulder, and for a blessed second all I felt was anger. Then, before I could say anything, I saw Skizi's face thaw and crumple. She gazed at me and blinked, and tears spilt out of her eyes and rolled down her cheeks.

'Sorry,' she said, so quietly I hardly heard her. 'Sorry. I didn't mean it.'

'Didn't you?'

'No. It was stupid. I just . . . I'm sorry.'

I kept looking at her, filled with an odd mixture of anger and pity. I'd never seen Skizi cry; it was like seeing someone else with the same face.

'Don't go,' she said. 'Please, Esteya, don't go. I was being stupid. I'm sorry, I'm really sorry . . .'

I stood still and silent. There was nothing I could say.

She came up to me, and leant her head against my shoulder, rubbing her face against my coat. 'Please, Esteya, I'm sorry. I'm grateful for the food, really I am. Don't be angry.' It was so unlike her that I almost pushed her away; but instead I lifted my hand and stroked her hair, very gently.

She raised her head and pressed her lips against mine, suddenly, surprisingly. I put my arms round her and pulled her into a better position. For a moment we kissed properly – and then I felt her start to sob.

I pulled back, staring at her. She glanced up, seeming to meet my gaze, but her eyes were blind, overflowing with water. She bent over, wrapping her arms round her ribcage, and wept. She cried and cried, as if everything in the world was broken.

I had never seen anyone cry like that. It made me think of the way Teddy had cried, on his knees in our hallway, staring at the blue-and-white fragments of his English tea set; but Skizi wept with a kind of abandoned, unself-conscious grief that resonated in my bones and made me feel bruised. I crouched next to her, patting her shoulder awkwardly, saying useless things like, 'Hush, Skizi, it's all right, it's all right . . .' But she didn't seem to realise I was there.

After a while the cold got too much. My muscles were aching and prickling, and I couldn't stay still. In the end I stood up, wincing as the blood flowed back into my legs. Skizi didn't notice that I'd moved; she was still sobbing, with a hopeless, adult note in her voice, as if she'd go on for ever. I'd never felt so alone in my life.

I wanted to sit down next to her and cry too; but that wouldn't help. I clenched my back teeth together and walked around her to the food that was still spread out on the tea towel. I picked it up and put it on her shelf. The sausage smelt of grease and garlic, and the cheese smelt of old boots; I despised myself for expecting Skizi to eat them.

I put the soap on the other end of the shelf, and went outside to fill her old metal bucket with water. The well-water was freezing, and my hands hurt so much it was hard to hold the handle. I was glad of the pain, though. It distracted me from Skizi's sobs.

I took the bucket back inside, built up the fire and put the water on to heat. I dragged the old hip bath out from its corner and put it in front of the hearth. Then I sat down against the wall with my knees up, waiting for the water to boil. After a long time Skizi quietened down, and her sobs turned to sniffs. I poured the water into the hip bath and went outside for another bucketful. When I came back inside Skizi was lying quietly with her eyes closed.

It took a long time for the water to get hot. By the time the second bucketful was boiling, the water in the bath was only just at blood heat, and it took four bucketfuls to fill the bath. But I didn't mind: I felt empty, content to sit and stare at the fire, adding bits of coal until I could feel the warmth slowly filling the hut.

When I'd finally filled the bath I said softly, 'Skizi?'

She opened her eyes, and then stood up, undressed and stepped into the bath, resting her hand on my shoulder to steady herself. Her bruises went right down to her waist, and there were more on her legs. She winced a little as she sat down. She rested her chin on her knees, clasping her hands around her shins, taking deep breaths. There was already a faint sheen of grime on the surface of the water.

I unwrapped the soap and gave it to her. She took it and sniffed it, and the corner of her mouth twitched. She raised her eyes to mine, and gave me a watery smile.

I smiled back, feeling a great surge of relief. I didn't say anything – everything still felt too fragile – but I watched while Skizi washed herself, rubbing the soap into her hair, bending forward to work it into the spaces between her toes with an earnest, concentrated look on her face. Then she handed me the soap and said, 'Can you do my back?'

I knelt down behind her, and ran my hands gently down her spine. I cupped my hands and poured water on to the nape of her neck, watching the wetness slide down over her vertebrae and her bruises. Anyone else would have thought it was ugly: Skizi's grimy, bony back, stained blue and purple . . . I ran the soap across her shoulders, and down, making my touch as soft as possible. The warm water made my fingers tingle. Skizi's skin was smooth – familiar and unfamiliar at the same time – and it made me think of wet clay, as if I was remaking her. I rinsed the dirt away and the shape of her bones shone pale gold in the glow from the fire.

'Thank you.'

For a strange, dreamy moment I didn't know if she'd said it to me, or the other way round. I said, 'Thank you,' and heard her laugh.

I leant forward and rested my cheek against her shoulder blade, feeling the rhythm of her breathing. I wanted to stay like that for ever.

Finally I felt her sigh, and the buzz of her voice in her skin as she said, 'Esteya? Did you bring a towel?'

'Mmmm.' I got up. The air was cold on my wet cheek. I picked up the towel, and when she stood up I wrapped her up in it, the way Mama used to do with me. She screwed up her face and grinned when I scrubbed her hair. I said, 'Are you warmer now?'

'Yes.'

'I'm stupid,' I said, 'I should've brought you some clean clothes.'

'For God's sake, Esteya, don't you think you've done enough?' But she was laughing as she said it.

'You could have my school uniform –'

'Shut up,' she said, and stepped out of the bath. 'Shut up shut up shut *up*.'

She put her arms round me, so that we were both inside the damp towel, and kissed me.

And it was the same as it always was – my hands recognising her body, knowing her, following the lines of her as if I knew her by heart – but it was different too. There was something new in the way she moved, a kind of need, as if for the first time I really mattered to her. She undressed me, fumbling with my buttons, breathing hard. Her wet hair clung to my cheek and mouth; I could taste soap and roses.

And then she kissed my eyes and my nose and my neck and my collarbone, working her way down my body, until I felt her lips brush my stomach. I put my hands on her hair, pushing my fingers into the tangles, as she went on kissing me.

We stayed there, wrapped in the blankets, for a long time. By the time I rolled over and sat up the fire had almost died. The light had faded, and there was a deeper chill in the air; I realised, with a shock, that it was late afternoon and Mama would be home.

Skizi yawned and stretched. She said, 'I'm *starving*. Did you bring me anything sweet?'

I stood up, passed her the jar of honey and started to get dressed. When I glanced round she was eating the crystals with her fingers. She looked up.

I said, 'What – what did happen to your parents?'

'They got taken away,' she said, as if she was talking

about the weather. 'By the police. A long time ago. They're probably dead.' She sucked one finger, and then scooped more honey out of the jar.

I nodded.

'We were . . . Back then, there were five families. We all travelled together. But people never liked us.' She shrugged. 'There was one day, my dad got drunk in the town and started a fight. That night the police came and burnt our camp and took everyone away.'

'Except you.'

'Yes, except me.' She stared into the bottom of the honey jar, but her eyes were blank, as if she was seeing something else. 'I ran away. I didn't want to get caught.'

I moved towards her, but she looked up and flinched before I could touch her. Her eyes were narrow and fierce.

'I survive,' she said, almost spitting the words at me. 'That's all I want. Nothing else matters, as long as I survive. Understand?'

'Yes,' I said, although I wasn't sure I did.

'If I need to run, I run. If I need to steal, I steal. Whatever I have to do . . .' There was a hard, intent look on her face. 'I don't care what I do, as long as I can walk out the other side. All right?'

'Yes, of course. I mean . . . of course. That's only sensible.' But I couldn't help feeling that I was missing something, that we were talking at cross purposes.

She stared at me for a moment longer, and then laughed and looked away. There was silence; I could hear the little moist sounds of her tongue as she licked the last of the honey off her fingernail.

'I should go home,' I said.

'Yes.'

'Goodbye then,' I said. But I couldn't bring myself to leave. If only she'd look up, say something or smile . . .

Nothing. I put my hands in the pockets of my coat, gave her a last look and went out into the field. The sky was dark grey, and the cold took my breath away. The smell of snow was in the air. I picked my way across the frozen ruts, moving through a mist of my own breath.

'Esteya!'

I turned round. Skizi was standing at the corner of the hut, still wrapped only in a blanket, her feet bare.

I paused. 'Yes?'

She took a few stumbling steps. I could see her shivering. 'Esteya –'

'What are you doing out here?' I said. 'Get back into the warm.'

'Tell me you love me,' she said, rushing the words so it took me a second to register what she'd said.

'Wh–?' I stared at her, and then took a deep breath. The air burnt my oesophagus, like acid. 'All right. I love you.'

'You mean it?'

'Yes, of course I – yes, I mean it.'

'Whatever happens?'

'Yes, of course, whatev–'

'No – *think* about it! Really, whatever happens?' She held my gaze.

I thought about it. I looked past Skizi, at the smoke trickling from the roof of the hut, at the skeleton of the olive tree, at the sky hanging low and heavy above it. I felt so helpless, so small, that I could have cried.

I said, 'Yes, whatever happens.'

There was silence again. I noticed a fleck of snow spin and settle on my sleeve, and when I looked up I could see the snow beginning in earnest, undulating and folding in on itself like a curtain.

'Thank you,' Skizi said. Her voice was very low.

I laughed. I was so tired that everything was starting to disappear into a kind of haze of absurdity. I said, 'You're welcome. Now can I go home?'

She nodded, turned away and ran into the hut without looking back.

I made my way down the hill, wondering vaguely what Mama would say when she saw how much food was missing, and what on earth I was going to answer.

Spring

Eleven

I sat on my bed, staring at the wall. I'd pinned up a couple of Leon's leaflets – the one with Angel on it, and one about the Great New Nation, and one about farming. I wasn't interested in farming, but it had a picture of women laughing, leaning on their hoes, their hair blowing out from under their hats. The sun was shining, and there was an overflowing basket of food sitting beside them. Now the paper had gone a funny jaundiced colour and was curling at the corners. The plaster behind it had cracked.

There was a knock on my door. I didn't say anything, but Martin came in anyway. He glanced at me, and went over to the window. There was water dripping from the eaves, and the breeze was blowing it against the pane. He opened the window and I felt the air swirl round me. It was – well, not warm, but only cool, not icy. I drew my legs up and rested my chin on my knees.

Martin sat down on the end of my bed, tried to flatten out the corner of the farming leaflet with his finger, and gave up.

'What do you want, Martin?'

'Just . . . bit of good news for you.'

'Oh yes?'

'There was a – the Party has . . .' He stopped and took a deep breath. Then he said, 'Esteya . . . are you all right?'

I looked at him, and then away, because I didn't want to see the sympathy in his eyes. I said, 'Oh yes, I'm having the time of my life, locked in my own house, not allowed to go *out* even, not allowed to –' I heard my voice thicken, and swallowed. If only I could have got word to Skizi . . . What if she thought I . . . ?

'Well, if you hadn't stolen all that –' Martin took another breath and rubbed the back of his neck. 'Honestly, Esteya . . .'

'Be quiet.'

He sighed. 'I wish I knew what was wrong with you. Ever since – well, since the summer . . . And now . . .'

'Leave me alone, Martin.'

And then, in spite of myself, I started to cry. It wasn't him. It was the thought of Skizi, waiting for me – or worse, not waiting for me. It was two weeks since I'd come back from her hut, to find Mama waiting for me, furious; two weeks since I'd refused to say what I'd done with the food. I'd never seen Mama so angry – or Papa either. It frightened me.

But I couldn't have told them about Skizi. In a way, it made it easier, not to have the choice: like a high wall, blocking me in, telling me where to go. I kept my mind on that wall, and kept my mouth shut.

And now I wasn't allowed to leave the house. And if Skizi was waiting, and waiting . . . Her voice went round in my head: *Tell me you love me*.

Martin shifted his weight, so the bed creaked, and I felt his fingers digging into my shoulder. 'Est . . . come on, Est . . .'

I fought to stop crying, and after a while it worked.

I stared at the leaflets – those laughing women in the sun – and blinked the last tears out of my eyes. I said, 'I'm fine.'

'Course you are,' Martin said, his voice resigned.

'So what was your good news?' I said. 'School opening again? No more food rationing? Another parcel from Leon?'

'Better than that.' Martin grinned. 'Remember Angel Corazon?'

'Of course I *remember* –' I said, before I realised he was joking.

'Well, he's coming to play here. The Party wanted to – well, Leon said they were sorry about what happened at your school, and they wanted to do something to make up for it, you know, a sort of celebration, and to mark the beginning of the pello season, and –'

'Propaganda,' I said.

'Well. Yes. Exactly.'

'Nuns getting killed by guards isn't good for the Party image. So they want to get everyone back on their side.'

Martin winced. I clenched my teeth and refused to look at him. 'Yes,' he said finally. 'I suppose that's it.'

There was a pause. I said, 'In any case, Mama and Papa won't let me go to a – a *celebration*. I'm in disgrace, remember?'

'Yes, they will. Everyone has to go. I mean . . . it's not exactly compulsory, but . . .' He trailed off. He scratched at the plaster, flaking it away from the wall with his thumb.

I caught Martin's eye. 'Oh. Not compulsory *but*,' I said. 'I see.'

'Leon at his megalomaniac best. Aren't you proud of him?' Martin said, and laughed.

A gust of cool air blew across my face, smelling of moisture and wet pavements. I felt my heart lift, a little. I took a deep breath. The winter had been hard, but now it was almost over, and then . . .

'Can I ask you something?' Martin said.

I shrugged.

'Are you in love with Angel Corazon?' He was leaning forward, so earnest . . . I snorted, and then started to giggle. It was the first time I'd laughed for weeks, and it felt good. He smiled reluctantly, and said, '*Are* you, though?'

'Martin, you're priceless. I've never even *met* Angel Corazon.'

'But you . . .' Martin gazed at me, and turned away. He stood up again, and pressed his hands into the plaster as if he wanted to knock the wall down. 'Ever since we saw him play, against the Bull . . . you've been so strange. And after the King's Cup final, when you ran away, and you said you were looking for Leon but I don't believe you, and . . .' He tailed off, and stared at the leaflets pinned above my head. 'I know it sounds stupid, but –'

'Martin . . .' It wasn't fair to laugh at him. He was right, in a way – although he was hopelessly wrong too.

'Tell me. Please. Esteya . . .' His voice was quiet, almost blown away in the soft, cool air from the window.

I leant back against the wall. It took me a second to realise I was shaking my head, rolling it from side to side in a slow, automatic refusal. Of course I couldn't tell Martin. It was the brick wall again, rising straight up in front of me. Of *course* I couldn't tell him. It was mad even to think about it.

I wished I could, though. If anyone would understand, it would be Martin.

I opened my mouth, not knowing what I was about to say. My heart was beating fast all of a sudden.

But I'd left it too long; Martin stood up, shrugging his shoulders. 'All right, not to worry,' he said. He grinned at me, just slightly too widely. 'Forget about it. You're such a sweet, innocent little girl that you couldn't possibly get up to anything anyway . . .'

'Little? I'm five minutes older than you,' I said. I could feel the same expression on my face: a grin, or almost.

'Better go and help with lunch. Make yourself useful. That way Mama and Papa might forgive you sooner.' Martin reached over and prodded me. I moved away, but he prodded me again. I pushed at his hand impatiently, but he kept on, and then we were struggling – scrapping, like we used to do – and I couldn't stop giggling and neither could Martin.

And afterwards, when I'd finally managed to kick him off the bed, and he was sitting against the wall, still laughing, I stood up, and went downstairs; and even though Mama was still coldly polite to me, I felt better than I had for a long time.

The day of the pello event, a week later, was spring. When I woke that morning, I was hot under my blankets and the room was bright and warm from the sun. It was already nine o'clock. I sat up, and for the first time in ages I felt pleased to be awake. Today I was going to go out; today I was going to watch Angel play pello; and today, if I could – if I was lucky – I'd see Skizi. It felt like the first day of the holidays – not the school-cancelled-until-further-notice holidays we'd been having, which left a sour taste in the mouth, but real, how-they-used-to-be, glorious summer holidays, like last year, when I'd spent months in the sunshine, running wild with Skizi . . . I felt my heart lift.

I dressed carefully. A year ago I would have worn my blue dress, my favourite, but it was too bourgeois now. I put on some old trousers of Martin's, and a shirt and waistcoat, and tied my hair up in a red handkerchief. When I looked at my reflection, I looked perfect: a daughter of the people, ready to shoulder arms at a moment's notice, androgynous and glamorous at the same time. It made me think of Elena, the girl who'd been shot in the street that day – and then, when I pushed that thought away, of Ana Himyana. I wrinkled my nose at myself. Like a film star *pretending* to be a Communist.

I went downstairs. Mama was in the study – I caught a glimpse of her through the open door, writing one of her endless letters to my great-aunt in America – and Martin was alone at the kitchen table, staring at his hands. When I came in he looked up, and raised his eyebrows. 'Revolutionary chic,' he said, grinning. 'You look like a propaganda poster.'

'Thanks,' I said, smiling back. 'You look like a peasant.' His clothes were practically identical to mine, as if we were wearing uniform.

'Thank you very much . . . Comrade,' he added, and we giggled. It was funny, how it still felt like a joke, like a game, even after everything. As if Martin and I were safe; as if all the things we'd seen were . . . not unimportant, but just not . . . about *us*.

'So,' Martin said. 'Angel Corazon, and that new player from Irunja, what's his name?'

I shrugged. I wanted to see Angel Corazon play, that was all; and then I wanted to find Skizi.

'I only care about Angel,' I said, and it sounded true. 'I'm not sure about pello any more. I just care about Angel.' Maybe it *was* true. If only I could have mentioned Skizi.

He rolled his eyes. 'Huh. Girls.' Then he grinned. 'Shall we go?'

'Now?'

'Come on. You don't want to wait for Mama, do you?'

I didn't, but it seemed amazing – a kind of miracle – that we could just walk out of the front door, into the street. I stood in the doorway, feeling a strange relief, as if I'd really been in prison. The street smelt of melted snow, and there was still water dripping off the eaves. It made a kind of tapping noise all around me, as if every stone had a heartbeat.

Martin looked over his shoulder and then walked down the street without waiting for me to follow. I took a last deep breath, and went after him.

We didn't see anyone until we got to the square in front of the church. Then there were hundreds of people, spilling out from the side streets, all with scarlet scarves or handkerchiefs or wide red belts. It was like a festival – people were eating and drinking, someone was selling pies – but no one was laughing, or dancing, or playing music. People were smiling, but with forced, cheerless smiles that faded when they looked around, scanning the crowd for guards or Party officials. Only the kids, running around and screaming, seemed normal. When we walked past the pie stall I heard someone say, 'Bread-and-garlic pies? Sacred Heart, when did meat get *that* hard to come by?'

Martin put his hand on my arm and didn't let go. I started to shrug it off, and then I was glad it was there.

They had put seating up around the square in front of the church, and there was a little group of men sitting outside the tavern, with their feet up on chairs, smoking. I saw, with a strange twist in my stomach, that one of them was Angel, looking heavier and older than I remembered him, and Leon was there too. Automatically I started to walk towards them, but Martin's hand on my arm held me back. When I looked at him, he shook his head. I rolled my eyes at him and sighed, but I didn't go any further. Martin was right: there was a sort of tension in the air, and their conversation was a staccato mix of pauses and raised voices. I saw Karl as well, drinking pastis out of a tiny cup and watching Leon in silence. Angel looked thoroughly miserable.

'Come on,' Martin said. 'I'll buy you a cone of sweets, if they haven't sold out already.'

The sweets were greasy and not very sweet, but they passed the time until the bell started to ring, summoning us to the beginning of the warm-up match. Everyone obeyed, but the enthusiasm was oddly muted, mixed with a kind of grimness like pupils having to go inside at the end of break. I kept hold of Martin's hand, not caring if it was babyish, and looked round for Skizi. Surely she'd be here, somewhere. But I couldn't see her. I lagged behind, ignoring Martin's tugging at my hand.

'Esteya, come *on* –'

I frowned and kept looking; then, when Martin shoved me forward and I found myself sitting on the bench beside him, I saw why he'd been trying to get me to walk faster. There were guards on both sides of us, eating pies full of strong-smelling garlic pap and laughing at their own jokes. They were the only people who were. The one closest to me pushed his leg against mine and gave me a wink. I gritted my teeth and looked straight ahead. But I couldn't keep it up; my eyes started to rake the stands again, searching for Skizi's face.

Martin said, 'What's up?'

'Have you –' I stopped, and then started again, in spite of myself. 'Have you seen – there aren't many – there haven't been many Zikindi around lately . . .'

He gave me a sidelong look, frowning, and shook his head. 'Don't think so. Not for ages. Haven't seen a Zikindi since . . . for ages. Not here, not since – oh, since we saw that girl, the day the Bull –'

'Course not,' the guard next to me said. 'We've been cleaning up, haven't we? Party orders.'

I turned to look at him. He was dark and spotty, and young. He had a sparse moustache and breath that stank of garlic. I said, 'What?'

'Zikindi clean-up,' he said, as if that explained everything. 'Get 'em out of our towns and cities. He who doesn't contribute to the state cannot expect to profit by it.' He put on a different accent for the last sentence; it reminded me of Leon's voice.

I felt my throat tighten. I said, 'Oh.'

'Weren't many here, actually. There was a clampdown last year and they don't try to come back here any more. Except – hey, Pauli –' The guard turned sideways to consult his friend. 'Last week, that tip-off you had –'

'Oh, yeah, that girl . . .' Pauli leered. 'Sweet little thing, so anxious to please . . .'

It took me a breathless second to realise that he was talking about the informer, not Skizi; then, with a wave of fury and relief, I thought, *Ana Himyana*. It had to be.

'Yes,' the first guard said, giving me a little smile as if he was doing me a favour. 'One of the convent girls, right?'

'Yeah,' Pauli said. He rummaged in his pocket for a cigarette, and then looked round, as if he was surprised we were still listening. 'She said there was a Zikindi girl living in the old Ibarra hut – you know, up on the hill – so we went up there and –' He broke off to light his cigarette. Somewhere a long way away I heard the referee blow his whistle for the start of the match, and everything went silent.

I couldn't move. In a strange, hoarse voice that didn't sound like mine, I said, 'Go on.'

'Well, we –' Pauli started, but the spectator on the other side of him jabbed his elbow into his ribs, and he scowled and shut up.

'What did you do?'

Martin nudged me. He said, in a low voice, 'Est–'

'What did you *do*?'

'Hey!' The spectator leant forward to glare at me along the row of seats. 'Let the players concentrate, Comrade!'

I glanced down at the court, where one of the players was standing ready to serve, taking deep breaths. It was stupid; in three seconds everyone would be shouting. The guards were looking down at the court now, as if they'd forgotten everything they'd been saying. As if a pello match was easily more interesting than the Zikindi girl they'd –

'Please,' I said, but there was a ripple of applause, and they didn't seem to hear me. 'Please tell me what happened to the Zik–'

Martin punched me.

It was on my shoulder, but I felt the impact all the way from my jaw to my buttocks. And it was *hard*; it made me catch my breath and then, after a second of numbness, clutch at my arm, the tears welling up automatically in my eyes. When I thought I could speak again, I opened my mouth to swear at him.

But he was already leaning towards me, looking worried. He said, 'Sorry, Est, sorry. Did I hurt you? I just needed to shut you up . . .'

'Why?'

'Because . . .' He hesitated, and looked round; but everyone was watching the game, and no one seemed to be paying attention to us. 'Please, Est, I don't think it's a good idea to ask too many questions. Not about . . . just don't. Please.'

My mouth was still open. He knew about Skizi – not her name, or exactly what had happened, but he'd realised why I was asking. I could see it in his face. Somehow he'd guessed . . .

I said, 'I have to go.'

'Not now. Go after the match.'

'But –'

'I know. I understand, honestly. But you can't walk out now. Look.' He pointed, keeping his hand low, so no one else would see. I followed his finger. The ranks of Party officials, in the stand near the referee. 'And there are guards everywhere.'

I looked at him. His eyes were very steady.

'All right,' I said. I dug my nails into my legs. I thought that if I could hurt, and keep on hurting, I wouldn't be able to think.

I stared at the court. *A Zikindi girl living in the old Ibarra hut . . . we went up there and . . .* I kept on staring, and the crowd made noises, but I stared and stared and I couldn't see anything.

* * *

The warm-up match ended finally. The noise was thick, like a wall, but it was restrained, polite, for a pello match. One player was standing in middle of the court, with Karl and another Party man I recognised only vaguely from one of Leon's leaflets.

I stood up. I wasn't the only one; people were shuffling out, going to buy another garlic pie, or stretch their legs. My knees were shaking. I had to lean on Martin's shoulder just to get myself to my feet.

He looked at me, and I felt him start to get up too.

'I'm going on my own,' I said.

'Esteya . . .'

'Please,' I said, and although I couldn't come up with any more words I thought Martin understood. He bit his lip, nodded and sat down again slowly.

I pushed my way along the row of seats. I was shaking more now, and my hands were fizzing as if they were crawling with ants. I shoved my way through the crowd, smelling garlic and sweat so strongly I had to cough to stop myself retching.

Then I was somehow out of the crowd and running through the alleys, and up the hill and towards the Ibarra hut, and my heart was beating in a kind of sickening blur in my chest, and I would have given anything, anything in the world, to see Skizi coming out to meet me, but she'd never done that, and this time she didn't either.

Twelve

I knew, of course.

I stepped in through the doorway, and grit and dead embers crunched under my feet, and I knew. Everything was smashed to pieces, burnt, scrawled with obscenities in ash and faeces. I was afraid to breathe, in case they'd killed her and not taken away the body. For a moment the fear was so strong that I smelt rotting meat – sweet, horrible – until I caught my breath, and there was nothing but the clean smell of faeces and charcoal, and I knew I'd been imagining it. At least, I thought, at least they'd had the decency to take her away . . .

I didn't want to go any further into the hut, but I did.

I was almost glad that they'd smashed everything: it was like walking into somewhere that reminded me of Skizi's hut but wasn't – definitely wasn't, couldn't have been – the same place. It would have been worse if nothing had changed. I didn't want to look round and think about the time I'd spent here, the hours we'd spent in front of the fire, in the bed, Skizi –

I felt my throat close, as if the air had turned to water and if I tried to breathe I'd drown. My legs started to give way. I stumbled to the wall and leant against it, my forehead against the plaster. Everything hurt.

They couldn't have killed her. They couldn't have . . .

But if they'd taken her away . . .

I heard myself cry out, a kind of hoarse, gasping noise, like someone falling. I couldn't bear it. Skizi, beaten up, taken away, imprisoned somewhere – in one of the camps, one of the work camps for scroungers and counter-revolutionaries that no one talked about and the Party claimed didn't exist but still, somehow, everyone knew about . . . There were people who belonged there – there were people who deserved it, who really did plot and subvert and sell black-market food, but not Skizi, not Skizi. I shut my eyes for a second and I could see the camp in my mind's eye, rows of white faces and grey blankets on the bunks and men with guns and everything smelling of grime and despair. I rocked forward, hitting my forehead on the wall, once, then twice, hard. Please, God, please don't let this be happening.

And I'd been . . . when they took her away, I was at home, sitting on my bed, reading or looking out of the window, thinking I was so strong, such a martyr for not telling Mama and Papa about the food, and . . . she must have thought that I'd abandoned her, that I was never coming back. She must have thought it was *me* that sent the gua–

I dropped to my knees, and then bent over. I felt myself retching and retching, tasted bile, felt my mouth gaping, stretched in a grimace. She must have thought –

I vomited on the floor, over and over again, until my ribs ached and my throat burnt with acid. My eyes were watering. In the end I caught my breath, sobbing with fatigue; and then, in the moment of silence between inhale and exhale, I started to cry.

* * *

When I stopped, finally, I was cold and shaking all over. I didn't feel any better, but the tears had dried up. I was thirsty.

I stood up. On the plaster next to me someone had written *LEECH*, in excrement. The *C* was smeared out of shape. I touched my face and felt the stickiness on my temple where I'd been leaning against the wall. It should have disgusted me, but all I could think about was how someone had managed to relieve themselves just at the right moment. Or perhaps they'd found the latrine pit at the edge of the field.

I raised my hand to wipe it off, and then thought I'd only get my hand dirty. I walked to the bed, or where the bed had been, letting my fingers brush the broken bits of furniture, the ash on the wall, the last smudged traces of Skizi's drawings. I remembered the first time I'd seen them. It seemed more than a lifetime ago. I could just make out the shape of a face, behind the new grafitti: *PERVERT* . . . I realised with a shock that it was my face, the dark-browed, unexpectedly beautiful face that had surprised me so much when I saw it.

PERVERT. It was a coincidence; they'd got everything else, *BITCH, SCUM, WHORE* . . . Above the bed someone had written *BOURGEOIS*, getting smaller to fit it on the wall. I heard someone laugh; I was on my own, so it must have been me.

I bent down and looked at the floor, searching for the floorboard with a knot in it. The floor was dirtier than I'd ever seen it, covered in mud and ash and with scorch marks where someone must have kicked the embers out of the hearth into the corners of the room, but it only took me a second to find the place I was looking for. I crouched, hooking my finger into the knothole the way

Skizi had done. It stuck – it must have swollen in the damp from the thaw – but when I pulled harder it came out, leaving the dark space underneath. I didn't know what I was looking for. Skizi had sold the rest of my mother's things ages ago, to buy food – we'd never mentioned it, but I knew, all the same – and she didn't have anything I wanted, not really . . . But there was something there, and I felt my heart speed up. Something pale, flimsy, folded up . . .

My old exercise book.

I'd forgotten about it. I hadn't seen it since the day I gave it to Skizi; she'd gone on drawing on the walls, on the spaces between paragraphs in the Party leaflets, on whatever else she could get her hands on.

I took it out, and opened it. It was sticky with moisture, and the pages clung together. I had to peel them apart, carefully, and even then they were wrinkled and fragile.

Drawings. Every page was full. Faces, figures, hands . . . I looked through, and the pain that had faded rose again, so intense for a moment that I couldn't see. When it died away, I was looking at myself. I swallowed, feeling a smile on my face that wasn't quite like a smile, and touched the charcoal lines, very gently. I was on the next page too – sitting with my back turned this time, my head leaning against the wall, watching a fire in the hearth. I recognised myself, somehow, in the shape of my shoulders. That was the way I sat – me, and no one else. I couldn't bear to keep looking at it. I turned the page.

There was a picture of a hand, a picture of a foot; and I realised, with a kind of pang, that they were my hand and my foot. They weren't beautiful – they looked like *my* hand and foot, after all – but they *were* too. As if she'd looked and looked, until she saw something that was worth drawing.

I flipped the pages, faster and faster. They were all me. My other hand; my knee, my elbow, my breasts, my navel.

She must have spent *hours* drawing me.

I would have cried again, if I'd had any tears left. But I didn't. I folded the exercise book over into a roll and put it in my pocket.

Then I left, walking down the hill without looking back, towards the noise of the festival. I walked slowly, because it didn't seem important.

Nothing was important any more.

The game was over. The streets were still heaving with people, and that strange joyless tension was still in the air, so that people grinned and shouted to each other and broke drunkenly into song without any of it sounding quite convincing. Or perhaps it was because of me that everything sounded fake, and actually they were all having a wonderful time. I didn't know, and I didn't care.

I glanced around for Martin. There were red handkerchiefs everywhere I looked, everyone in the same trousers and shirts, dressed like peasants. It was hard to spot anyone; they all looked the same. I caught sight of some girls from school, laughing with their heads together. It made me think of Ana Himyana. *That tip-off you had . . . that girl . . .* I felt sick. I turned aside, afraid someone would notice the expression on my face.

I found myself face to face with Martin. He was leaning in a doorway, frowning. When he saw me he straightened and moved towards me, but his face didn't change.

'Est. Are you all r–'

I looked at him, and he stopped and swallowed. I watched his face, somehow shocked by how quickly he seemed to know what had happened. I didn't realise my own face was that transparent.

I said, 'Don't ask me anything. Please?'

He blinked, and nodded. He held out his hand, as if I was a child, and I took it, holding on as if he could help.

'He lost,' he said. 'Angel Corazon lost.'

'Of course he did,' I said. I felt as if I'd known already, from the moment when I saw Skizi's hut all broken and empty. Of course Angel had lost.

Martin opened his mouth and hesitated. He said, 'Let's go home,' but I thought it wasn't what he'd meant to say.

I let him tug at my hand, leading me home. The streets were emptying already, the crowds receding like a tide, slipping back into their houses as soon as they decently could, leaving little pools of guards and Party members and drunkards. One of them called out as I passed: 'Hey, gorgeous, give us a kiss!' I should have felt vulnerable, but I didn't quite believe in my own existence. Martin gave me a sidelong glance and didn't say anything, but he sped up.

Then we were back at our own door, and inside the house, the thick walls cutting out the noise from the street.

Martin stood looking at me, in the dimness of the hall. I could smell the filth on my face, and the acrid scent of ash.

'Est . . . what happened? Are you all right?'

I stared back at him. I could have told him; I could have told him everything, and he would have understood. But if I told him, I'd cry, and it would all be real, and Skizi would still be far away, in a labour camp or raped or dead.

I heard myself laugh, a long shuddering laugh that sounded like the symptom of a disease. I turned away and started to climb the stairs. Without looking over my shoulder, I said, 'Long live the revolution, Comrade.'

I don't remember very much about the rest of that spring, or summer. The only thing that's clear is the letter I wrote, a few days after Skizi – after the pello game that Angel Corazon lost. It was to the Comrade Captain of the People's Guards, who happened to be one of Papa's friends. I didn't sign it.

Dear Comrade, I thought you should know that Ana Himyana has Anarchist sympathies. She spends all her time trying to distract the Communist guards and is a bad influence.

The second draft said, *Dear Comreyde, I thort you should no that Ana Himyana has Anakist simpathys. She spends all her time triing to distract the Communist gards and is a bad inflooence.*

But in the end I just wrote: *Ana Himyana is an Anarchist.*

I shouldn't have sent it, but I did.

Later I told myself that they would have taken her away even if I hadn't.

After that, the summer, when I think about it, is a blur of dust and thirst and politics. I didn't care; nothing seemed to make any difference to me. It was as if I'd left my life behind in Skizi's hut, and there was nothing left of me but a kind of hopeless determination to carry on. And hatred, of course. I used to sit on the edge of my bed, thinking about Ana Himyana, wishing I hadn't written that letter so that I could have the pleasure of doing it all over again. It gave me something to hang on to, something to think about, something to *feel*.

School had stopped for good, and we hung around, running errands for Papa, waiting for news from Irunja, sleeping during the day through sheer boredom. For a few weeks everyone was supposed to work in the fields, but the farmers got angry when we didn't know what to do, and after a while fewer and fewer of us went. We wore the same clothes every day – the Communist uniform of trousers and shirt and kerchief – and I cut my hair short with kitchen scissors, because bothering about how you looked was bourgeois, and dangerous. Not that I cared about the danger, but my hair made me hot, and now Skizi was gone I wanted to be ugly. One of the Ibarra boys taught me how to shoot a rifle.

There were more food shortages, and now Leon sent us nothing, not even letters. We ate lentils and oranges. The water kept being cut off, and we had to get our water from the stream, carrying it in buckets like peasants. Gatherings of more than ten people were banned; then more than five; then there was a curfew. The King's Cup was cancelled. No one played pello any more, not even kids in the street, because if too many people stopped to watch all at once they might have been arrested.

But people were arrested anyway.

Ana Himyana disappeared in the middle of August; but she wasn't the first, by a long way, or the last. I heard about it from Miren, who lived near the Himyana place. She sent me letters sometimes – her father came to visit Papa, to give him news and smuggled antibiotics – and I remember taking the envelope and opening it in the garden, in the shade of the wall, the place where Skizi and I had first talked. It was so hot that there was sweat dripping off my forehead and on to the paper before I read it.

Dear Esteya, I really miss you . . . Things are horrible here and I'm so bored!! My skin is all pimply, I'm so glad you can't see me, I think it must be the lack of vitamins. Mama says oranges are packed with nutrients but when that's absolutely all there is to eat I don't think they're enough, do you? And garlic soup for dinner and supper every day! If I see another garlic clove I shall DIE . . .

Papa's friend in Irunja says things are bad there too – the streets are quieter, but it's because everyone's leaving, and going over the border or into the country to find food. The water keeps getting cut off there too – I never thought I'd be glad I lived somewhere with a well . . .

How are things in town? Papa says a lot of people are hiding inside with the shutters closed, but I expect you're all right, aren't you? I mean, no one would dare to arrest YOU! Did you hear about Ana Himyana? There were guards on the road in the middle of the night a few days ago, and then we got woken up by someone pounding on the door. We were pretty scared, I can tell you, but when Papa opened the door it was only Mrs Himyana in hysterics, saying they'd taken Ana away. I never would have thought it, she was always so thick with the guards. I thought she was like you, not needing to be scared like the rest of us.

There was more, but I didn't read it. I sat, feeling my heart pound, fiercely pleased. It was justice, that was all. She deserved it. I thought about how it must have been: the guards pulling her from her bed, her hair tousled, her eyes red with sleep, not looking like a film star any more. Or did they wait downstairs for her, with insolent good manners, or pat her bottom as she walked out with them, head held high? I hoped not. I wanted it to have been horrible for her. I hoped they'd trashed the Himyana house while they were there, and spat in Ana's mother's face and hit her father with the butt of a rifle. I hoped they'd put Ana up against the wall and ripped her shirt off her and –

I put my hands over my face, feeling sick. I hated Ana. I did. I hated her. This was what I'd wanted. Wasn't it?

I took deep breaths. I felt exhausted, empty. I realised, distantly, that I *didn't* hate her, any more. I was too tired to hate anyone.

And then, in a flash, I was afraid. If I wasn't angry any more, I wasn't sure I was *anything*.

I stayed where I was for a long time, until the heat had lessened. Then I went upstairs, to where Martin was sitting at his desk, reading one of the bourgeois novels that he'd wordlessly refused to surrender. I stood in the doorway until he looked up.

I said, 'Ana Himyana.'

He blinked, and nodded. Then he stood up and went over to the wall, stepping over the mess on the floor. He wrote her name on the plaster, the most recent name in a long list.

I watched him write it. He spelt it wrong, with two *n*'s, but I didn't say anything. Then he stood back and looked at the wall. He opened his mouth, as if he was going to say something, but he didn't. He just looked.

I followed his eyes, and for a strange split second, instead of seeing Martin's wall, I saw the wall of Skizi's hut. Instead of Martin's neat handwriting, I saw the scrawls of excrement. *LEECH. WHORE. BOURGEOIS.*

I raised my eyes to the space at the top, too high for Martin to reach easily, above the names. Skizi's name should have been there; Skizi's name should have been there, first on the list. But there was just a blank space. No one would even know there was anything missing. When everyone else disappeared, they left their names at least; but it was as if Skizi had never existed.

I reached out and grazed Ana Himyana's name with my fingertips. Glamorous Ana, flirting with the guards.

I said, 'At least they get it right once in a while.'

Then I went and sat in my own room, on the bed. I got the pello ball that Skizi had given me out from under my pillow. And I threw it against the wall, over and over again, like a prisoner in solitary confinement.

The list grew longer and longer, spreading across the wall like mould. From time to time I went into Martin's room to look at it. It was always the same; he would be at his desk, reading, and I would pick my way over to the wall and read the new names. Sometimes I knew about them already; sometimes one would be a surprise.

Then I'd leave again, without saying anything.

But for some reason it never occurred to me that it was dangerous, just for the names to be there.

Autumn

Thirteen

The summer died slowly. The weather cooled, going straight from white-hot to grey, and autumn came, the storms giving way to endless, misty rain. The shops had notices in the windows. *NOTHING OF NOTHING.*

And then, one afternoon in October, Miren's father came to see us, unannounced. I was in the attic with Mama, sorting through clothes to find some that were shabby enough to wear but still thick enough to keep us warm, and I heard the door open and close. The sound was faint but unmistakable; so few people came to see us that Mama and I both froze, sharing a look. If it was one of Papa's patients, they would have knocked at the door to the dispensary, at the side of the house . . .

We stood up, without a word, and clambered down the ladder to the landing, careful not to make any noise. Then we heard Miren's father's voice, and grinned at each other in relief.

Papa said, 'Come in, I was just sorting some –'

'Are you alone?'

'Well, I –' In a lower voice he said, 'My wife and the children are upstairs, but I don't have any patients here, if that's what you mean.'

'I must talk to you, Anton.'

'Certainly,' Papa said.

'And your son – none of your son's Party friends – you're sure no one's here except your family –'

'Yes,' Papa said, 'as I said, only my wife and the children are here. Bernardo, are you feeling quite all r–'

'Good, good,' Miren's father said, interrupting him. He was speaking too quickly, as if he was running out of breath on every word.

I heard my father open the door to his study, and two sets of footsteps as they went in. The door shut.

Mama took hold of my wrist and pulled me towards the top of the stairs. When I turned to frown at her, she put her other finger to her lips and pointed down through the banisters at the door of Papa's study. She breathed, 'Come on . . .'

It took me a second to understand; then I said, too loudly, 'You want us to *eavesdrop*?'

She smiled. Suddenly, disconcertingly, I saw what she must have looked like when she was my age; but it only lasted for a split second, and then I saw the new creases round her eyes, the strain in her expression. 'You know Bernardo,' she said softly. 'If he knows there are women listening, he won't say anything sensible.'

'But . . .' I wanted to laugh – at her, at how shocked I was.

She started to walk down the stairs quietly. She didn't look back at me, but she didn't let go of my arm either, so I had to follow. She had grey in her hair; I hadn't noticed that before.

When we got to the hall, she let go of me and leant to put her ear against the crack between the study door and the door frame. I stood there, watching her face.

She seemed to have forgotten I was there. Very faintly, I heard Papa's voice, forced and jovial, as if Bernardo was one of his patients.

' . . . on then,' he was saying. 'What's the trouble? More shootings in Irunja? More corpse pits?' His tone was brisk and businesslike, as if he was enquiring about a rash of pimples or a nasty cough.

Mama closed her eyes, as if that would help her to hear better.

'More arrests here, in town,' Bernardo said. 'Mainly Socialists and Anarchists, couple of Catholics . . . business as usual . . .' He laughed, but the sound of it made me wince, and I imagined Papa frowning and glancing quickly at his medicine cabinet. I might have been right; at any rate, after a few seconds I heard the clink and glug of pouring, and the chink as Papa put the brandy bottle back on the sideboard.

Papa said, 'Pull yourself together, man. Drink this and calm down.'

'Calm down? Anton – do you know why I've come? Not to chat about the news in town, I can tell you! It's . . . You know Miren, my daughter Miren –'

'Of course I know –'

'She talks to the guards a little bit, trying to keep them on our side, you know, not everyone has your adv–' Bernardo stopped, as if he was suddenly uncertain of what he was saying, and I heard him gulp. 'Talks to them, calls them "comrade", never really approved but she was right to do it, Anton . . .'

'Certainly,' Papa said, but he wasn't agreeing, only trying to keep Bernardo on track.

'She gets to hear things that way, you know, things that aren't in the newspapers, well, nothing *is*, these days, is it?

But the gossip, the talk in the Party, things trickle down from the top, never thought Miren would be so useful, of all people . . .' He started to laugh again. I crouched opposite Mama and put my ear to the door. I couldn't help it.

'All right, Bernardo, stop it!' Papa had raised his voice, and he caught himself and took a deep breath. There was a pause, and another glug and clink: he was pouring a drink for himself. He never drank alcohol during the day. I didn't look at Mama.

In a quieter voice, he said, 'Come on. You want to tell me something, don't you? It's all right, Bernardo. Whatever it is, spit it out.'

'They're coming for you,' Bernardo said.

I thought I heard the rattle of glass against teeth. Then there was a sharp click, as if Papa had put his drink down.

'Nonsense.'

There was another silence.

'They are,' Bernardo said, and that painful note of mirth was back in his voice. 'Us, too, because we've got a well in our courtyard and they want the water. But they're coming for you, soon.'

'Where on earth did you get that idea?'

'The talk . . . the gossip in the Party . . .'

'From Miren? Honestly, she's simply being over-imaginative. I may not be proud of my – of Leon, but I –' he hesitated – 'I thank God every day that his protection is allowing me to go on with my work.'

'Leon is the problem, Anton. They say he's not . . . He's being edged out . . .'

'Nonsense,' Papa said again. 'You think the guards know more about the situation than Leon himself? We would *know*, Bernardo.'

Bernardo didn't answer. I looked up and met Mama's gaze, but her eyes were empty, as if she hadn't heard. I put my head against the crack again. I felt strange, as if everything was very distant and cloudy.

'Come on,' Papa said, and laughed; but his laugh had something in it like Bernardo's, as if the hysteria was contagious. 'We mustn't let things get blown out of all proportion. The Party is taking preventative action against civil war, that's all. I mean . . .' He faltered. 'I don't mean the arrests are *right*. But there's logic in them. You said yourself, Anarchists, Socialists . . .'

'Catholics, Royalists, Zikindi, people who've been a bit rude to the guards . . .'

'Yes, all right!' Papa broke off and was silent for a moment. When he spoke again his voice was wet, blurred. 'What I'm saying is that *we* are safe. Even if we didn't have Leon, we'd have no reason to –'

'You're not listening, Anton. Leon has enemies. That means that *you* have enemies. You're *not* safe.'

'Oh . . .' Papa blew out his breath, and his footsteps crossed the floor to where the window was, looking out into the courtyard. 'It's kind of you to come all this way to say this to me, Bernardo, but you'll forgive me if I don't pack up immediately and run away from my responsibilities here. We're all under a lot of pressure and it's very easy to blow a few bits of gossip out of all proportion.'

'Anton . . .' I could hear the frustration in Bernardo's voice, but it was mixed with fatigue, and a kind of resignation. 'We're leaving. We're going to my aunt's place in the country, and – you won't mention that to anyone, will you, Anton? – with any luck we'll find a way to get over the border, I've got a cousin who lives there . . .'

'No, I won't mention it to anyone,' Papa said.

Then there was silence, apart from creaking floorboards as one of them shifted his weight.

'Anton . . . you're sure . . .'

'Yes,' Papa said, cutting him off. 'Thank you for your concern. And I'm very glad to have the opportunity to say goodbye, before you go. I shall miss you. But I don't think we need to worry about ourselves.' It sounded as though he was reading the words out of a book.

'Thanks for the drink.' I heard a little click as Bernardo put his glass down; then there were footsteps crossing to the door. I stumbled backwards, grabbing for the handle of the door to the drawing room and pulling it open just in time. Mama leapt up and together we half waltzed, half scuffled through it. It should have been funny, but neither of us was laughing.

Bernardo paused in the study doorway, and then his footsteps went back into the room. I heard him say – clearer than before, now that the door was open – 'Oh, Miren gave me a letter for Esteya. Shall I leave it on the hall table?'

Papa murmured something, and Bernardo came out, walking past the drawing room and putting the envelope on the table with a crisp papery sound. He let himself out, and the front door shut behind him heavily. The silence in the hall was very thick, like syrup, or dust.

Mama didn't look at me. She took a deep breath and went into the hall, then into Papa's study without knocking. I couldn't bring myself to move. I leant against the wall and listened. At first I couldn't hear anything; then Mama raised her voice, and I heard her say, 'But – Anton, the children – if he's right, and Leon is in trouble . . .'

'How dare you listen to my private conversations!' The door slammed, muffling Papa's voice, but it was still audible, just. 'You know what Bernardo's like – scare-mongering, full of his own importance. Please don't –'

I put my hands over my ears, not quite knowing why.

But Papa was right, wasn't he? If something had happened, with Leon and the Party . . . we'd know. If we were in danger, Leon would have told us. And even with that list, growing and growing on Martin's wall, I didn't believe that *we* could be next.

My parents' voices rang and blurred in my ears. I made an effort not to understand what they were saying.

I couldn't stay where I was. I crossed the hall, picked up Miren's letter and sat down on the bottom step of the stairs to read it. It wouldn't be anything very interesting; the usual things, news that wasn't really news, complaints, maybe with a little sentimental bit at the end to say goodbye. The thought of it gave me an unexpected pang. Once Miren was gone . . . She'd been my best friend, for years, all through school. It was only when I met Skizi that everything had changed. And poor Miren had hardly noticed.

The flap of the envelope peeled up cleanly. I took out the sheet of paper and scanned it, already almost bored.

We're leaving, although Papa says I mustn't tell you where. I don't exactly want to go, but I'm always afraid now, and maybe there I won't be. I'll miss you, Esteya, even if we don't see each other very much and you don't even answer my letters. Remember the fun we used to have at school?

Papa is going to visit your father to tell him about what the guards said to me, about your brother, so I expect you know already. There isn't much to say, except that there are rumours that he's not as central to the Party as he was, and that other people are writing the leaflets now. But from the way the guards were saying it, it sounded as if he was in trouble, and they were pleased – you must know that lots of people don't like your family because of Leon and because you all had food over the winter and special privileges and that sort of thing . . . So please, please be careful. I never thought I'd have to say that, but please, Esteya, I'm frightened for you.

In a way, though, I'm glad I can give you this warning. That's because I've got something to tell you that you might be angry about, but honestly I had to do it. I needed to make friends with the guards, in the spring, because Papa kept saying things about the Party, and Mama asked me to . . . And, a long time ago, ages ago, last summer in the holidays, I saw you going up to the Ibarras' hut on the hill-side and you were with a Zikindi girl and I saw you both there together and that she was living there, and so when I was talking to the guards I told them about her, because they had targets for undesirables. I don't know if she was still there when they went looking for her. I could have asked them, but I didn't. Anyway, I'm sorry. But now I'm warning you about Leon, and that makes us quits, doesn't it?

Please don't be angry with me. It was just that I had to give them something – information, I mean – to make them like me.

And when I saw you together I thought she was leading you astray, and –

I folded the letter along the crease and put it back into its envelope. There was something about doing it that made me feel queasy. For a moment I wasn't sure why; then I realised it made me think of the letter I'd written, about Ana Himyana. I shut my eyes and tried not to think. From the study I could hear snatches of words: 'For the children's sake, then, Anton!' and Papa replying, 'Who is the master of this family?'

Leading you astray . . . She hadn't, she didn't. If anything, it was the other way round; because it was always me who loved more, who wanted more, and Skizi who went along with it, because she might as well . . .

And I'd loved her so much that I'd – when I thought it was Ana Himyana who'd told the guards – I'd –

I put my hands over my eyes, pressing until my head started to ache. I didn't want to think about what I'd done. *Ana Himyana is an Anarchist.*

And Miren . . . I wanted to be angry with her. But I wasn't. She was only protecting herself, and I understood that. Or maybe I was just too tired; maybe I'd used up all the anger I had, and now there was nothing left, like a container with only dry dust in the corners.

Somewhere behind me, Mama and Papa both raised their voices at the same time, and there was a thud and a crash, like something smashing against a wall. I'd never heard my parents argue before; it seemed a good time for them to start. I thought I heard Martin's bedroom door opening upstairs, and the creak of his feet crossing to look down over the banister. He called down to me, but I didn't look up.

I'd killed Ana Himyana, as surely as if I'd borrowed a rifle from one of the guards and shot her myself. And I'd known it, when I wrote that letter. I'd known exactly what I was doing.

Ana Himyana is an –

Ana Himyana –

I clenched my jaw, pressing my back teeth together. I couldn't move. If I stayed still, I wouldn't exist.

‘Est!’ Martin hissed down from above me. ‘Est? What’s going on?’

I stood up. Everything felt a long way away. I took a few steps forward, opened the front door, went into the street, shut the door behind me and walked down the narrow strip of sunlight between the houses. It was chilly, and I felt the skin on my neck prickle. I thought I heard Martin call my name again, but I might have imagined it.

I walked up past the church – it was empty, the windows smashed, the doors wrenched off their hinges, the pews taken away for firewood – and through the network of alleys that led to the edge of town. They were full of rubbish, scraps of fabric and dirt I didn’t want to look at. Everything was quiet.

And I went to the only place I could think of.

Fourteen

No one had been in the hut for months; at least that was my first impression, when I pushed my way in. The door was stuck, entangled in weeds, and most of the roof had come down and was on the floor, in great grass-covered mounds. You wouldn't have known where Skizi's bed had been. The scrawls on the plaster were still visible, and I took a careful breath, somehow expecting to smell faeces and ash, as if it was only yesterday that Skizi had been taken away; but the air was clear and didn't smell of anything.

But I hadn't been the last person in the hut. I saw – feeling nothing – that the guards, or partisans, Anarchists or Socialists, had left three rifles stacked in the corner, and there was a dog-eared pile of leaflets on the shelf, which had slid down the wall and was at an odd, lopsided angle. I picked up the top page: *A Letter to the People* . . . They were home-printed, hardly legible, and the grammar was all wrong. I looked round, imagining candlelit meetings, arguments, and then . . . They'd left their rifles here, and there were cobwebs strung across them like ribbons. They must have been arrested.

I picked up one of the rifles. The stock was cool and clammy, and it was heavier than I remembered. But it was the same model that the guard had taught me to load, and to fire. I leant it against the wall and walked back to the door, wiping my hands on my trousers, and stood looking out. The breeze ruffled my hair.

Once, a long time ago, Teddy had told us about his friend in the trenches in the Great War, who'd put a rifle barrel in his mouth and pulled the trigger with his toe. It wasn't cowardice, Teddy had said, it was just fatigue. He was too tired to go on living.

I sat down in the doorway, not caring about the damp chill that soaked into my trousers. I put my head against the door frame. One evening last summer – more than a year ago – Skizi and I had sat side by side squashed into this doorway, passing a cigarette back and forth, savouring it as if it was a fine cigar. She'd got bottle of cheap vodka from somewhere – we'd drunk it earlier that afternoon – and the world was soft-edged, not quite real. I could still taste the thin, fierce alcohol, the tobacco smoke and warm evening air, and see the stars coming out slowly in the sky. The memory sat in my stomach like a live coal.

I stood up. The sun was going down. I was shivering, but I didn't feel cold. I watched my hands shaking and they didn't seem to belong to me.

I went into the hut. I picked up the rifle again. It was loaded.

I wondered what Ana Himyana would tell me to do.

I slept there that night. It was freezing, but the cold didn't seem to touch me, not really. I was hungry too, but I didn't mind. I wanted to stay still, frozen and curled into myself like someone that hadn't been born yet.

I dreamt of Skizi. At least, I think it was a dream; but I

was so cold that I was in a kind of lucid place between being asleep and awake. It was very quiet and simple, more like a memory. She was standing in front of me, still wet from the bath I'd given her, with her hair dropping tiny gems of water on her shoulders.

'I survive,' she said. She'd said the words to me before, but now her voice was different – soft, clear, as if it was something she wanted me to understand. 'That's all I want. Nothing else matters, as long as I survive . . . If I need to run, I run. If I need to steal, I steal. Whatever I have to do . . . I don't care what I do, as long as I can walk out the other side. All right?'

I was too cold to move, or breathe. I wanted her to stay where she was, even if she was only a memory.

But she didn't. It was too much to hope for; after all, she was dead, wasn't she? She gave me a long look – and for that strange, suspended moment, I was afraid and full of a kind of joy – and then she was gone.

I closed my eyes again, and I was back in the dark. But now the cold had started to reach me, and I felt real again. It wasn't a good feeling, but it was better than being far away, watching myself through a film of shame. And after a while, I slept.

When it got light, I unfolded myself painfully and got up. I was hungry. At home there would be hot water and ersatz coffee, coarse bread and lard, maybe a little scraping of jam.

As I walked past the rifles, I paused; but it was too cold to stand there for very long, and in the end I went out, leaving them where they were.

The sun was coming up. All the shadows were thin and long, and the light was silvery. I went down the hill, my hands in my pockets, not hurrying, my head empty and clear and cold, like the sky.

The streets were still deserted. I walked back the way I'd come, past the church. The pello wall in the square was covered with peeling posters, men with their fists in the air, women laughing with their hair blowing over their faces. I stood there for a moment, thinking about the morning I'd come back from Skizi's hut that first time.

Suddenly, irresistibly, I wanted to tell someone about it. I imagined putting it into words – leaning forward, searching for the right way to say I loved her, I loved her, I *loved* –

When I got home, I could tell Martin. If I was brave enough; and I felt brave.

I could even tell him about Ana Himyana.

I turned the corner and walked down our street, blinking in the sudden darkness between the houses. Blue and purple spots danced in front of my eyes.

There was a pello ball in the gutter in front of me. I went to kick it out of the way, but something seemed to stop my foot, and I paused, looking down. There were shards of glass around it, glinting and catching the light, like jewels. And the ball was . . . familiar. I bent down and picked it up.

The pello ball that had killed the Bull . . . Angel Corazon's ball, Skizi's ball. My ball . . .

There was a peculiar, shivery feeling on the back of my neck, as if a cloud had gone over the sun; but I was in the shade.

I looked up at my window. There was sunlight catching the top corner of it, in a jagged, toothy edge. The glass was broken, as if someone had thrown the ball out while the window was still closed.

I felt my throat tighten. The glass crunched under my feet as I took a step forward.

Our front door was open. Just a little way open.

I found myself looking back over my shoulder, as if there was someone there who could help. But there was no one, just the quiet street. It looked flat and shadowy, like a stage set after the lights had gone out.

I took a deep breath, trying to make it last as long as possible. I wanted to stay here, in the moment before I went through that open door and saw what had happened. I squeezed the ball in both my hands, pressing the seam into my palms until I knew it had left a pressure mark on the skin.

Then, when my lungs were empty again, I put the ball into my pocket, and went into our house.

There wasn't much out of place. There was only the silence, and perhaps I was imagining that. It felt as if I was the only person in the world.

There was nothing missing. Nothing had been taken away; only the hall table was at an angle, and a bit of the plaster had been knocked off the wall behind it. Someone had struggled; or just been clumsy . . .

Papa's study door was open. I looked through the doorway without going in. The medicine cabinet was empty. There was a smashed bottle on the floor and a heavy, volatile smell.

I went up the stairs. I ought to have been hurrying, but my body wouldn't move fast enough. It was as if the space around me was thick, like molten glass. I couldn't breathe properly. The doors on the landing were open too. Mama and Papa's bed was rumpled, and the wardrobe door was swinging. Maybe the guards had let them get dressed, before they took them. There was a pale, lost-looking boy looking back at me from the mirror, his ragged hair sticking to his temples.

I felt as if I was stuck to the floor. I had to make an effort to turn on my heel and leave the room.

I went up the last staircase. Martin's room. It always looked as if it had been ransacked; there was nothing different now. Only –

My heartbeat hiccupped.

The wall.

There were new names.

I picked my way across the things on the floor – books, leaflets, a dirty shirt – to the wall, the way I'd done hundreds of times before. Something crunched under my foot, and when I lifted my shoe there was the broken barrel of Martin's fountain pen, and a mess of dark purplish ink. I noticed with a kind of distant interest that there were crumbs of plaster on the nib. I looked at the new writing. The letters were rough and difficult to read; they'd been half written, half scratched on to the wall. I thought it must have been awkward to hold the fountain pen at the right angle; it was stupid of Martin not to use a pencil instead, like he had for the other names. In spite of myself, I saw him stumbling over to the desk, rummaging desperately for something to write with, and scribbling the names on the wall with whatever came to hand, not caring if it spoilt the nib of his pen . . .

I didn't move my eyes, but suddenly the letters came together, and I was reading the words, without wanting to.

Anton Bidart. Veronika Bidart. Martin Bi

He hadn't had time to finish writing his own name.

* * *

I went into my room. The sheets had been dragged off the bed. They'd looked for me then. There was a cold breeze from the window. Someone had cut themselves on the jagged edge of glass; there was a sprinkle of red on the windowsill. I hoped it was one of the guards, and not Martin, but there was no way of knowing.

I sat down on the bed. I didn't mean to exactly, but everything swayed and flickered darkly, and when it cleared I was sitting down.

I stayed where I was, frozen. I didn't feel anything. It was like that moment when you find the right wavelength on a radio. On either side of me there was the hiss and scream of noise; but where I was, exactly in the middle, there was nothing. As long as I didn't move, I'd stay in that narrow band of clarity, safe.

I'd been here before; this time it wasn't real, it couldn't be real. For my whole family to be gone, like a magic trick . . . This time there was no scrawled graffiti, or ashes or smeared excrement; just the absences, just their names on Martin's wall, as if he'd known I'd come back and look . . . The guards were practised by now – bored, even – and they'd done their job efficiently, without malice. Even if it was Martin who had left his blood on the window, it was probably an accident, like the dent in the plaster downstairs . . .

Nothing moved, nothing changed. The breeze from the window touched my forehead, my eyelashes, my lips. If I moved I'd feel it, so I kept still.

I stayed where I was for a long time, staring at the wall until the sun shone on it directly, so bright my head started to ache. Then, slowly, I realised that I couldn't stay where I was. I didn't know whether the guards came back to check for the people they'd missed. I couldn't believe that I was that important – but then, hadn't Papa said the same yesterday? The memory made me shake uncontrollably, and I had to close my eyes and hug my knees before I could go on thinking. I remembered that someone – one of the old police chiefs – had been released, a few weeks ago, but it had been a mistake, a clerical error at the prison, and the next day the guards had turned up at his house to arrest him again. Maybe they would come for me now . . .

But if Mama and Papa and Martin and Skizi were all gone . . . where was I supposed to *go*?

I had to take a deep breath, because of the panic that rose up inside me and threatened to engulf me. This couldn't be happening, it couldn't have happened.

It was like looking at a wall, a wall so wide and high that I couldn't take it in properly. There was no way past it, or over it, or around it. It was just *there*, unnegotiable, merciless. My life was on the other side of it.

I opened my eyes again, staring at the real wall, where the leaflets were peeling away from the plaster and the laughing peasant women had faded to the colour of old teeth. I'd left the bedroom door open, and it swayed a little in the draught from the window. The chill prickled on my skin.

I heard Skizi's voice in my head, soft and unexpected. *I survive*. And suddenly I thought I knew what she was trying to tell me. She wasn't going to let me give up.

Leon. I still had Leon.

I stood up, stuffed a few things into a bag and left the house. And I made my way to the train station, keeping to the back streets, out of sight.

* * *

I bought a ticket with my cap low over my face, frowning and hunching my shoulders so that I looked like a boy. I waited behind a low wall, until the Irunja train had drawn up at the platform; then I ran for it. At the first stop – Zuberi – I got out of the train, walked to the ticket office and then turned on my heel, ran back and swung myself up into a different carriage just as the train started to move off. No one who'd got off the train changed their mind when they saw me; one woman gave me a strange look, but that wasn't surprising really. I dropped into my seat in the new carriage sweating and out of breath, but almost sure that no one was following me. I didn't know if I was relieved or disappointed.

There were guards at Irunja station, checking papers, but they were giving everything a lazy, cursory glance that made me suspect that they didn't even bother to read the names. They let me through without a problem, although I heard them whistle and laugh amongst themselves after I'd gone past. I felt the air rush into my lungs with relief, but I made myself keep walking, in case they were watching.

The streets were quiet, and everyone I saw was walking quickly, head bent, as if they were on an urgent errand and couldn't stop to talk. It felt like a foreign country. I kept seeing abandoned motor cars, some burnt to blackened shells, some only vandalised, their windscreens smashed. I wished I'd thought to look in Papa's study for a map of the city; but now all I could do was keep walking, trying to remember where we'd gone, the Sunday of the King's Cup more than a year ago. From the station I thought it was left along Museum Street, towards the student quarter, but I wasn't certain. If only Martin was here . . .

For a moment the ground sucked and heaved under my feet, and I stumbled. If Martin was here . . . I would have given anything, anything at all, for him to be here with me – or instead of me. I couldn't bear it. I stopped where I was, in the middle of the pavement. I couldn't go on.

But after a while I discovered I *could* go on. So I wiped my face on my shirtsleeve, and went on.

The street names had changed. I couldn't remember what they'd been before, but they'd been whitewashed and painted over: Revolution Street, Marx Street, Liberty Avenue. Someone bourgeois had painted in an apostrophe after the *s* in Workers Road. I walked past a little mews called Magnificent Uprising Avenue, and couldn't stop myself giggling. I felt drunk with adrenalin and exhaustion and misery.

After a while the revolutionary fervour seemed to die out, and the streets had no names at all. But I thought perhaps I recognised the houses I was passing; and if I was right, Leon's old rooms were over to my right, not too far away. There were posters of Our Glorious Leader everywhere I looked. I turned a corner into a wide, sunlit street. I stood swaying slightly, feeling nauseous, wanting more than anything to sit down on the pavement and fall asleep. The building opposite was draped in red banners and more Our Glorious Leaders, but it seemed familiar all the same. After a few moments I realised it was the Royal Museum – although it wasn't royal any more, of course, and everything that made it a museum had been smashed long ago.

I turned slowly on my heel and scanned the buildings on this side of the street. Leon's rooms had been in one of those . . . I didn't think I knew which one, but my feet walked me to a door and I thought I recognised it. It was open, and I caught a glimpse of broken tiles on the floor, peeling paint, and posters that were sagging off the walls. It was where Leon's rooms were – or had been . . . Now it had an indefinably official air, and there was a guard lounging just inside the door, clicking and clicking at a battered cigarette lighter. I stopped dead, started to turn away, then faltered and turned back. It was stupid to come all this way and not even ask for Leon . . . and they'd know where he was, wouldn't they? He was *famous*.

I walked up to the doorway and put my head around the door frame. But before I could say anything, the guard said, 'You on Party business?'

'Not – not exactly, but –'

'Then bugger off.' He hadn't lifted his gaze from his stunted cigarette.

'I need to find Leon Bidart.'

The grimy thumb flicking at the lighter paused, and he raised his eyes to mine. 'Sorry,' he said, with an edge in his voice. 'Can't give out addresses for Party officials. You could be an assassin.'

I said, 'I'm not.'

He looked me up and down, taking in my short hair, my trousers, the bag slung over my back, and his eyebrows twitched. There were footsteps behind him, but he didn't seem to hear. He gave me a grin full of a personal, pointed malice that I didn't understand. He said, 'All right, sweetheart. Number one, Pello-Heroes Street.'

'Where's that?'

His grin got wider, until it was almost a grimace. 'Oh . . .' he said. 'Go down Icons-of-the-Working-Class Road, turn left on to Loyalty-to-the-Proletariat Road and it's on the corner of Liberty-from-Tyranny Street.'

'Shut up, Bernardo.' The voice was sharp and thin, with an educated accent, but the man who stepped into the light was hefty and bearded, with a few greasy curls escaping from a flat cap. He looked at me, and somehow even from metres away I could smell his exhaustion, as strong as the odour of sweat and stale clothes. 'Who're you?'

'I'm just . . . one of Leon's friends, from home.'

He gave me a look. He didn't believe me, but he said, 'He's in pr– he's working in the prison. I don't know if they'll let you see him.'

I swallowed. 'And that's . . . in the north, beyond the Queen's – the Red Park? In –' I glanced at the guard – 'Pello-Heroes Street?'

The bearded man clenched his jaw and shot the guard a foul look; but he only said, 'No, that was a joke.'

'And . . . Icons-of-the-Working-Class, Liberty-From-Tyranny . . . ?'

'No. Just follow the road outside, until you see the towers. Big place, you can't miss it.' He gestured, as if he was eager for me to leave; as if he might have said too much already.

I nodded. There was a tight knot of unease in my stomach; I didn't understand why the guard had lied to me about the street names. If he was really joking, he could have thought of something funnier.

Silence. The bearded man stood staring at me. That was it, obviously; I wasn't going to get any more help.

Pello-Heroes Street. I didn't know why that made me feel so horrible. I didn't know what I was scared of. It wasn't the prison; it wasn't the way the man had almost said Leon was in prison, before correcting himself. It was something else, something more. The look on the guard's face . . .

Pello-Heroes Street.

I said, 'Thanks, Comrade,' and started to run.

The man was right, the prison walls and watchtowers loomed above the street like a fortress. You couldn't miss it.

The gate was massive, wood reinforced with iron, as much for keeping people out as keeping them in. And it was shut.

Then, with a kind of frozen hope, I realised that there was a littler door set into the big gate. I laid my hand flat against it, almost too afraid to push, in case it was locked. But it gave under my weight, and I stumbled through it, catching my foot on the lower rim and nearly falling. Inside the gate it was dark and cold, and I blinked as my eyes adjusted to the light.

'Criminal or subversive?' someone said.

I looked round. There was a guard sitting at a table, rolling a cigarette on a pile of black ledgers. He raised his eyebrows at me, and said again, 'Criminal or subversive?'

'I'm here to see my brother,' I said.

'*Yes*,' he said, and sighed so strongly the cigarette paper fluttered and specks of tobacco littered the desk. 'Is he a *criminal*, or is he a *subversive*? Criminal visits are eleven to twelve weekdays, subversives you need written authorisation from a Party offi–'

'He works here. At least . . . Leon Bidart. Minister for Information. He *is* a Party official.'

'Oh,' the guard said. He didn't exactly snap to attention, or sit up straighter, but he did stop rolling his cigarette. 'Er . . .' He looked round, as if he was hoping someone would tell him what to do.

I felt a wave of anger so strong it took all my strength

not to overturn his table and smash one of the heavy black ledgers into his face. I concentrated on breathing. I said, 'I want to see him, please, Comrade. Now.'

'Yes, well, I . . . ye-es . . .'

'Where is he?'

'In the . . .' He gestured helplessly to the right. 'Past the waiting room. The tower, around the yard . . .'

'Thank you.' I walked away, forcing myself not to run. I heard the guard behind me say something else, but I ignored it, and although my back tingled under his gaze he didn't follow me.

There was another guard in the doorway of the tower, but I walked past without a word. There were more guards at all the intersections of the corridors, but when one of them caught my eye and opened his mouth I said, 'Long live Our Glorious Leader,' and by the time he'd said automatically, 'Long live the Republic,' I'd turned the corner, leaving him behind.

I'd lost my bearings, but there was a spiral staircase in front of me, with a square of barred sunlight falling on the wall. I went up. The guard at the top of the stairs looked at me, frowning, but he didn't say anything. I pointed at the door opposite – it was thick wood, without a window, and not, I thought, the door to a cell – and said, 'Is Comrade Bidart through there?'

He licked his lips, and gave the same glance around that the guard at the gate had, as if he was looking for help. In the end he said, 'Yes. But I think – he's probably . . . not seeing anyone.'

'He'll see me,' I said. 'He'll *definitely* see me.'

'Are you on Party business?' His voice was unconvincing, as if he had no idea what to do about me and didn't want to get it wrong.

'Yes,' I said, and pushed the door open before he had time to ask any more questions.

Leon was there. He was sitting at a desk, looking out through barred windows at a brick wall. But there was a shaft of afternoon sunlight coming through, cutting a bright parallelogram on the floor, and when he looked up the sun flashed on his glasses, and the dust in the air swirled and sparkled. He said, 'Esteya . . . ?'

And then he stood up, stumbling against his desk, and walked towards me. I couldn't move. He put his arms round me. I breathed his smell of tobacco and ink and felt his shirt against my cheek; and I relaxed and started to cry, in spite of myself, and for a second I thought everything was going to be all right.

Fifteen

Leon helped me walk to his bed. He sat down next to me, keeping his arm around me, and let me cry. It was only when I'd quietened down that he said, 'Hello, Esteya.'

'Mama and Papa,' I said, fighting to make the words intelligible. 'Martin . . .'

I felt him stiffen. 'Yes?'

'They took them – Leon, they took them away, I came home and no one was there. Martin, on his bedroom wall, Martin put his name . . .' But Leon wouldn't understand about the list on Martin's wall. 'Leon, please . . .'

Leon didn't answer. His arm seemed to have turned to stone. Then he stood up and went to the window. He shouted, without looking at me, 'Get away from the bloody door!' I jumped; then I heard footsteps retreating down the corridor and realised he'd been talking to the guard outside.

'I *warned* them,' Leon said, his voice hoarse and flat. 'I sent them letter after bloody letter. Get out of the country, I said, it's only a matter of time. The stupid bloody *fools*. How could they? I don't believe it.'

'We didn't get any letters,' I said. My insides felt thick and sticky, like something congealed. Leon would be able to help. He'd be able to do something. He *would*. 'We thought you didn't have time to write.'

'But I –' Leon spun on his heel, spitting the words, and then swallowed and took a deep breath. 'I wrote and *wrote*. Smuggled out a letter with every single bloody guard. Bribed them all. Every *single* . . .' His voice cracked, and he stopped.

My insides got heavier and heavier, dragging everything down. I said, 'You have to get them out,' but my voice didn't sound right. He'd had to *bribe* the guards? So he was a prisoner here, or nearly; and that meant he wouldn't be able to do – *anything* . . .

He must have seen the expression on my face, because he laughed. It made me flinch; it didn't sound like him.

'Oh, don't worry, Est, the guards are here to *protect* me,' he said. 'After the assassination attempts on Karl, the Party wants to make sure I'm *safe* . . .'

'And Mama and Papa and Martin? You have to help them, Leon.' My voice sounded high and panicky.

He turned back to look out of the window, staring as if he could see more than just a blank square of wall. He said, in the same tight, flippant voice, 'What do you suggest? Smuggle them a pie with a rope ladder baked into it?'

'But you're – you're in the Party, you're important, Minister for Infor–'

'Yes,' he said, and gestured at the little room. 'Yes, I'm exactly *this* important. Important enough to be stuck here, waiting for someone to come and –' He stopped, the muscles in his jaw flexing. 'I can't do anything, Esteya. I'm washed up. No more leaflets, no more writing speeches for OGL, no more sending you food parcels . . .' He shook his head, his face suddenly contrite, as if the food parcels were the most important thing in the world. His eyes were vague.

'But Leon –'

'Only a matter of time,' he said. 'When they get round to making a decision . . . chucked in with the other poor buggers, in the death pits . . . Not supposed to admit to the death pits, but everyone knows . . .'

I took a deep breath. The dust danced in the sunlight and I focused on it. '*Leon*,' I said, 'you have to find out where Papa and Mama and Martin are, and get them *out*.'

'Stop saying that!' he said. 'I can't.'

I stared at him. It was as if he didn't understand what I was saying; as if I was telling him to change his shirt, or have a shave. 'Leon –'

'For Christ's sake!' He swung round, and I saw how white his face was. '*I CAN'T*. Listen to me! I *can't*.' He stumbled to his chair and dropped into it. 'Don't you think . . . Don't you think I would, if I could? Mama and Papa and Martin, oh *hell*, all of them. If I could walk out and offer myself instead, don't you think I would? I tried, I warned you all – I tried to warn you – and now everything's . . . everyone I care about, it's all . . . Oh hell, damn it, damn it all . . .' He dropped his face into his hands. For a moment I thought he was going to cry; then he lifted his head again and said, 'Stop *staring*, Esteya . . . You look just as bad as I do, you look a mess. What the hell did you do to your *hair*?'

There was a silence. I looked away sharply.

'Sorry . . . I've been . . . There's no one really to talk to. I daresay I'm not completely . . . ever since they put me here . . .'

'But you can have visitors,' I said.

'Yes, but who would want to visit me? Everyone I know is in the Party, and now that Karl – now I'm not – now . . .' He tailed off, into a kind of laugh. 'Now that . . . ever since we . . . He's mad, Esteya. He's gone funny in the head. He sees plots, conspiracies everywhere. Someone tried to shoot him and ever since then, *before* then, ever since things started to go wrong, he's been . . . You wouldn't believe . . . and I had to, if we didn't agree he said we were liberals, weren't committed to the new order, and I had to, I had to, I had to –' He stuttered, saying the words over and over like a cracked record.

I glanced over my shoulder in spite of myself, checking the gap under the door for the shadow of someone lurking on the other side. I didn't think there was anyone there. Leon followed my gaze, nodding as if I'd asked a question. He looked mad himself – mad, and old. I wanted to stand up and walk out; but where would I go?

'Want to know what I did? Why good old Karl turned against me? Want to know? I told him he'd gone a little bit too far, in my opinion. He's a bloody madman, he's paranoid. There are things . . . things he did, told people to do – *madness* – and I took him to one side and told him he'd *gone a little bit too far* . . .' He laughed, gurgling. '*In my opinion*. That's it. That was bloody it. Not that he'd liked me for a long time. People read my leaflets, you see, that was the real problem – they knew Karl was the psychopath and I was the man of the people. I was a bloody good minister, he was just . . . just . . .'

There was a pause. The sunlight had moved. The wall opposite was in shadow.

'Remember Hiram Jelek, and the young one, the blond one . . . ?'

A pause. I didn't answer; I wasn't sure he'd really said it. Maybe my mind was wandering, and I'd imagined it.

'Pello player . . . The other one. A kid. Won the King's Cup, the last King's Cup, remember, we were there, the day the Revolution started? Best player ever, people said. Only a kid. Only a kid . . .'

Pello-Heroes Street. Whatever Leon was going to say, I didn't want to hear it; but I couldn't stop myself. I said, 'Angel Corazon.'

Leon shut his eyes; and I had the impression that he knew the name perfectly well, he just hadn't wanted to say it. He said, 'Yes. The kid. The . . . He was a hero. He was in a gun battle, the first day of the Revolution . . . An icon of the working class . . . poor sod.'

'Yes, I know,' I said, but I don't think he heard me.

'Lost the game, at home, remember? The pressure got to him, he was only a kid . . . But Karl thought he'd done it on purpose, thought he hadn't tried . . . and then the crowds . . . People care about pello more than politics, course they do, but Karl thought . . . Karl got worse and worse.'

I didn't know what he was trying to say. I said, 'Leon . . .' but I couldn't make myself change the subject. *Pello-Heroes Street . . .*

'Telling OGL that the games were a security threat, all that, and then . . . The kid couldn't handle it, being an icon. He couldn't make speeches or say nice things about the Revolution, of course he couldn't, he was just a pello player, for God's sake, just a kid, and . . .' Leon shook his head and then opened his eyes, looking at me like someone waking up. 'House arrest,' he said. 'We put them under house arrest, for their own protection. So they wouldn't get involved in any kind of uprising. Karl said they were a danger to security . . . House arrest. *Room* arrest. An old place, dark. They put them in the top rooms, nurseries. There were bars . . . bars over the windows . . .'

'You mean . . .' I swallowed. 'Hiram Jelek and – and Angel Corazon . . . ?' It made my heart pound, just to say his name.

Leon frowned and nodded, like a schoolmaster with a slow pupil. 'House arrest,' he said again. 'The kid . . . Funny, Jelek was how you'd expect – shouted, tried to bribe the guards, pleaded, had his wife go to OGL and beg . . . But the kid . . . had a ball in there with him . . . that was all, just the ball against the wall, over and over, all day, *thud thud thud*. Used to drive the guards crazy . . .'

I clenched my teeth. It was stupid – I didn't even *know* Angel Corazon – but even now, after everything, it made me feel sick, to think of him shut up in a dark room, throwing a ball against the wall. I said, 'Couldn't you get him out?'

Leon didn't seem to hear me. 'And Karl . . . didn't understand. Hated him, really *hated* him, used to listen through the wall, *thud thud*, used to shout at him, like he wanted the kid to know he was there . . .' He laughed. 'Like it was a fight, and the kid was winning. He'd tell the guards to go in, rough him up a bit, but the next day the kid would be back to it, *thud thud thud* with the ball . . .'

I sat silently, watching the shrinking diamond of sunlight on the floor.

'Then Jelek got ill, and it was just the kid left, and . . . they started to interrogate him – Karl's orders. The kid used to get letters from all over the country, people who didn't even know him, piles and piles; he was a hero, even though he was just a kid bashing a ball against a wall . . .

Karl was sure it was some kind of conspiracy, made the guards sit and read the letters, underline anything suspicious, and then they interrogated . . . they . . . and he didn't know anything, of course he didn't, he was just a kid . . .' There was something blank in Leon's voice, slurring the words, as though he'd said this so many times before that he'd smoothed the edges off the consonants. I imagined him saying it to himself, telling himself this story over and over again, and wished I hadn't. He swallowed, and I thought he'd fallen silent; but in the end he went on speaking. 'And then . . . Karl – he was mad, paranoid. If you criticise it's the end, no one dares to open their mouth . . . but he was obsessed with him, with the kid, *obsessed* . . . and so . . . I tried to stop it, but it got worse and worse. I did try to stop him . . . but they . . . the poor kid, they . . .'

I was frozen. I thought I knew what he was going to say.

'They . . . it was the only thing he had, and they – they took the ball away . . .'

I shut my eyes for a moment, then opened them again, because the blankness of my eyelids was worse than the real world.

'Took him away, knocked him out, put him back in the room without the ball, and just *watched* . . .'

I looked at the sunlight, and the shape of it seemed to burn into the back of my eyes. In my head I could see a boy stepping out from behind the fountain in the square, his hair golden, a kind of glamour hanging about him like a halo. I tried to keep hold of the image, because if I let go of it I might believe what Leon was telling me.

'And he . . . he tried, the poor bloody kid tried to go on –' Leon paused. He took a deep breath, as if the worst was still to come; then he bent his head, and started to weep. I'd never heard a man cry like that. I thought I knew what it was like to lose everything; but this was different. I should have gone to comfort him, but I was paralysed, repelled, as if he had some disfiguring disease.

He was saying something else, or trying to, but his mouth was the wrong shape to form words and all that came out was noise. Then he said, 'Mad . . .' and I thought he was talking about Karl again, until he forced out more consonants. 'Played with an imaginary ball, throwing and catching it, like he was desperate, like it was the only thing keeping him –' The tears rose again, cutting him off.

I found myself on my feet, stumbling to the door as if I could escape the sound of Leon's weeping. I leant my forehead against the wood.

'Thought he'd go on like that for ever . . . bashing an imaginary ball . . . watching it bounce . . . but he . . . he –' A long breath in, as if there was only one thing left to say. 'Killed himself, didn't he? Only a kid. Drowned himself in his own p–'

'Shut up! Shut *up* –'

I'd spun round to shout at him. We stared at each other, shocked, trembling. There was silence, a kind of fragile, shivering silence that I was afraid to break.

He opened his mouth. I said, 'Please, Leon, please don't . . . I don't want to know any more.' It felt like cowardice, but I couldn't help it.

Another pause; then he sniffed, with a great snort of snot, and wiped his nose. I remembered suddenly – irrelevantly – how he'd given Angel his shirt, that day when he beat the Bull. Poor Leon.

'Est,' he said, 'you have to leave.'

I stood up.

'No, I mean –' He shook his head, laughing a little. 'Leave the country. Cross the border, over the mountains. I'll give you the address of someone I know, who can get you out.'

'But I –'

I don't know what I was going to say, but Leon smacked his hand down on the desk, making everything shudder. '*Esteya*. You are going to *go*. Do you understand? Everyone else in this family has ended up in prison, and I want – please, I just want *one* of us –' He looked at me, and I saw that he was crying again; but this time his face was still, and only his eyes overflowed.

'I can't . . .' I felt shivery and sick, as if I was ill. 'Where would I go? I *live* here. This is my home. I can't just run away.' It was stupid, to be more afraid of starting again somewhere else, on my own, than I was of staying here and getting arrested; but I was. I thought about what it would be like to cross the mountains and live in a foreign country. I didn't even speak the language. 'Leon, it can't be that bad . . .' I had a sudden, unwelcome flash of memory: Papa, telling Miren's father that we were safe.

But if I ran away now, I'd never see them again; I'd be giving up on them . . .

I shut my eyes, thinking of Mama and Papa in prison, in the death pits – *no*, that couldn't happen, it couldn't . . . Martin, in a cell underground or with a barred window, thinking of me, praying that I'd find a way to get to him . . . My breath caught in my throat, like a sob. There had to be a way, didn't there? Surely . . .

'Esteya,' Leon said, and I heard him exhale. 'Do you know how many people disappear every day? And most of them . . . most of them get put up against a wall straight away and . . . you can't do anything. If you try to find them, if you stay here for another week, another day, it'll be suicide. Do you think Mama and Papa would want you to stay and look for them? *Do* you?'

'No, but –' My voice was thin, unconvinced.

There were footsteps, crossing the floor, and suddenly I felt hands on my shoulders, spinning me round. When I opened my eyes I was staring at the wall. The paint was grimy, institutional off-white, bubbling with damp. Leon was behind me; I could feel his breath on my neck. I tried to wrench away, but he was stronger than I expected. He said, 'Look.'

'What?'

'It's a wall, isn't it? Look. At the bloody wall. Suppose I told you that Mama and Papa were on the other side of it, and all you had to do was to knock it down and they'd be free. Suppose I told you that.'

I twisted again, but he held me still. I said, 'Then I'd – I'd knock it down, wouldn't I?'

'Go on then. Knock it down.'

I glanced at him. He was serious, his eyes blazing. I put my hands up and pressed against the cool rough surface of the paint. There must have been a metre of plaster and stone and mortar behind it. I leant my weight on it. Without looking at Leon, I said, 'This is stupid, Leon, this is –'

'You can't do it.' I felt the warmth of his hands on my shoulders disappear. He walked away. 'You couldn't do it, no matter what. There are some things you just *can't do*. And getting Mama and Papa and Martin out of prison, even if you knew they were still alive, even if you knew where they were, Esteya, you wouldn't have a hope in hell. You'd be arrested too. You'd be mad to try, you'd be *mad* . . .'

I turned round. I raised my voice, and shouted at him,

'Shut up! I can do it, I can *try*, at least. You're just cowardly. It's all your fault anyway. If they're dead you killed them – don't tell me what to do, I'll do it, you'll see, I'll find them, I'll get them out, I won't just *forget* them, I can, I will, I bloody will, just you try to st–'

Leon came towards me. He swung his hand back and slapped me.

I fell back, and my skull hit the wall with a *crack*.

Leon's mouth opened. He reached for me, grabbing my arm to keep me on my feet. 'Esteya – I'm sorry, I only wanted to – are you all right? I'm sorry, I'm sorry, really, forgive me, I didn't mean –'

I shook my head and my knees gave way. I slid down the wall, until I was sitting in a heap on the floor.

And then I started to cry; and this time I was crying like Leon, without hope, full of grief and guilt and an awful shame, because I knew he was right.

The sunlight had disappeared from the floor, and the wall outside the window was in shadow. I didn't know how long I'd been here; I felt painfully tired, as if I might fall asleep and never wake up.

There was a kind of scratching sound, like an insect. When I looked up, Leon was writing something on a scrap of paper. He caught my eye and pushed the paper in my direction. I didn't move, so he walked over to me and put it on the floor in front of me. I let the words blur into a long line of black.

'Memorise it,' Leon said very softly.

'What?'

'Memorise it. The guards might search you, and he's a friend of mine.'

I blinked, and read what he'd written.

Eli Apal, 2a, 144 Universal Brotherhood Street, Irunja.
I said, 'Who is he?'

Leon winced, and gestured at me to keep my voice down. He murmured, 'To get you out of the country. Go and find him – be careful, you'll probably be followed when you leave the prison – and tell him who you are. He runs people over the border. God knows, he owes me enough favours . . .'

'Leon . . . are you sure –' My throat clogged up and ached. 'I mean . . . there really isn't *any* chance . . . ?'

Leon sighed, shook his head. 'There's nothing you can do, or me. But sometimes . . . Listen, Esteya. You should leave. I know that's the right thing for you to do. Mama and Papa and Martin are almost certainly dead, or will be soon . . .' His voice was matter-of-fact, but he broke off and ran his hand over his face. 'Maybe there'll be a miracle. But that's no reason for you to stay and get arrested yourself. Do you understand? It's horrible, and I'm sorry. But any kind of heroics would be suicidally stupid.'

I nodded. I knew already that he was right; I just wished he wasn't.

'My brave little sister,' Leon said, and tried to smile.

For a second he looked like Martin. I felt grief punch into me. I looked down, staring at the address, pronouncing the words silently in my head, trying to distract myself: *Eli Apal, 2a, 144 Universal Brotherhood Street, Irunja*. I said, 'I don't know where that is.'

Leon leant forward without saying anything, and drew a rough map. 'It's easy,' he said. He added writing: *Behind what used to be the Royal Parade. Big building, all apartments. Ask him if he remembers his grandfather's shed, when he kept contraband vodka in it.*

I nodded again. I wanted to think of more questions. I remembered how when I was small and Papa was helping me with my homework, I'd pretend to be stupider than I was, to delay the moment when he sent me away. He was always surprised when I got good marks at school.

'Leon . . . would they really stop you, if you tried to leave?'

'Yes,' he said, and even though the silence went on and on he didn't add anything else. In the corridor I heard footsteps, a quiet, cut-off laugh, and the clunk of a metal chair as someone sat down on it.

'Esteya . . . you should go. If you go now, he might get you out by tonight, or tomorrow morning.'

'*Tonight?*' I hadn't realised it would be so soon.

'Have you got this by heart?' He pointed at the paper.

'Yes – but –'

Leon picked it up and put it into his mouth, grimacing as he chewed. Black ink ran and stained the corners of his lips. He looked at me and grinned, shaking his head. 'Yum yum.'

For a second he was Martin again. I couldn't speak. I suppose something must have shown on my face, because Leon's grin died, and he chewed and spat the grey pulp of paper into a bucket in the corner of the room. Then he came and put his arms round me, the way he had when I first walked into the room. It made me feel strange – as if we were going to start again, say and do everything again, exactly the same.

Leon gave me a final squeeze and then pushed me away, holding me by the shoulders to look into my face. He said, 'You remember the address?'

'Yes.'

'And you're – you'll be all right?'

'Yes.'

'No heroics. Promise me, Esteya. For Mama and Papa and Martin. Promise me you'll survive, no matter what.' The way he said it reminded me of something, but I couldn't think clearly.

'Yes.'

'Good girl.' He kissed my forehead, the way Papa would have done; and then punched me lightly on the arm, the way Martin would have done. It was as if he heard the thought; he screwed up his face and added, 'Call your first son Martin.'

I stared at him, and a bubble of misery rose and burst in my throat.

'Don't cry.'

'I'm not crying.'

He gave me a long look, and smiled. It was a warm, generous, affectionate smile, as if he wasn't keeping anything in reserve. I wished I had a camera; but then, he'd never smile like that for a photo.

'Go on. Stop dithering.'

'Yes.' I went on tiptoes to kiss his cheek. The skin was rough and smelt sour, and I paused for a split second, breathing in the odour, not wanting to let go of him. 'Goodbye, Leon.' I turned away, and banged on the door. I heard Leon move behind me – I think he went to his desk and sat down – but I didn't look; and when the guard opened the door and stepped aside to let me pass, I left the room without a backward glance, because I was afraid that if I looked back I wouldn't be able to leave.

Sometimes I dream about that moment. I dream I'm back in the cell, just after I've kissed Leon goodbye, and the guard opens the door to let me out. And in spite of myself I *do* turn to look at him, wanting to know for sure whether he's at his desk, or at the window, or leaning his forehead against the wall with tears streaming down his face. In the dream, I'm glad I'm going to look – that when I leave I can take the image with me, that I'll always know exactly what he was doing, the moment when I walked out of his cell for the last time.

And I turn and look, and he's gone. The cell is empty, and suddenly I know the only person in the prison is me.

Sixteen

Eli Apal, 2a, 144 Universal Brotherhood Street, Irunja.

The guards did search me, half-heartedly. Their hands lingered on my buttocks and breasts, and the one who checked my pockets stood too close and breathed the smell of tobacco into my face; but they didn't check my socks or my underwear or the fold of my collar. Their hands didn't bother me. I thought they could have undressed me and pushed me up against a wall and I wouldn't have felt anything. I stood there like stone, not caring what they did, and after a while they lost interest, or realised that I wasn't hiding anything. When they stopped, I said, 'Can I go now?' as if I was at school talking to a nun, and they looked away, shrugging their shoulders.

Leon had told me to be careful in case I was followed, so I left the prison and turned at random, walking the streets without taking any notice of where I was going. When I looked over my shoulder there was someone there – a dumpy woman with a shopping basket – and she stayed a street-length behind me, never catching up or dropping behind. I imagined a whole army of followers waiting at the prison, ready to nip out at a moment's notice to track whoever seemed interesting. I felt a rush of anger, mixed with a kind of amusement: no wonder the country was so badly run, with so much energy and manpower spent this way. I wanted to call out to her, but I'd promised Leon no heroics. Instead I sped up, ducked round a corner into an alleyway, then sprinted to the other end of it and round into another alley that led to a wide quiet street. I paused, listening, and eventually heard the woman breathing heavily as she jogged a little way into the alley and then stopped and stood still, looking for me. She waited there for a long time – until I was almost sure she'd gone and I was imagining the rasp of her breath – and then I heard her footsteps go back the way she'd come, and a muttered stream of obscenity that got fainter and fainter. I took a deep breath, but I hadn't been afraid; I was still in a grey, numb haze.

I kept walking. I wanted to put off going to Eli Apal for as long as possible; while I was still wandering aimlessly, I could tell myself that there was still time to change my mind, to go and pound on the doors of every prison, asking for Mama and Papa and Martin. Or I could go to the guards' headquarters at home, and give myself up. I felt myself smiling, without amusement, at the thought of what Leon would say. *Promise me you'll survive, no matter what.*

And suddenly I realised what it was, that had niggled at me, when he'd said that.

Skizi. He'd reminded me of Skizi. As if she – as if her ghost – was speaking to me through his mouth, loving and fierce. As if I would be betraying her, as well as Leon, if I stayed.

Call your first son Martin . . .

I thought, I *might* have children, one day. I *might* have a son called Martin.

I shut my eyes, and pictured the map Leon had drawn me.

The building, when I finally found it, was a great soot-darkened apartment block, with balconies and shutters that had been grand, once. Now the windows were covered in cataracts of grime, and the stagnant air that met me as I opened the main door was damp and rancid. Outside the air was cool, with a cold bite to it when the breeze blew; but inside it was icy, and I started to shiver the moment I crossed the threshold. It occurred to me for the first time that I'd have to cross the mountains, and it was October already, and there'd be snow. I clenched my teeth together to stop them rattling, and went down the dark little passageway to find the door to 2a.

I paused at the end, where the corridor turned a corner, and tried to read the plaque on the door in front of me. The light was thick and murky, like a soup you wouldn't want to eat. 3a. I looked round, wondering if I'd gone past it, or if the numbers weren't in the right order.

A door opened at the far end of the passage, and a young couple hurried out, the woman tucking something into a little leather purse. The man was laughing nervously, in a kind of loose, hysterical voice, and the woman pushed him on the shoulder, propelling him down the corridor towards me. She said, in a low voice, 'Shut up! Let's go. If we don't make it to the car in time –' Her voice had an odd kind of lilt, as if she was putting on an accent. It resonated in the narrow space and made my stomach clench.

'All right, all right! I'm just . . . God, I hope he's straight, don't you? Or –'

'Shut *up*!' She hurried after him, clumsy in her high heels. She was wearing a flimsy dress with a red handkerchief around her neck, and her hair was so dark it blended in with the shadows.

The man stumbled past me, still with that hiccupping laugh bubbling in his throat. He was younger than I had first thought; hardly older than me. He had the same impossibly black hair as the girl, and I wondered if they were brother and sister. I didn't move, and he didn't seem to notice me. He was very pale, with beads of moisture on his forehead, and he smelt of sweat and anxiety. He got to the doorway and turned to call to her. 'Esta!'

For an odd, dislocated moment I thought he was calling my name; then she said, 'Yes, coming,' and I realised it was hers. She was standing in the corridor, peering through the dimness. I started to follow her gaze; then I realised she was staring at me. I couldn't see her properly, but there was something in the way she was standing, the angle of her shoulders . . .

She opened her mouth, and said something; but the boy called again, '*Esta!*' and whatever she said was lost in the echo.

I said, 'Go away. Go.' My voice was small and childish. I didn't know why I felt so strange, so quivery and afraid; but there was something about her. She reminded me –

She took a little step backwards, then forwards again, wobbling on her high heels as if she wasn't used to them. I despised her for her dress, her jet-black hair, the lipstick that was like a bruise in the dim light. She looked like she slept with Party members for black-market nylons.

The boy called, 'Esta! For God's sake, we have to go, the car is goi–' He seemed to notice me finally, and broke off. He lowered his voice, even though she was further away from him than I was. '*Esta*. Come right *now*. Or I'll go without you.'

She opened her mouth, but nothing came out. She'd gone white, a white that gleamed through the shadows like ivory. She said, 'All right, Jack, I'm coming.' She tottered towards me, and I caught a whiff of cheap perfume. Something turned over inside me as she went past.

I heard them go out, and realised I'd been holding my breath. I let it out slowly; but then I heard her heels clacking in the doorway, coming back. When I turned, she was outlined against the light, the shape of her legs showing through her dress. She called something to me, but the echoes blurred the consonants and I wasn't sure what she'd said. Something beginning with M . . . She called again – the same thing – and I realised that it was a name. Marina? Miren? Madeleine. She was calling to me because she thought I was someone else.

She started to say something, but the boy shouted at her, grabbed her wrist and pulled her out into the street, and I turned away. No wonder she'd stared at me like that. I wondered who Madeleine had been, and when she'd disappeared, and why.

But the encounter had shaken me. The girl's voice seemed to ring in my ears, singing like a glass about to break. *Madeleine* . . . I trailed my hand along the wall, in case I lost my balance, and stood trembling in front of the door marked 2a. In the end I had to knock three times before it was hard enough to make a noise.

After I'd knocked I stood there for a long time, hearing shuffling from behind the door. Finally it opened a crack, jerking against a chain, and half a brown, leathery face peered at me through the gap. 'Yes?'

'Are you Eli Apal?'

'No,' he said, and started to close the door.

'My brother Leon says do you remember your grandfather's shed when he kept contraband vodka in it?'

He'd shut the door halfway through the question; but now it opened again, and he gave me a long look and slipped the chain off. I had to squeeze past him to get inside, and I felt his eyes on me, assessing me. He said, 'Name?'

I wondered if I could trust him; then I decided it was too late to worry about that. I said, 'Esteya Bidart.'

'Another Esteya,' he said, with a short laugh, and then went silent, as if he'd been indiscreet. I knew already that I *didn't* trust him. 'What can I do for you?'

'I need to get out of the country.'

He narrowed his eyes, considering me. 'Can't do that.'

'What?'

He shrugged. 'I have a friend who might be able to help. If you've got enough money. A thousand should do it. More if you want papers.'

'I don't have –' I stopped, and swallowed. 'My brother said you took people over the border. He said you owed him.'

He sighed heavily. 'He's wrong. I don't.'

'But –'

'I don't take people over the border. More than my life's worth.' He paused, rooted in his pocket for a packet of cigarettes, and lit one. After a long pause, he added, 'I occasionally conduct business with the Communists in St-Jean-Pied-le-Mont. I'm authorised to do that. It involves a short drive over the mountains – my petrol is all legal and accounted for, by the way – and I tend to stop to have a piss just after the marker stone. The lock on the boot of my car is broken.'

I stared at him. I said, 'So . . .'

'Can't stop people getting in and out, you see. It's in a garage, on Red Street. Number sixteen. Big green motor car, with a Party flag on the bonnet.'

I nodded slowly. I said, 'Is that the same car that – those people, who just left – I suppose they won't be in there as well?'

He held my gaze, and then the corner of his mouth twitched. 'No, sweetheart. I don't know where they're going. Rich little kids like that don't get the personal touch. But my friend'll look after them. Now they've got their papers, they're all set up.'

I nodded. They hadn't seemed rich; I thought of the girl's cheap scent and flimsy dress, her dyed hair and lipstick . . . No, she'd been working hard for that money, and I could guess what she'd been doing. I felt a pang of something that hurt too much to be pity; a mix of pity and resentment and jealousy, as if I was pitying myself. 'Well then. Now I've explained that I can't help, you'd best clear off.' He gave me a level stare, and a wink. I wondered how he'd managed to survive this long, and if that would change, now that Leon was in prison.

He sat down noisily at a desk in the corner of the room, dismissing me. There was faint light spilling from the window behind him, catching the things on the desk: no papers or books, only a bundle of banknotes – American dollars, I thought, green and white – and a mess of little trinkets. Payment for the false papers and the introduction to his mysterious, useful friend . . .

I imagined the couple I'd seen, emptying their treasures out in front of him, hoping it would be enough. A string of bumpy pearls, a gold-plated cigarette lighter, a crucifix, a little heart-shaped silver box –

A little heart-shaped silver box.

It must be really hard, a voice said in my head, *fighting to survive in a world where you don't even have a gold crucifix or a little silver box shaped like a heart . . .*

I stared at it. Eli followed my gaze, and started to scrape the treasures off the desk into the drawer. I took a step forward, without thinking. 'Wait –'

He frowned, and paused, his hand cupped protectively over the heap.

'That box – I – please – let me see –'

He gave me a suspicious look, but he held it up, between finger and thumb, so that I could see it. I knew that if I reached out for it he'd jerk it away, but that didn't matter. I didn't have to see it more closely. I knew it by heart: the filigree, the lacy shell of silver over silver gilt, the flaw on the straight edge above the hinge. I even knew the inside: the cushioned red velvet, worn and soft, like the core of a rose. I had dreamt about that box, when I was little. It was the thing of Mama's I had wanted most of all.

And when Skizi had stolen it, there had been a part of me that was glad she had it: as if it had been mine, after all, and I had given it to her. Even if she never knew how much I'd wanted it. As if it was a gift.

A gift to Skizi. That box.

I looked and looked. I couldn't move. The world blurred and ran with water.

'Are you all right? Look, if you're going to throw up, there's a WC in the corridor . . .' He got to his feet, putting the box down. 'Or – deep breaths, there's a good girl, don't worry, you'll feel better in a sec, always gets a bit close in here . . .'

'That girl,' I said, forming the words thickly with my teeth and tongue, as if they were lumps of clay. 'That girl, she brought you that box . . .'

He looked sideways, then at me, licking his lips. 'Not for *me*, nothing dodgy, just for . . . safekeeping . . . Course, I'll check with the authorities that there's nothing . . . dubious . . .'

I felt myself smile, because I didn't care what he said. I knew that she *had* brought it to him. The girl I'd seen in the corridor, with the dyed hair, the high heels, the lipstick . . .

Skizi.

I started to laugh.

Skizi. She'd walked right past me, and I hadn't realised. Skizi was alive. She was alive. She – *Skizi* – was *alive*. I said, 'She's *alive* . . . Oh thank you, thank you . . .' The giggles rose and rose, taking control, until I bent over, unable to speak, and tears rolled down my cheeks and dripped off my chin. Skizi, my Skizi, was *alive* . . .

'Look, you can't stay . . . I'll get you a glass of water, and then you'll have to go . . .'

And I'd seen her and not known. I'd seen her hair and her lipstick and nothing else – but no, I'd seen the way she moved, I'd heard her voice. Part of me *had* known, hadn't it? My heart had turned over when I heard her speak, even with that fake accent . . . I shook my head, laughing, crying, as if she was in front of me. I would've wanted to kill her, if I hadn't been so glad that she was alive. I should have known, I should have known . . . She'd said, hadn't she? *I survive*. I should have trusted her.

And she'd recognised me. She'd called my name, hadn't she? And then something else, something more – that name, that girl's name . . .

The giggles subsided. I straightened up, and suddenly the room was cold, the damp settling on my skin.

She was leaving. They'd been running for the motor car, to cross the border. I'd never see her again.

What had she *said*? But all I could remember was the first consonant, the lightness of the word on her tongue . . . Madeleine, Miren, Miriam, Maria . . . But she knew my name, didn't she? So what was she trying to tell me? It could have been *her* new name – but she'd called herself Esteya, hadn't she? That gave me a tiny flush of pleasure; but it wasn't important. *Madeleine. Miren.* But they didn't mean anything, or nothing that made sense. I felt the tears rising again. If she was alive, but I never saw her again . . . Why hadn't she said something *real*?

If I'd only listened. If I'd only let her speak to me . . .

I swallowed. Eli was just coming back into the room with a cloudy glass of water. I already knew what it would taste like: metallic, like blood. He said, 'Ah, you feeling better now?'

I took a deep breath. 'Yes.'

'Good. Shut the door on your way out.'

I nodded. I had to move, or I'd die here, frozen, on my feet. I turned and opened the door. I felt as if there was something I had to ask him – a prickling, niggling feeling that there was a question, the *right* question, that would tell me what Skizi had meant to say . . . But whatever it was, it was gone. I couldn't think. I said, 'Goodbye.'

'Garage sixteen. Nice car. Green, with a Party flag.

There's a little bit of twine on the inside of the boot, to hold it shut. Otherwise it rattles like mad, going over the pass.'

'Yes,' I said. 'Thanks.' I felt as if the top layer of my skin had been removed, and everything hurt. I wanted to be numb again, the way I'd been when I said goodbye to Leon.

I went out and shut the door behind me.

I think perhaps I should have been afraid, walking through Irunja that afternoon, looking for the garage on Red Street. I might have been in more danger than I realised, wandering alone in the gathering dusk, making myself hurry, even though I knew, somehow, that I was going to find the garage, that everything was going to work like clockwork. There were burnt-out motor cars on the corners, and smashed windows, abandoned buildings . . . but I don't think I saw any other people, and I felt strangely safe, as if all of this had happened before and I already knew how it ended. Or, I suppose, I just didn't care. If a car had driven down the pavement towards me at seventy miles an hour, I might not have bothered to get out of the way.

I found Red Street almost by accident. It was a narrow little mews, with a row of garages but only one that had a door. I thought for a moment it would be locked, but when I pushed it the damp wood groaned and creaked open. The car was there – green, with the red flag on the bonnet – and I picked my way around it to get to the boot. It was like getting into a coffin, and for the first time since I'd left Eli's rooms I felt a deep stab of fear. But when I hesitated, I thought it would be worse *not* to get in and have to go home again. There was a torch and a bottle of cheap wine sloshing in the corner, and a length of twine trailing from a little metal thing on the inside. It looked as if Eli had done this before. I checked that it didn't lock; then, when I'd run out of things to look at, I got in. I pulled the lid of the boot down, until it was almost closed, and once my eyes had adjusted to the light coming through the crack I managed to tie the two ends of twine together to stop it bouncing open again. The line of dim light coming through was comforting. I lay there, curled up, and although I should have been excited and afraid I just felt empty and quiet. I think I might even have slept.

When I woke, it was because the engine was roaring and the car trembling underneath me. The car moved, pressing me against the awkward corners of the boot. The line of paler darkness flickered and re-established itself. After only a few metres the car stopped again; I heard a door open, footsteps come round the back of the car, wood scraping on the ground, and then the slam of the car door as the driver got back in and accelerated again. He must have closed the garage door, I thought. I realised with an uneasy feeling that I didn't know who was driving the car. It might not be Eli; it might be a guard, driving me to prison . . .

But we drove for a long time, so I was sure we'd left Irunja. The road curved and the momentum dragged me from side to side. We were climbing, and I heard a sibilant patter on the metal over my face. It was cold in the boot, and my whole body was aching. When we went over bumps in the road, the lid of the boot jerked and pulled against the twine, banging loudly. There was an icy draught blasting through the gap. I took deep breaths, but my stomach was full of a mixture of hope and terror, fizzing and sickening. I pressed my hands against the bottom of the boot, shut my eyes and tried not to panic. If this was a trap, if something went wrong . . . I felt tears of frustration prickle in my eyes. What was I doing here? How could I have been so stupid? I reached out, fumbling in the dark, until my fingers touched the jerking piece of twine. If I untied it, I could jump out of the boot, while the car was moving; I'd hurt myself, probably, but anything was better than staying put, not knowing where I was going – almost sure now that it was all a trap. I said, 'It's all right, calm down, it'll be all right . . .' but the noise of the car drowned out my voice. The car slowed, grumbling, and I thought it was going to stop; but it accelerated again, and I gritted my teeth, half relieved, half disappointed. I felt the car go on climbing, and wondered whether we'd passed a checkpoint. If we had, it wouldn't be long before we were safely over the pass . . . I waited, feeling my pulse in my mouth, counting the heartbeats. I'd count to a thousand, and then I'd jump out, whatever happened . . . But my heart was racing so fast that I kept losing count. I went back to five hundred over and over again, until I thought I'd lost the ability to think. Soon, I'd jump out soon . . . before it was too late . . .

Suddenly the car slowed again; and this time it stopped, and the engine cut out.

There was silence. I heard my own breathing, fast and irregular, and the world swayed underneath me as if the car was still moving. The door slammed.

The air squeaked sharply in my throat. But nothing happened. My skin prickled with tension, waiting for someone to open the boot and drag me out. But no one came. The twine was slack between my fingers, and the outline of light around the lid of the boot was silver, and steady. The air coming in through the gap was cold and smelt of earth and snow.

What had he said?

I tend to stop to have a piss just after the marker stone. The lock on the boot of my car is broken . . .

With tentative, trembling fingers, I fumbled at the twine, undoing the knot. My hands were cold, and the jerking had tightened it, and for a second I thought I wouldn't be able to do it. Horror took hold of me, like a hand squeezing the breath out of me; but after a while it passed, and I could feel enough of the knot to pick at it with my nails until I felt one of the strands loosen. It gave way. I heard myself sob, and for a moment I couldn't move, paralysed with relief and fear. I was shaking uncontrollably now.

It was hard to get enough leverage to push the boot open, and even harder to summon the strength. It took me a long time to do it.

And then I was leaning – aching with stiffness and cold, breathing hard, my teeth chattering – against the car, weak at the knees and suddenly sick with hunger and relief, my bag at my feet; and there was a moonlit expanse of snow and silver sky, two humped peaks on my left and in front of me nothing but the path sloping downwards. I had never seen so much open space. It was like being on the moon.

Over to my right, Eli was standing with his back to me, pissing. The stream of liquid caught the light, like glass, and steamed. His shoulders stiffened, as if he felt me looking at him, but he didn't turn round.

So he was trustworthy after all. I glanced back over my shoulder. A mile away, in the snow, I could see the little black box of a checkpoint. We'd passed it without stopping then; they must have recognised him. The thought of what would have happened if they'd searched the car made my heart skip.

Still without looking at me, Eli raised an arm and pointed sideways, to the track. It was covered with a faint dusting of new snow, but the line of it was clear.

I opened my mouth to call out to him – to thank him or wish him luck – but in the end it seemed too dangerous, even now. And the silence was so huge, so heavy, that I was almost afraid to rupture it. So I turned away, and started to walk.

It was a relief to move, even though I was still aching and cramped from being curled up. The air was so cold it seemed to sting my windpipe as it went down, and my lungs started to burn. I walked briskly, trying to warm myself up. I knew that sooner or later I'd have to decide where to go . . . Sooner or later I'd have to start the complicated business of living. But for now, there was only one road, leading down the slope, and I was free not to do anything but follow it. The sky was full of silver light, drowning the stars, and when I looked up it was like staring into a chasm, unbelievable space and depth. I had never felt so alone, or so free; it was frightening.

The track went up over a hump in the landscape, and when it started to descend again the valley was spread out like a cup, wide and bleak and featureless. I hurried forward, conscious of how small I was, how anyone there would see me without even having to look. As I went down the slope I saw that there was a little wall ahead of me, beside the track. It was shorter than head-height, and only a couple of metres wide, and for a while I assumed it was the remains of something bigger. But as I walked past I realised it had been built like that on purpose, like a little screen: a hide for hunting, or – no – a shelter for anyone caught in the snow, something to huddle against to stay alive. A life-saving wall, just big enough to shield a person.

I looked at it for a long time. I got colder and colder, but somehow I didn't want to move. It made me think – I didn't know why – of a pello court, the wall that isn't built to keep people in or out, but for something else, something *good* . . .

I thought of Angel Corazon. I thought of him bashing his ball against the wall of his cell, over and over, until they took it away and left him to go mad. I thought of him drowning himself in his own piss. I thought of how he'd played, the day he defeated the Bull.

He liked walls, I thought. If anyone looked at walls and saw more than just something to keep thieves out, or hold up the roof, it was him . . .

I had his pello ball in my bag: the ball that Skizi had given me, the ball that killed the Bull. I got it out of my bag and pushed it into the snow that had drifted against the bottom of the wall. I would have liked to bury it, but the earth was frozen and my hands were too cold to dig. For some reason I felt as if I was standing at a graveside – Angel's grave. A wall in a white moonscape . . . He might have liked it, I thought, looking around. It would have been a good place to rest. Clean as a page, as blank plaster, as a bed. A faint sparkle of snow drifted across my face on the wind and clung to my nose.

A good place to rest . . .

The euphoria I'd felt as I walked had faded. I was so tired. I only had to stumble down the mountain, but it didn't seem worth it, somehow. What was there to go on for? Mama and Papa, Martin, Leon, everyone I cared about was dead, or would be soon. Even Skizi had disappeared. I'd never see her again. She was alive, but that meant she'd go on living and fall in love with someone else and be happy, without me. She'd never even know it wasn't me who betrayed her.

I was crouching already; now I let my legs crumple underneath me and sank sideways into the snow. After a few seconds icy water started to soak into my trousers, but it didn't matter, nothing mattered. I could close my eyes, I could go to sleep. It didn't seem such a bad way to go. The pale sky looked down at me, empty.

I shut my eyes. A spasm of shivering went through me but I forced myself to relax into it, and it passed. A trickle of snow-melt ran down into my collar. My hands were already numb. It was supposed to be a kind death, cold . . .

I should have been afraid, but I wasn't. I tried to think of Skizi, and my family, but their faces were blurred. I'd see them soon, anyway, if I fell asleep here . . . I let my mind drift, and I saw the wall of Martin's bedroom, with all those names. The Ibarras' hut, my own face in charcoal. The graffiti on the wall next to the church, *WE RISE* . . . And I saw myself the day Angel Corazon had played the Bull, the day I first saw Skizi; I saw us all, when we were still innocent, before . . . A cheerful crowd, sunlit, breathless with excitement –

And I thought of Angel.

I saw him in the moment of victory, blazing with triumph, set on fire by the sun. I could see him so clearly; the purity of it took my breath away. The way he'd looked around at us, the delight in his eyes, the pride, the way he knew he'd made something glorious with nothing but his hands and the laws of physics. He'd won; and no matter what happened later, no matter what –

That had been real too. The victory was real.

I opened my eyes. The silver sky glared down at me, but I could still see Angel in my mind's eye, faint as an after-image against the curtain of the Milky Way. I was cold. I was too cold to stay where I was, too cold to fall asleep.

He'd won, that day. No one could change that.

Angel *won*.

It didn't make sense; but it forced me to my hands and knees and then to my feet, hissing through my teeth. The shaking took hold of me again and I wrapped my arms round myself. I steadied myself with a hand on that little wall.

Then something – my last scrap of energy – forced me to walk away, following the track without looking back.

I walked for hours. It must have been later than I thought, because the sun rose before I'd got to the foot of the mountain. After the sunrise it seemed even colder. I was frozen to the bone, hardly able to walk. I followed the track until it joined a road, and then I stood and looked at the signs, blind and dazed with fatigue.

St-Jean-Pied-le-Mont, 6 km. La Magdeleine, 10 km. Bailarain, 12 km.

La Magdeleine.

I stood and stared, reading it over and over. I mouthed the consonants; then I said it aloud. But it wasn't my own voice I heard; it was Skizi's, calling down that dark, echoing corridor to me. *La Magdeleine*.

I breathed out until my lungs were empty. The vapour

from my breath hung around me and melted away. My eyes stung, but I was too cold to cry.

'La Magdeleine,' I said again, and laughed.

I was too tired to feel very much; but at least now I knew where to go.

About the author

'Collins is one hell of a writer'
Mal Peet

B.R. (Bridget) Collins is a graduate of both university and drama school. Her first novel, *The Traitor Game*, won the Branford Boase Award in 2009. Her books for Bloomsbury include *A Trick of the Dark*, *Tyme's End*, *Gamerunner, The Broken Road* and *MazeCheat*. Bridget lives in Tunbridge Wells, Kent.

To find out more about Bridget, visit her at
www.jugjugjug.blogspot.com

Also by B.R. Collins

Tyme's End is more than just a deserted house.
And anybody who enters must prepare themselves
for terror . . .

OUT NOW